Nice Woody

By Gerry Stimmler

A prequel to:
Margie's Murder Mysteries

Copyright 2013

Other Books by Gerry Stimmler

Margie's Murder Mystery series...

Dropped Dead in Kona © 2011

An Invitation to Murder © 2012

Eleanor Avenue Press
St. Paul, Minnesota

1st Printing, July 2013

For Paula, Liz, and Paul

Authors Note:

Two titles were attached to this story at various times. *Nice Woody* was always my favorite, but *My Favorite Vacation* was also considered. I decided on *Nice Woody* finally because although *My Favorite Vacation* is more genteel, it's not nearly as much fun.

A Very Rough Start

As Hawaiian Airlines flight 398 completed its turn and leveled off for its final approach to Kona International airport I assumed my customary landing position: head up, shoulders back, feet braced firmly on the legs of the seat ahead of me, anaconda grip on the arm rests, eyes tightly shut, and repeated my landing mantra in my head: *we are not going to crash, we are not going to crash, we are not going to crash.*

I suppose there are some who would label me a coward based on that. But I don't think that's fair at all. A coward, according to my dictionary, is 'somebody lacking courage.'

I don't lack courage. In fact I have done many courageous things in my life. I saved a number of people from drowning the summer I was life-guard at camp, and I told a supervisor to go f–k himself after he gave me a lousy performance rating just two years ago.

The problem is simply that I've never fully accepted as possible that something the size and weight of a modern aircraft can actually stay aloft. How can eighty tons of aluminum stay up there? It's air for Pete's sake. Air!

Everyone tells me it's a matter of physics of course. "So what" I say? Physics and I have never been on friendly terms. My college physics class ended my aspirations of becoming an astronomer and spending my life gazing at the heavens. Why should I like physics?

I'm convinced that someday flying will be exposed for what it is – a fraud – and when all the great minds have come together and accepted *that* logical conclusion, all the planes in all the skies all over the world will fall like rocks and we'll go back to using trains and ships and sensible travel machines to get around.

I do not intend to be in the air on that fateful day of course, and toward that end I watch the news and read the papers so I'll have a heads up before it happens.

And so it goes without saying that I'm not a happy flyer. And the part that rattles me more than any other – the part I really, really hate – is the landing.

A friend of mine once referred to landing a plane as a 'controlled crash.' Some friend. The point is, I never forgot the implication. Or forgave my friend.

And so it is that I have never actually witnessed a landing, which is too bad because on this particular flight I might have seen from my window seat the breathtaking landscape of the Big Island of Hawaii as the last rays of sunlight bathed earth and sand and sea and sky with a golden hue that Michelangelo would be hard pressed to duplicate.

This display was only fitting, of course, since our destination was known as Hawaii's Gold Coast, the playground of the rich and famous and all those who wished they were.

But, as I said, my eyes were shut to all this splendor.

Likewise, I missed the small melodrama taking place down on that stretch of highway 19 that circles the Big Island – also known as the Queen Kaahumanu Highway – where a vintage powder blue 1966 Thunderbird convertible with white leather seats and chrome everything was speeding along in an incredibly long line of bumper-to-bumper northbound traffic.

I know it sounds fanciful, but had I been watching I would have known for certain it was a woman at the wheel. A real looker. You could tell that even from way up here. I would have seen the T-bird pull out to pass, then brake and slip back in ahead of on-coming traffic only to pull out again, then back in once more.

Finally I would have seen it pull out one last time, accelerate like crazy, and soar past three SUVs, a panel truck, and two sedans before slipping back in line to avoid a southbound limo.

And I would have seen the police car dogging the T-bird a half mile back, mired in heavy traffic, its blue lights flashing. It too pulling out to pass then darting back in, then trying once more.

A betting man would have given odds the police car would never catch the T-bird, but I'm not a betting man, and like I said I saw none of this because my eyes were shut and I was repeating my little protective mantra.

Of course had my eyes been open I would also have seen the goings on in the cabin, where my wife, Jillian, bored senseless by our fourteen-hour flight out of Chicago with stops in L. A. and Honolulu, thumbing her way through one of those in-flight shopping magazines in a final attempt to find that one item – a digital rain gauge? a talking thesaurus? – that she hadn't seen before and that we (she) couldn't possibly live without a second longer.

But I didn't see that either.

I did hear the terrifyingly loud *bang* as the pilot lowered the landing gear, and I did feel that long final plunge as we dropped fast during those last seconds of flight as the pilot throttles back on the engines and the airplane glides until the wheels contact the ground and catch the earth, an action that is followed quickly by violent shaking and rattling as the pilot reverses thrust and the engines howl until the plane reduces speed to a modest crawl and the pilot engages the brakes and we turn off the runway and make for the terminal, and I breathe again.

It was at this point, as my heart rate slowed and my jaw fell slack, that I opened my eyes, pried my hands from the arm rests, and allowed myself to peer out the window at a spectacular tropical sunset that glinted off the small Polynesian-style buildings, palms, and whatnot of Kona International airport. But paradise? I couldn't see it. Where was the thick vegetation? The verdant hills? The tropical rainforest?

Jillian glanced quickly outside. "Not much to look at is it?" she said critically, echoing my thoughts.

"Where's the guide book?" I asked, and pulled my carryon from under the seat and dug around for the 'Guide to Hawaii' that I knew was there but which had suddenly vanished.

Jillian was on another track. "Where's *my* carryon?"

It was in the overhead since its massive size prevented it from fitting under any seat on any airplane in the world. And since we had come to a stop and the little bell had gone 'ding,' I stood and pulled her carryon free and handed it to her and we both crowded into the aisle with all the other passengers, even though the door was still shut and we weren't going anywhere at the moment.

I watched in disbelief as Jillian pawed through her purse and extracted her cell phone.

"You brought that?" I whined unhappily. I hate cell phones. Always have and always will, and I loathe the idea that someday it will be as necessary to have one of my own as it is necessary to fly on airplanes. Modern conveniences. Bah!

Jillian made a face, squinted at the phone (she needs reading glasses but refuses to consider them), pressed the button that retrieves her messages, and plugged her free ear so as to be able to hear above the din of the cabin.

I shook my head and pondered the repercussions of taking the phone and pitching it right there and then. I knew it was not a practical solution, and would be an unforgivable sin. And I was not in the position to commit unforgivable sins.

She must have had a lot of messages or one long message, because she listened long and hard as we shuffled toward the exit and began our trip down the gangway and onto the tarmac under a swiftly darkening tropical sky.

I noted the aromatic mix of flora and jet fuel, which I hoped was only temporary, and silently thanked God for having once again allowed me to violate the laws of nature and finish my flight before physics was exposed as the con I knew it was.

We were half-way to the gate when Jillian finally pulled the phone from her ear and announced almost gleefully: "I've got to go back to L.A.!"

"No problem," I replied, misinterpreting the immediacy of the request. "We'll call and get your ticket changed when we get to Jack and Margie's."

L.A., you should know, has become Jillian's home away from home so I wasn't surprised they wanted her there after our vacation.

"No. I have to go now! There's a ticket waiting for me!" Jillian said.

You know how it is when you hear something you don't want to hear? You pretend you didn't hear it right even though you did.

"What?" I said dully.

Jillian ignored me and began speed-walking toward the arrival gate, her eyes searching the crowd for an agent. I was doing a quick two-step beside her with the carryons trying hard to keep up.

"You can't be serious," I blurted with astonishment, though to be honest I wasn't all that surprised. Jillian's new job had become her life and it was as much

5

responsible for the troubled state of our marriage as anything.

"We just got here," I said as if that were a forceful objection.

Jillian gave me that look she gives me when I've stated the obvious but the obvious to her is completely different than the obvious to me.

"I have to go to L.A. for *work*. You remember *work*."

"Yes," I volleyed back, panting from the exertion of keeping pace with her. *What in God's name did she have in her carryon?* "I remember work," I said. "Do you remember our vacation? Let someone else do it. We've been planning this for months."

Jillian's eyes lit on a gate agent and she made for her like a fly for a filly.

"You know I can't do that," Jillian spat. "Besides, it'll only be a day or two. I'll be back before you know it."

"And just what am I supposed to do with *your* friends for two days? I've never even met them."

Jillian wasn't listening. She was talking to the agent and a moment later we were headed to gate 7B where the L.A. flight on which Jillian was ticketed was already boarding.

"Joe, you'll be fine." Jillian assured me, though her voice didn't sound sincere. "Honestly, sometimes you act so helpless."

Me? Helpless? Well, that might be true sometimes, but... This time the circumstances were bizarre. My mind was racing in its effort to find an argument that would change her mind. Something. Anything. Finally I cried out: "So, you're just going to abandon me?"

We'd arrived at the gate and Jillian showed another agent her I.D. and got her ticket.

"I'm not abandoning you, Joe," Jillian snapped. "Margie and Jack will meet you at the luggage carousel. They'll take good care of you."

She said the last line a little too condescendingly but I let it go. I knew it was over. Arguing was not going to change things. Reasoning was not going to change things. There it was. Jillian was as good as gone, so I did the manly thing and accepted my fate.

We stood together silently until the P.A. system sputtered out a mumbled last call for United 505 to L.A.

Jillian started for the gate, stopped and came back. For a moment I let myself think: *She's changed her mind.* But of course she hadn't. She'd just forgotten her carryon which she took from me and dashed toward the now-waiting plane. No kiss goodbye. No nothing.

"I'll be back in two days!" she yelled without turning. "Two days. I promise."

I watched numbly as she crossed the tarmac and climbed the ramp. I watched her disappear through the hatch, and I watched it close. I waited as the ramp drove off and the plane's engines fired and the jet turned slowly. I stood in silence as the plane taxied to the end of the runway, paused a moment, gunned its engines, raced down the runway, and leapt into the night sky.

But it was not until the running lights were out of sight and the golden glow of 'paradise' had turned muddy brown that I finally turned away and started toward baggage claim wondering if perhaps it was time for serious marriage counseling.

***

Ten minutes later I was sitting on Jillian's suitcase outside the airport near the curb under the orange-tinted glow of a streetlamp trying to recall the events that had brought me here and exactly what was supposed to be happening but wasn't.

The plan was simple. A vacation. A vacation to rekindle a struggling marriage. Two weeks away from snow and cold and the work-a-day world. Two weeks of sun and surf in a tropical wonderland with Jillian's friends.

To be precise, we were to be the guests of Margie and Jack Geanosa, of Los Angeles, California.

Margie Geanosa was Jillian's old college roomy, best friend, and confidant of all collegiate secrets during their sojourn at UCLA, where to hear the stories Jillian told they were like Frick and Frack, Thelma and Louise, Mutt and Jeff... you get the picture.

But like most dynamic duos they had gone separate ways after college and grew apart and lost touch.

Then about a year and a half back, after Jillian got her dream job scouting commercial locations for a mammoth Chicago advertising firm, they'd reconnected in a fateful way.

Because Jillian's duties took her to L.A. on a weekly basis, it happened that she found herself working with a local producer who turned out to be none other than Margie's husband Jack. Surprise and excitement. Small world and all that. And magically Margie and Jillian were best friends once more.

So eventually it transpired that Margie and Jack invited Jillian and me – though I'm not sure they cared one way or the other if I came along – to visit with them in Kona where they had a *spectacular* vacation home.

Now vacationing with friends, especially those I don't know, is not the sort of thing I relish. But Jillian pressed for it, and I came around finally after she agreed we could have our own condo. I acknowledged how beneficial it would be for us to get away and spend time together with a couple who was getting along as famously as Jillian claimed Margie and Jack were getting along.

Jillian spoke incessantly of Jack's devotion to Margie and Margie's devotion to Jack and so I got comfortable with the idea of staying with strangers and even excited about the whole Hawaii thing after reading a travel book about Kilauea volcano, night diving with manta rays, deep sea fishing, gorgeous beaches, and perfect weather.

Unforeseen, of course, was the prospect of Jillian being called back to L.A. Likewise unexpected was that Margie and Jack, who Jillian had promised absolutely would be at the luggage carousel to meet me, were not at the luggage carousel or for that matter anywhere else in sight. And finally unanticipated was that my luggage would be lost. Jillian's luggage made it, but mine? Lost? Stolen? Gone to Greenland?

I tried to think positively and thanked the Supreme Being that I still had my wallet, my credit cards, and a pack of gum. Had I known that at that moment I was being watched and that within 48 hours or so I'd be the prime suspect for a murder, I might not have been so hasty in my thanks, but since I'm not psychic nor omniscient I was oblivious to my future dilemma. I had enough trouble as it was for now.

So I sat in the night and felt the warm tropical breeze and pondered what I might do. Drinking occurred to me immediately, but the only bar available at the airport was behind the security doors so that wouldn't work.

I couldn't call Jillian on the plane. Her cell phone would be off. And I didn't have Margie and Jack's phone number. Why should I have their number? I didn't need it; Jillian had it! Of course it was conveniently *not* listed in the Big Island phone directory.

I began to think that perhaps I should have taken a greater interest in these friends of Jillian's.

In my own defense I can offer only the fact that all the 'get-togethers' with them took place in L.A. and I was in Chicago, so there was little opportunity to get to know the Geanosas.

I do recall a few phone calls from Margie, but I don't think I answered any of them. The exclusivity of communication by cell phone made it hard for me to get in the loop.

It wasn't until Jillian was in the air and I'd exited the secure area and made my way to baggage claim that another realization struck me. I didn't even know what they looked like! I didn't even know what they sounded like!

And so I stood by the luggage carousel waiting for my luggage that didn't arrive and the people who never arrived until I realized I was all alone, and I made my way out to the curb and sat down, determined to wait a reasonable time for Jack and Margie to appear and if they didn't appear, to take a taxi to some hotel and find a bar and... do what?

As I pondered that question, my attention was drawn up the street by the squeal of tires and I watched as headlights raced toward me until a powder-blue T-bird screeched to a halt directly in front of me and a *gorgeous* young blonde popped out of the car and darted 'round it in one hell of a hurry.

Blonde and beautiful, with a dancer's body: slender, athletic, small breasted, but not flat-chested. She looked to be five-three to five-five and twenty-seven, twenty-eight tops.

She looked a little slutty, but tastefully so. Women don't understand about that, but men know what I mean.

Like a cross between the sweet girl next door and the pole dancer at the strip club. Or maybe it's the pole dancer that looks like the girl next door. I guess what I'm trying to say is she looked like Lolita all grown up.

In any event, she was wearing a white dress that was conservative and sexy all at the same time. I don't know what it's called, but it was one of those things with a scoop neck and no sleeves that hugs the body down to the waist then blouses out in soft pleats, like a tennis dress, only longer. I think it might be called a sundress, but don't bet on it. It emphasized her figure and her long legs as did a pair of tiny, size 5 taffy-colored sandals with two inch heels – not that she needed to emphasize anything.

Her curly blonde hair was partially covered by a large straw hat that matched her sandals and which, because of the breeze and her haste as she dashed around the car, she had to hold onto with one hand. The hat, together with the blonde curls, framed a small, girlish face, with pouty lips, wide eyes, and one of those upturned movie-star noses. Her expression said 'I'm late! Oh, my. I'm late.'

In her right hand she carried a pair of white gloves, which is something you don't see much anymore – white gloves I mean, not people carrying things in their hands – and in the crook of her arm were a half dozen leis and a straw handbag that matched her hat and complemented her shoes. Around her neck was a string of faux white pearls – 'faux' I'm sure, unless pearls are available the size of grapes – and she had matching 'pearl' earrings.

I know it sounds peculiar, but for some reason watching her prance around the car looking as she did and dressed as she was reminded me for all the world of a young girl late for church.

It's important that you know I'm not one of those guys who gawks at every pretty thing that goes by. Jillian may have gained a few pounds over the years and she may be showing a little wear, but I'm not interested in 'trading up' as some men put it. Jillian's just what I'm looking for.

But this woman was a real show-stopper and if you were male – and maybe even if you weren't – you couldn't help but watch.

Of course I took an instant dislike to her.

'Hold on. What?' you say. 'That seems odd.'

It's really not. And while I'll agree it may not be the norm and that most men would have a different reaction, my experience with stunningly beautiful women, like my experience with physics, has not been positive, and 'Size 5 Sandals' was about as stunning and beautiful a woman as I'd ever seen in real life. The women in *Playboy* and the swimsuit issue of *Sports Illustrated* are not real are they?

In any event, her appearance evoked painful memories of my limited encounters with gorgeous women, the first of which was back in college days when I made my living as a shoe dog. For those of you who don't know, a shoe dog is someone who sells shoes; I did it in the shoe department of a large department store. They actually had people who sold shoes back before everything became giant warehouses where you get everything yourself. But that's not the point.

Anyway, it was late one evening when this *vision* walked into the place. A flawless beauty, lavishly dressed and perfectly coiffed (do they still say that?). Makeup, if indeed she was wearing any, was applied so skillfully that she glowed with a beauty and an inner light I had never seen outside an airbrushed magazine photo. I was stunned. Flummoxed.

She had my testosterone gushing – college boys have loads of that – and I was sweating and stammering before I timidly asked: "Can I help you?"

Now don't get the wrong impression. I'm not shy around women. Never have been. At least not normal women. But this stunner had me mesmerized, and try though I might I couldn't help but wonder who she was and where she'd come from and what was she doing in my boring corner of the world.

Despite my sweating and stammering, I managed to show her several pair of expensive shoes that fit her size seven AAA's to perfection. None of them pleased her, however, and for some inexplicable reason all I wanted to *do* was to please her. Even if it was only with a pair of alligator pumps or glove-leather flats.

I tried to make conversation, but all that ever came out of my mouth was: "How do those feel?"

Cute huh?

She showed no interest in me except for my skill at fetching shoes and slipping them onto her feet. It wasn't that she was impolite, just disinterested.

I was in agony.

Eventually I found a pair of taupe Ferragamos she didn't hate and as I was ringing up her purchase my brain raced like a Ferrari to think of something smart to say that would make her notice me. I finished the transaction and handed her the bag. I opened my mouth and said: "You are the most gorgeous woman I have ever seen."

That's it? That's what my 3.5 lbs of intellectual muscle put together? "You are the most gorgeous woman I have ever seen" was all my brain could think to say?

As soon as I said it, I knew it was lame. I think it was so lame that she couldn't believe I'd actually said it out loud because she just stared at me for a few seconds with a bewildered expression on her face, and I think she was trying to figure out the meaning of my faux pas. Was I making a pass at her?

Whatever she was thinking she gave up, shook her head as if I'd just said the most feeble thing – which was true – and turned and walked away.

I was crushed. Devastated.

Though I was only a lowly shoe clerk and she was a goddess, would it have been too much for her to respond with something pleasant such as: "That's very sweet of you" or "Thank you" or even "I get that all the time."

No. She dismissed me as if I didn't matter at all!

And I never forgot that.

Years later I had a similar encounter in a hotel bar when I was getting a drink and found myself next to what I could only believe was one of those international fashion models. She too was blonde and incredibly beautiful and had an engagement ring the size of a tennis ball. I made the same mistake as before of telling her bluntly how attractive she was. You would think I had told her I had doggy doo doo on my shoe and wanted to share it with her! She gave me a look that could not only have shrunk a violet; it could have wilted a whole garden!

Now I know you're saying: "It's three strikes and you're out, Joe!" But not for me. I decided those two encounters were enough. I swore off beautiful women, and decided a more proactive stance was justified: that of complete contempt for them and the men who loved them. Hence my strong aversion to Size 5 Sandals.

As I've already mentioned, she was in a hurry, moving fast and not paying attention to anything and certainly not to me. So when she rounded the trunk and her head went down and she opened her purse to look for something I knew it was trouble.

I was 'under her radar' as they say. Invisible. She hadn't noticed me at all and it was obvious that if she didn't change course she was going to plow right into me.

You know the human brain always impresses me. Even an average one like mine. In the space of a nanosecond (I don't really know what that is, but I do know it's a very small part of a second.), I considered my options. One, I could sit and do nothing and let Size 5 Sandals plow into me, which would teach her to watch where she was going when she was hurrying like a maniac, which in some small way might repay me for the snub those other two lovely ladies had foisted upon me.

Two, I could be a gentleman and get out of her way, which would not be all that easy since Size 5 Sandals was moving fast and I would have to stand, pick up Jillian's suitcase, and shuffle right or left or... Well, you get it.

As it turned out, I did neither because fate intervened with a third option when a loud *voice of authority* barked from down the street: "Hold it, lady! You can't park there!"

It was a female voice. At least I thought it was a female voice. Powerful and forceful like a mother scolding her child, and it was commanding enough to halt Size 5 Sandals like a dog tethered to a leash. We turned – Size 5 Sandals and I – toward the voice and found that it belonged to a dark, boxy-looking TSA agent who bustled over with stern disapproval on her face.

"You have to move your car," she barked vigorously.

"I'll only be a minute, I'm just meeting..." Size 5 Sandals started with an apologetic and beseeching voice.

But 'Boxy TSA Lady' would have none of it. "Move your car. NOW." The raised tone was clearly meant to intimidate, but it didn't really seem all that intimidating since Boxy TSA Lady was barely five feet tall.

Size 5 Sandals started to argue but stopped when Boxy TSA Lady started to talk into her shoulder.

You know what I mean. Everyone in uniform today carries these microphones clipped to the epaulets of their shirts or jackets and they kind of lean their head over and talk out of the side of their mouth into them. It's very dramatic, and very television.

Size 5 Sandals crossed her arms and began to tap her foot, looked quickly at her watch, and then looked toward the arrival area. I looked too.

Who might *she* be meeting? A friend? A lover? I spotted an engagement ring and a wedding band. Her husband? I was quick to acknowledge it could still be one of the previous two.

Another flight must have landed for a steady stream of vacationers dribbled out of the doors from the secure area headed toward baggage claim. Size 5 Sandals danced nervously or excitedly – I'm not sure which – and looked intensely at the gate as she waited for Boxy TSA Lady to stop talking into her shoulder.

It was at that point, and almost as if by magic, that a police squad car appeared and pulled in at the curb to block the T-bird.

I smiled wryly. *The plot thickens.* What do they do to people who don't move their cars in post 9-11 Hawaii I wondered? Jail? Thumbscrews? I was eager to find out.

Since I was certain the arrival of the police would up the ante in terms of making Size 5 Sandals squirm, I was surprised to find it had the opposite effect. As a 'Stern-faced Officer' climbed out of his car and headed for Boxy TSA Lady, Size 5 Sandals brightened noticeably and skipped over to meet him. And as soon as Stern-faced Officer saw Size 5 Sandals, he became 'Smiley-faced Officer,' which I noticed upset Boxy TSA Lady to no end as she hurried to intercede.

I was too far away to hear and I'm not good at reading lips, but my take on the discussion was this: Smiley-faced Officer knew Size 5 Sandals and took up her cause, which, if I'm correct, was to convince Boxy TSA Lady that it *was* okay if Size 5 Sandals left her car at the curb for a minute or two while she met someone.

Boxy TSA Lady was clearly unhappy with this development, both because her authority was in question and because Size 5 Sandals looked like Size 5 Sandals and Boxy TSA Lady looked like Boxy TSA Lady. I couldn't say I blamed her. I was rooting for Boxy TSA Lady 'cause as I said I had this dislike for Size 5 Sandals from the get-go and the way she was flirting and smiling at Smiley-faced Officer made me a kind of queasy. Or was that envy?

Why do beautiful women get away with everything? There ought to be a law.

As the confrontation in front of the squad car continued, a new occurrence caught my attention that seemed to provide proof that no ill deed be left rewarded. Or something like that.

It concerned a stout woman in her mid fifties – dyed red hair, twenty-five pounds overweight – who made her way across the street behind the T-bird carrying a small dog under her right arm. She was quite interested in the disagreement going on and when she got to the curb she stopped to watch, not paying any attention to the fact that I was now watching her watching them.

The dog under her arm appeared to be a Yorkshire terrier. I say 'appeared to be' because it was big for a Yorkie – at least the Yorkies I knew – and it had floppy ears; not those pointy ones you generally think of when you think of Yorkies. But it had the Yorkie markings and Yorkie hair – though the thing was in need of a good trim.

Anyway, as the woman climbed the curb she stopped and looked at the squabble up the street. She looked quickly at me, and I looked away so I could pretend I hadn't been watching her.

Then she did the oddest thing. She took the Yorkie and set it on the front seat of the T-bird, brushed off her hands as if ridding herself of something infected, gave me another quick glance – which I saw from the corner of my eye since I wasn't going to let her see me watching her – and walked quickly away toward the departure area.

I waited a long moment and then turned around. She was gone. Nowhere in sight. Vanished!

I couldn't help but smirk. '*What will happen now?*' I pondered. This was better than dinner theatre. Although I must admit I could have used a bite to eat.

When I turned back from looking for the vanishing woman, the quarreling trio was breaking up. Boxy TSA Lady looked mad enough to throw something and stood hands on hips arguing fiercely with what was once again Stern-Faced Officer.

You could tell Size 5 Sandals had won because she was headed my way with a noticeable skip in her step, one hand on her hat and the other filled with leis and that purse I told you about.

As Size 5 Sandals passed the passenger door of her T-bird, the Yorkie stood up on the seat and barked. This of course drew Size 5 Sandal's attention.

It was wonderfully satisfying to watch Size 5 Sandal's face change so quickly. One minute she's a winner, the next she's a ... What was she?

Size 5 Sandals looked at the dog then she looked at me, probably because I was the only person close to the scene. I smiled politely and nodded hello. It was arguably the wrong thing to do, but I couldn't help it. It seemed so right.

Size 5 Sandals misunderstood my acknowledgement.

"Do you mind?" she said smartly. She said it nicely enough but with a hint of impatience, and I took her to mean 'will you please get your filthy animal off my nice clean car seat' or something to that effect.

It was a pleasant voice, softer and gentler than she'd used before, and it was clear she thought that I was supposed to know exactly what she was referring to. Of course I did know, but I wasn't going to let her know that I knew.

"Not at all," I said, not moving a muscle.

Size 5 Sandals stood looking at me for a moment, then looked back at the Yorkie as if *that* might make her request clearer. "Well?" she said, her voice an octave higher and noticeably vexed.

"Well, what?" I responded dully, and quite convincingly, as if I had no idea what she was referring to. At least I thought so. *'That'll teach you to ignore me!'* I thought triumphantly.

Size 5 Sandals took a deep breath and said with all the force her hundred-pound frame could muster. (I don't mean it literally. I'd have guessed her weight at one ten, maybe one fifteen. Like I said, she was slender and athletic looking, like someone who did a lot of aerobics and yoga.) "Would you please get your dog out of my car?"

I was having the most fun I'd had since last June when my boss fell off the podium in the middle of his annual safety lecture. I wanted to make it last.

"That's not my dog," I said coolly. Her look of confusion was classic.

"Well whose dog is it?" Size 5 Sandal's voice rose noticeably and suspiciously.

I shrugged. There was no way I was gonna tell. I'd take that secret to my grave.

I'm sure she didn't believe me, but she didn't have any place to go. She looked around for someone else to confront. Except for Stern-faced Police Officer and Boxy TSA Lady, we were pretty much alone. It was a slow night out at the curb; the bags from the last flight hadn't arrived yet.

Size 5 Sandals suddenly tired of the game. She looked at the Yorkie, she looked at me, she looked at her watch. She sighed and without another word she raced past me toward the arrival gate.

I smiled the satisfied smile of a chess master announcing checkmate and turned to watch her go, noting the lilt in her step was completely gone.

Okay so I wasn't nice. Still, I didn't feel guilty. She'd steam-rolled poor Boxy TSA Lady and that wasn't nice. She had it coming. At least in my book.

Suddenly I was alone again and certain now that Jack and Margie had forgotten me. Clearly something had gotten screwed up and since the free entertainment seemed to be over I decided I'd better find a hotel and a bar. A Dewar's sounded right. A double. Maybe a triple.

I stood, gathered Jillian's suitcase, and started for the line of taxis. But before I'd gone two steps the P.A. system delivered the words I'd been waiting to hear: "Jillian Thomas, please come to the Hawaiian ticket counter."

Help had finally arrived. I turned on my heels and headed for the ticket counter as fast as a five-year-old for the candy store.

When I arrived at the ticket counter, Size 5 Sandal's was there talking to one of the agents, a local man I thought with lots of tattoos and a long ponytail. Too bad for him I thought – although 'Tattooed Agent' seemed to be enjoying himself.

Size 5 Sandals noted my arrival and gave me a 'look.' I could have said a sneer, but it really wasn't. It was just a look.

What could I expect, really. I hadn't been very helpful about the dog and all.

I gave her a 'look' back, and Size 5 Sandals returned to her conversation with Tattooed Agent.

I bellied up to the counter where a studiously pretty, dark-haired local girl was on the phone. She motioned me to wait and I complied.

It wasn't a long wait and a moment later 'Agent Island Girl' hung up the phone and gave me the standard: "Aloha. May I help you," as though she really, truly meant it.

"Yes," I said. "I'm Joe Thomas. You paged me. Or rather, you paged my wife."

Well, you could have heard a pin drop.

A Kiss and a Growl

Just in case you haven't figured it out, let me spell it out for you. Size 5 Sandals was Margie, of Jack and Margie, and it took only a second for her to adjust to the reality that the rude man at the curb, the man who refused to give her any information about the strange dog in her car, was her best friend's husband.

I anticipated a cool reception, and after the way I'd behaved, I deserved it. But Margie apparently was not one to hold a grudge, so following a brief, if slightly uncomfortable, conversation in which I told her what had happened to Jillian and she told me a similar tale about Jack — he too had been called to L.A. "probably for the same stupid commercial" — Margie threw a beautiful and pungent lei about my neck.

I expected I was in line for the ritual peck on the cheek, but to my surprise Margie threw her arms around me, pulled herself up, and gave me a smack right on the kisser!

That's right! It was a real smooch! Right on the lips.

Now this was definitely unfamiliar territory for me, and I didn't know what to do, especially with my arms which were just hanging there, but since she didn't let up right away I finally folded them around her and gave her a nice hug. The kiss might have gone on even longer but the wind came up suddenly and Margie had to chase her hat, which was being tossed along by the breeze toward the street.

While Margie chased her hat, I pondered the following: *What kind of woman kisses a stranger hello like that?* I licked my lips self-consciously. Strawberry? Cherry? It was hard to place. She hadn't smelled of liquor. I was understandably baffled.

Margie returned, hat held firmly in place again atop her blonde curls, and she studied me a moment with her sapphire blue eyes and said enthusiastically: "Welcome to paradise, Joe."

I couldn't think of a single thing to say so I just cleared my throat. Which Margie accepted as a 'Thank you,' and we were off.

"Come on," Margie ordered. "I'm parked..." she stopped and laughed self-consciously. It was a very winning laugh that was half giggle and half chortle, if you get my drift. "Of course you know where I'm parked," she laughed again and waved me along.

Margie was ten steps ahead of me and out of earshot before I realized we were in motion. I picked up Jillian's bag and my carryon and hurried along.

"I'll bet you're beat. How many hours is it from Chicago?"

She really wasn't interested in an answer for although I answered her question she was miles ahead of me talking a mile a minute about how much fun 'we' were going to have and how glad she was 'we'd' finally made it and I remember wondering who the 'we' were because it was just her and me and 'we' were strangers after all even if she had just given me a smack to match that one that sailor gave the nurse in Times Square at the end of WWII. It was on the front page of the New York Times I think. I'm sure you've seen it.

We arrived at her car and Margie stopped and looked at the Yorkie who was waiting for us. He wagged his tail as Margie patted his head.

She turned to me. "You really didn't see who put this dog in my car?" Margie asked skeptically.

Of course from where I'd been sitting it was nearly impossible for me *not* to have seen, but I stuck with my previous answer.

"Nope," I lied. I felt guilty doing that, but I lied just the same. I was in too deep to tell the truth. And what was the point? "I was watching the little drama between you and the TSA lady and the cop," I said. At least that was partially true.

"I can't believe someone would just abandon the poor thing," Margie reached in the car and scratched the little guys chin. He rolled over for a tummy rub. Margie obliged.

"Isn't he adorable?" Margie cooed and picked him up and made funny faces at him the way people do with tiny infants. Why do people do that? Do infants think it's funny? He tried to lick her face, but she held him just out of reach.

"No tag, no nothing," Margie said. "He looks healthy. Why would someone just leave you?"

He didn't respond except to try again to lick her face.

I pulled my suitcase up to the trunk and waited for Margie. She eventually noticed.

"The trunk's a mess. Just put it in the back seat," she ordered.

I did as instructed and climbed into the passenger seat as Margie ran around and got behind the wheel. She started to pass the dog to me to hold while she drove.

Since I'm a dog person, I had no objection to this. However, it seemed the dog did. So it appeared that while this Yorkie liked blond, blue-eyed female strangers, he did not like brown-eyed, brunette male strangers and displayed his displeasure with small, pointy teeth and a throaty growl.

"Oh, my," Margie pulled him back onto her lap. "I don't think he likes you."

24

That was obvious, but I refrained from telling her so. What bothered me was that it presented something of a conundrum. Dogs always like me. Dogs and children and little old ladies were always drawn to me and that's my circle. It wasn't much of a circle and it hurt to think I'd lost the dogs. Even one of them.

"Don't you like dogs?" Margie asked with a penetrating stare. "They can sense..."

"I love dogs!" I countered and reached out to the Yorkie. "Come on boy, I won't hurt you." I got the same response as before and was beginning to see why someone might want to leave him behind. Margie examined me closely again with her baby blues which I noted had flecks of gold in them.

"It's him, not me," I said defensively. "Just put him in back"

Margie shook her head. "He can't ride in the back. Someone's got to hang on to him. Besides there's no room in the back with the suitcase." Margie paused a moment. "And I won't put him in the trunk!"

"I didn't suggest that." I said quickly, dismayed that she'd even think that I'd think of such a thing. "Look," I said. "I'm willing but he's not."

"Then let's try it this way," Margie said. "Just put your hands at your side."

I put my hands on the seat next to my thighs and Margie set the dog on my lap. He didn't snarl or growl. He didn't look happy, but he didn't try to bite.

"Maybe it's not a personal thing," I said. "Maybe he's a 'lady's' dog. I've run into a few of them. Hate men, love women." Actually now that I think of it, I've run into a few women like that as well. Hmmm.

"Just sit still," Margie ordered. "Let him get used to you."

I was willing to try that, and if he didn't get used to me, how much damage could he do? He was a Yorkie after all.

"Okay, Magoo. Take it easy," I said, trying to sooth him with a calming voice.

"Magoo?" Margie reached over and roughed Magoo's head. "That's a terrible name. No wonder he doesn't like you."

"Okay," I said. "What do you want to call him. He's your dog. Dogs need names."

"My dog?" Margie giggled. "He's not *my* dog. I'll take him to the vet tomorrow and see if he's got a chip in him and then we'll return him to his owner."

"And if his owner doesn't want him?" I asked. Based on my observation of the owner she would not take the little cur back under any circumstances.

"Don't be silly. Who wouldn't want a cutie like him?" Margie rubbed Magoo's head again and he panted excitedly. "I love dogs but Jack has allergies. Lots and lots of allergies," she said sadly and looked into the windshield pensively.

"Well until you give him another name, he's Magoo," I said.

It wasn't because the name reminded me of anything, but just because for some strange reason it had occurred to me from nowhere and it seemed to fit. It's not a flattering name I know and I guess Magoo knew that because he snarled at me whenever I shifted my weight or moved my hands. But he did tolerate me so long as I didn't try anything fishy, like scratching my nose.

Margie started the car and pulled away from the curb almost as quickly as she'd arrived; the G-forces pushed me back and Magoo teetered a moment and dug his claws into my pants till he found his center of gravity and relaxed. Her driving was a little unnerving, especially so since she only kept one hand on the wheel. She had to hold her hat on with the other. But I've ridden with Jillian many times while she talked on her cell phone, which might be worse. I don't think it's my karma to die in a car accident. A plane. That's how I'm going to die.

And so it was that I arrived in Hawaii and met Margie. And Magoo. I didn't know it at the time, but it was then that I began the most fascinating adventure of my life. Up to that point at least.

And Since I hadn't a clue why anyone would be interested in following me, I didn't notice the small, white, 4-door coupe dogging us from a reasonable distance. Nor could I have identified the guy behind the wheel. I was just happy to be on the ground and headed to my condo where I hoped to get a good night's sleep and maybe a drink along the way.

The Road to Kona

As we roared down the airport service road toward the highway, Margie began a Gatling gun commentary and thumbnail sketch of this, that and a whole lot of other things. I use the term Gatling gun because that's the way it seemed. She talked as fast as she drove and asked a lot of questions but never waited for an answer, and although I know she must have stopped for air, I couldn't detect any pauses. She was blessed with a great set of lungs. "The airport doesn't make the greatest first impression on visitors I'm afraid. It's built on an old lava flow and the scenery leaves loads to be desired don't you think? At least they stopped burning garbage mauka – that's Hawaiian for up the mountain, did you know that? Anyway, it used to absolutely stink when you drove between the airport and Kona at night. I'm sure people wondered where the paradise they'd read about was. But when we get to town you'll see. It's really very different. Of course all the vegetation is due to irrigation. We get very little rainfall in Kona. Hilo – on the other side of the island – gets loads. Or did you know that? Did you plan any activities? Jillian and I made a list and I put everything on a calendar so we won't miss a thing, but if you've got something else you want to do, just let me know. I was thinking that maybe we would stop at a watering hole on the way to your condo, but what with the dog and you looking so beat... You do look weary, Joe. How many hours is it from Chicago? Oh, I already asked you that didn't I? Anyway I think I'll just take you to your condo so you can relax and get settled. I picked up a few items for you and Jillian. They're in the trunk. It's just some liquor and some chips and something for breakfast. Jillian said you drink scotch so I got some scotch. I bought something called Glenlivet.

28

Is that what you like? I hope it's okay. I'm glad you're not a teetotaler. I'm certainly not. I'm not an alcoholic by any stretch, but I do like adult beverages. I must confess that sometimes I'm concerned that I'm drinking too much but I never get behind the wheel if I've had more than one drink. You don't drink and drive do you? It's so dangerous. If you *are* hungry we can stop. There's the typical fast food places here and we've got some really yummy sandwich shops. Are you hungry? I wonder if Magoo is hungry. That's such a silly name. What made you think of it? Are you hungry little guy? Oh look at that hitchhiker. I'd stop, but where would we put him? Well I hope he doesn't get hit. It's very dark out here. People really shouldn't hitchhike though You never know who's going to pick you up. I don't pick up hitchhikers when I'm alone of course. That's just asking for trouble. Jack doesn't like it when I stop for them, but I just tell him that there are people in this world that need a lift. I think you should help people when you can. Don't you agree? Well, here we are." Margie paused and took a breath.

As you can undoubtedly appreciate I was exhausted just listening to her so I was glad for the break and took a deep breath myself. 'Here' was in reference to a significant change in surroundings because the view had changed from bleak black rock with tufts of hardy grass to one that was lush and green and scented.

Margie took a right onto a broad well-lit boulevard lined with palms; an attractive sign set in the median read "Welcome to Kailua-Kona." I pondered briefly why communities put up such signs, since I can't imagine anyone arriving here without knowing where it was they were, but I decided it wasn't a question worth asking.

"Notice how much nicer it is now," Margie had reloaded and was off again. "You can smell the flowers and the soil and the ocean. I really don't like all the lava, but it can't be helped. I mean the whole island is just one big mountain of lava with a little dirt spread over it. It's a wonder anything grows at all. You can hardly dig a hole any deeper than a few inches. But it's enough for the grass and the bushes and the trees I guess. I'll drive along the waterfront so you can see the ocean and the town – at least the touristy parts."

We passed strip mall stores that lined either side of this boulevard, and Margie pointed out the ones she frequented and those she disliked and would never go to again. I paid close attention in case there was going to be a quiz later – which there wasn't.

This street wasn't very long and a few blocks down we hit water. The ocean actually. The Pacific Ocean to be exact.

"That's the King Kamehameha on the right," Margie said as she turned to avoid driving into the ocean. "It's been there forever. It's recently been renovated. Nice beach out front, especially for kids. And that's the 'Radiance of the Seas' I think," Margie nodded at a cruise ship in the bay, its lights dancing off the calm water.

"I can't keep the cruise ships names straight. But they dock every other day or so and fill the coffee shops and restaurants and snorkel cruises and other places with people. We're going to go snorkeling. Jillian said you would like that and I've got a friend who is a guide so you'll get to see things most people don't. We could scuba. I scuba. Have you ever scubaed? I really prefer it to snorkeling but..."

We were paralleling the ocean now and the Hawaii I'd anticipated was all around me. The narrow street we traveled was lined with colorful shops and signs and lights and inviting restaurants, an old church – "oldest on the islands" Margie told me – and across from it was a Royal Palace, which was "a great place to learn the hula" if I was interested in learning which I probably wasn't but maybe Jillian would want to because it was a lot of fun and the instructor was "this really wonderful old Hawaiian."

I tried to pay attention to Margie, but it was hard and like I said it took my breath away. So instead I people-watched, which is what I enjoy whenever I get someplace where there are people to watch and here there were a lot of people to watch. And I especially liked the view by the seawall and the huge banyan trees that leaned over the road and the palms and breadfruit and all the other flora that I couldn't name but which filled all the spaces between buildings.

I noticed that the breeze carried a mixture of scents including surf and earth and flowers and sand. A nice change from Chicago in winter.

"This is more like it," I said when Margie stopped to refill her lungs.

"Everyone says that," Margie agreed. "The airport ride is pretty grim. Even worse in the daylight. It's too bad you get it coming and going."

Someone called out Margie's name and Margie waved enthusiastically. "Hi Bradley," she called to a clean-cut surfer dude at one of those kiosks where they sell discounted adventure packets and flights on helicopters.

"That's Bradley," Margie said, adding nothing to my volume of knowledge since she'd already called out his name. I didn't feel obliged to know more.

We drove slowly now because of traffic, both pedestrian and vehicular, which was fine with me after the highway blitz. And we carefully maneuvered around a horse-drawn carriage and got stuck at a 3-way stop sign while a few hundred people crossed the street.

I felt a sudden longing for Jillian when a large man with a big white beard, white socks and sandals, and a cowboy hat walked across the street in front of us. Had Jillian been there, I would have pointed out that there were people in this world who dressed worse than me, but that only reminded me that I had nothing to wear since my bag was in limbo with all the other limbo bags somewhere in the Bermuda Triangle.

We finally got a break and made it through the stop sign and then a hundred yards on we passed a small bay so close to the road that you could almost reach out and touch the water and you could feel the spray as the waves crashed against the rocks.

I was thinking for the first time since my trip got weird that I was glad I'd come.

"There's Huggo's," Margie nodded toward a busy restaurant that sat right next to the water. "That's Jack's favorite place for dinner. The best stuff on the menu at Huggo's is the seafood I think. Jack is partial to steak and I suppose you are too. Most men like steak even though it's really horrible for you. They have a really yummy filet mignon that comes from cattle grown right here on the island on what used to be the largest privately held cattle ranch in the United States. That's up in Kohalo. Though I prefer a little town up there by the ranch called Havee. It's spelled H..a..w..i but pronounced Havee. There's a small artist community and .... That's Jake's." Margie pointed across the street to a busy open air restaurant. "At least that's what it was called last time I was there. I go there for coffee sometimes. Like everywhere else in the world the businesses come and go. I guess clients are fickle. One day you're up the next you're down. That's kind of true for everything don't you agree?"

I knew she wasn't really expecting answers, so I didn't respond.

"I suppose you're hungry, but I thought maybe we'd get you to your condo first. We could also pick up a sandwich or something..." Margie paused to dodge a surf board that suddenly blocked half the lane.

"Where was I?" She didn't have a clue. Nor did I.

"A sandwich would be fine," I responded. "What I'd really like is a drink though."

"Jillian said you were a scotch drinker. Like I said, there's a bottle in the trunk," Margie smiled. "I prefer rum or sometimes gin, depending on the time of day, or vodka. We'll go to the condo and then go up to this little shopping center and have a sandwich or something and you can pick up other stuff. There's a nice grocery store there and a few small restaurants."

I told her that sounded fine since I had no pressing engagements.

She gave me a curious look then smiled. "Of course you don't, you're on vacation!"

It was soon apparent that we'd passed through the thick of tiny Kona but Margie kept up her running commentary. We left the ocean for a bit and continued along Alii Drive, which Margie said was the name of the road we were on, and she pointed out what was new and old and fun and a few scary places and the beaches and condominium developments. The ocean returned on our right and we passed more building and homes – both small and large – and numerous condos, a few quiet beaches, shops, and stores and restaurants and even a few hotels.

She continued to point things out but my ears were tired and so I watched the scenery and smelled the air and pondered the future.

Finally we turned mauka, after passing Kahaluu Beach Park which Margie insisted was "absolutely the best" place to snorkel. It didn't impress me at all at the time.

At the top of the hill we took a right and Margie slowed. "This is the place," Margie said. "Look for 2023. That's your unit."

I could see a line of condominiums behind a tall hedge and spotted a stenciled '1013 - 3026' on the entry to a driveway a short way along. "There," I pointed and Magoo growled at my sudden movement.

Margie turned and we found a parking spot marked for unit 2023 and she came around and got Magoo so I could extract myself from the car and straighten my cramped legs. I took a quick look around. It looked like a very nice place.

"You're on the third floor," Margie said as she juggled Magoo in one hand and a shopping bag she pulled from the trunk in the other. "You're on the 16th hole and you should have a view of Keauhou Bay. That's all I know for sure. Sheila left a message."

She did not explain who Sheila was, nor did I ask since Margie was once again out front, walking fast, talking faster. We climbed stairs. Jillian's bag was heavy, so I was slow going up.

Margie stopped at the top of the stairs. "Oh, oh," she said uncertainly.

Margie's warning peaked my curiosity. "What's the matter?"

"There's a big rip in the screen door." Margie moaned. "Oh, well. We can get them to fix that."

Margie put Magoo and the shopping bag down and fumbled in her purse till she produced a scrap of paper. "Let's see..." She picked up the lock box and started pressing numbers. A second later it was open and Margie held up the key for me to see and smiled as if she'd just performed a magic trick that had stumped Houdini for eons.

I wasn't impressed, but I smiled at her to be polite.

The screen door creaked as Margie opened it but the key fit and a moment later the door was open and Margie reached in and turned on the lights.

"I don't believe it!," Margie cried, and before I could even get a peek inside, she slammed the door and picked up Magoo and the grocery bag and started cursing. "Just wait till I get hold of that bitch! 'The best one,' she said.' The best one, my ass. I can't believe it!" Margie took two steps forward. I was blocking her way.

"Go...go...go," Margie motioned me with her head to turn around and go back down.

"What's the problem?" I asked, as I did as directed, dragging Jillian's suitcase behind me.

"Bugs!" Margie said. "And there was a stain on the carpet. And the place smelled like garbage! Just wait till I get hold of Sheila. I'll ream her a new..." Margie paused and took a deep breath. "I'm sorry, Joe. I don't usually get so upset. I just...."

We'd reached the bottom of the stairs.

"You'll stay with me till I sort things out," Margie insisted. "I can't believe it. I just can't believe it."

We repacked the car and climbed back in, again with Magoo on my lap, and Margie took off like Mario Andretti. Three minutes later we arrived at the gate to 'Hawaiian Hills Estates,' which I knew was the gated community in which Margie and Jack had their place.

"Are you sure you're okay?, Margie looked me over. "I heard you shriek when I went through that yellow. I was..."

"No. No. I'm fine," I lied and tried not to shake. "I was just a little concerned that big yellow truck was going to hit us. But I guess three inches is as good as a mile."

Margie looked at me as if I'd farted, then sloughed it off. I made a mental note not to comment on her driving. Clearly it ticked her off.

There was no guard at the shack so Margie punched in her secret code. "It's 4789," she said. "The same as our address. We should come up with something different, but I can never remember which code goes with what. Do you have the same problem?"

Since there was a pause at this point it seemed that she did want an answer so I agreed that I did have the same problem and promised not to tell any terrorists or criminals what her code was.

Margie smiled politely at my attempt at being witty and we drove through the gate into a *very* upscale neighborhood.

As you probably know, the Hawaiian Islands are mountains in the sea, and because of that most of the real estate has a slope to it. If you've been to San Francisco or anyplace in the mountains, you know what I mean. The housing developments have a terraced look about them, and Margie's neighborhood was like that.

On my right, the bushes, trees, and other greenery obscured my view of the homes other than rooftops and an occasional glimpse into a side yard. To my left, however, where the houses stood overlooking the street, I got a good look at the architecture.

Most of the homes were quite large and almost all had swimming pools out front – one really nice place had a pool that overflowed its wall, the water cascading down to a second, smaller, pool. Margie told me that was called an "infinity pool" and since I didn't know anything about pools I didn't argue with her. But I did like it.

I could see into many of these homes, at least those that had lights on. I wasn't peeping, it was just that they were pretty wide open and you could see into the main living space. But because the houses were higher than the street, you could really only see the vaulted ceilings with big fans to circulate the air and the artwork on the walls. Still, it was a nice glimpse of what the upper class enjoyed in Kona.

I'd been in nice homes of course, but that was in Chicago where they were closed up tight for winter cold and summer heat. Here the homes were designed to take advantage of the moderate climate and the aim was clearly to bring the outside in. Most of the homes had the whole front wide open with big floor to ceiling louvered doors pushed back so you could feel the breeze and see the views. No screens, no nothing.

"Don't people worry about bugs?" I asked, amazed at how 'open' some of the homes were. In Chicago in the summer if you left the door open you had more bugs than you could handle.

"Not really," Margie confided. "At least not the flying, biting kind. I sleep with the windows and doors open all the time. Of course we have the Orkin man in on a regular basis. I wonder if that's good for me? I see these dead bugs and wonder what all those chemicals are doing. But then I have a drink and I don't worry about it."

This was Margie's second reference to her drinking and I made a mental note to observe her liquor consumption. Jillian had said nothing about alcohol addiction.

Margie took a quick right, and we dropped down a short, steep driveway sandwiched between a house on the left and a rock wall on the right. In the headlights, I caught a glimpse of thick, well manicured landscaping and a stucco house the color of creamed coffee.

"Here we are," Margie said, just in case I couldn't figure that out for myself.

She hit the garage door opener, which opened the garage and turned on several lights.

"I'll just leave it out," Margie said, turning off the engine. "I've hit Jack's car too many times trying to squeeze mine in. I only put it away when I'm sure it's going to rain."

There was a space in the garage large enough for a semi, but Jack's car was a Volvo so I understood that they might not want to dent it up too often.

Margie hopped out and came around for Magoo, who jumped into her arms as if she were a lost cousin. I got out, pulled Jillian's suitcase and my small carryon from the back and followed Margie toward the entrance to the Geanosa mansion.

"Welcome to Shangri-La," Margie said happily as she unlocked the big double doors and stepped aside for me to enter. A small plaque near the door read 'Shangri-La,' so I guess that was the name they'd given their place.

I stepped past her and into a small foyer, and Margie followed me in and closed the door behind, kicked off her sandals, and scooted past me. I noted a pile of shoes and sandals and a little sandal-shaped tile on the wall that read: 'Please remove your shoes!' so I kicked my loafers off next to Margie's sandals.

"Make yourself at home," Margie said, slipping Magoo down on a nearby ottoman where he stayed briefly and then jumped to the floor.

"Just drop the bags anywhere, I'll show you the guest room later." Margie rushed to the far end of the place,

38

leaving me and Magoo to sniff around. "I'll make drinks. How does a Long Island sound?"

"Sounds fine," I said, gawking at the size and luxury of the place. "As long as there's alcohol in it."

"Oh, there's plenty of that," Margie acknowledged as she pulled several bottles from the liquor cabinet.

Their place was amazing! I mean it was really fabulous!

I'm not much of a detail man, and I don't have that ability that women all have to describe things well, but I'll do my best to fill you in on what I could see.

First of all it was big. At least it seemed big compared to the Thomas condo. Part of this was because you could see all the way through the living area to the out of doors. The ceiling was at least fifteen feet high and held a dozen fans with big stylized leaves for paddles.

The foyer itself was spectacular: a small landing, where we'd left our shoes, then a little tiled bridge across a small pond with floating plants. Water shot from an artist's rendition of 'ole man Sol' on the wall and fell into the pond to add sound to the sight. A dozen or so brightly colored koi swam to the surface and sucked air, hoping I'd come with food. Which I hadn't.

I crossed the bridge and arrived at the upper level of the split-level living area which was maybe ten feet deep by twenty feet wide. A lower level – which was just down two broad steps – was probably twice as deep.

I'll say the decor was 'Asian' because the upholstered furniture, oriental rugs, vases, and wall hangings all had eastern prints and colors. But there was no single theme. I saw a carved turtle that looked 'Hawaiian,' and other items that looked like they could belong in almost any home anywhere.

Both levels of the great room had seating arrangements with sofas and easy chairs, lamps and low coffee tables that said 'hey, this is a nice place to sit and relax and read or talk to friends.'

The lower level was open at the far end, and I didn't see any doors folded off to the side. Margie told me later all their doors were pocket doors so they were hidden unless the house was closed up.

Beyond the living room, out-of-doors, was a small yard, an invitingly blue pool which was lit from beneath so that it reminded me of a giant daiquiri. There was also a table and chairs and – at what I assume was the edge of their property – a line of tall, thick bushes. And beyond that there was only night, except you could see the ocean in the distance, sparkling under the stars.

On the upper level where I stood taking this all in was an oval coffee table with a dark blue porcelain porpoise that appeared to be leaping through the glass top. It seemed a bit out of place with the motif of the room, but I was sure it was expensive.

I looked up and saw Margie on the move, waving an empty bottle. She must have seen me looking at the dolphin.

"It's a 'Whalen' piece," she explained, as if I should know what that meant. "Everyone's got something like it. Don't ask me why. Personally I think it's gaudy."

Margie took a hard right and disappeared through a dark doorway toward what I assumed was the pantry and probably the kitchen as well.

"We're out of vodka down there," she called. "But I'm sure there's more. Go out by the pool. We've got a million dollar view. Jack likes it, so I put up with it." The last comment I'm certain was in reference to the coffee table, not the million dollar view.

I followed Magoo down the steps toward the pool but took my time getting there. I wanted to take in the place in

40

case Jillian asked what it was like. I knew she'd yell if I just said: "It's nice." Anyway, I wanted to get a feel for it. I've discovered you can tell a lot about people by how they live.

I took comfort in the observation that the nose of that dolphin breaking the surface of the coffee table was sporting a woman's gold bracelet. There was also an open copy of *Barron's* on the same coffee table. I'd heard of Barron's but admit I've never read it. Was that Margie's or Jack's? Jack's I decided; Margie didn't look like a Barron's reader. I suppose that's sexist. Oh, well, that's what I thought.

I spotted an empty cereal bowl and a half-empty juice glass on a lamp table over in the corner with the remains of a Sunday *L.A. Times*. There was an empty wine glass on another table next to one of the big arm chairs and Magoo had settled next to a pair of women's tennis shoes and socks near the sofa. He looked quite happy.

I assumed the socks and cereal bowl were Margie's and that she was also the L.A. Times reader. Though again I have no idea why.

It's funny the assumptions you make and your reasons for making them, but it's downright eerie how often they are right.

All these items said one thing clearly to me: 'Yes, we live in a palace, but this a home. Relax. Enjoy yourself. Leave your socks anywhere.' Which was good because I'd been concerned that since Margie and Jack had money, they had everything in order and a place for everything. I've been in homes like that. So nice that you felt you were messing them up just by sitting in a chair.

Margie appeared suddenly at my side. "That's where we hide the telly." She swung a fresh bottle of vodka toward a large mahogany cabinet against the living room wall that

I'd just passed. Her bad attempt at a British accent came out of nowhere and she didn't try to explain it.

"Do you watch a lot of TV? she asked. "Jack watches sports. All the time sports. Golf, tennis, hockey, football, baseball... You don't do that do you?"

Before I could answer, Margie rolled on. "Why dooooo men do that? It's such a waste of time. You can read the score in the paper! I understand *playing* sports, but watching them hour after hour, day after day..." Margie was on her knees digging in the liquor cabinet for something. "But just watching them? What's with that?" Margie came up with a shot glass. "I'm rambling aren't I?"

"Not at all," I said graciously. Of course she had been. "Your place is incredible. Jillian will be green with envy."

"We've been lucky, Jack and I." Margie stood and started pouring vodka into the shot glass. "I try to appreciate that every day. It's too easy to take things for granted. Don't you think?"

I agreed and was glad she felt that way. Too many people that have a lot think they deserve it. It's just luck most of the time as far as I'm concerned, but of course I didn't say any of that out loud.

Margie finished filling a tall pitcher with a splash of vodka and stood back to look at it as though she were trying to decide if she was really done.

"You're still inside?" she said with a hint of surprise. "Shoo! Go grab a chair out by the pool and get comfortable. I think there are some pupus in the fridge."

"Pupus?" I asked. That didn't sound like something I wanted to eat.

"Don't you know what they are?" Margie laughed and shook her head till her curls bounced. "Hors d'oeuvres. Pupu is the Hawaiian name. It sounds awful, but I think it's fun. I thought everyone called them that now."

Margie raced off for the kitchen and I stepped outside. It really wasn't much of a transition, except the ceiling was a *lot* higher and there were no fans.

I walked to the far side of the pool where a table and six chairs sat in the shadow between the pool and the hedge. What a view!

Margie reappeared, dropped the pitcher of drinks and glasses and a tray of pupus on the table, and then sidled up next to me. I got a whiff of the perfume she was wearing, at least I think it was perfume. I was still wearing my lei so it could have been me.

"So what do you think?" Margie asked. I could tell she was very proud of the view and she had every reason to be.

"It's fantastic." I said truthfully.

There was a quarter moon over my shoulder so I could see some details and the moonlight added to the grandeur.

Just beyond the hedge was a golf course fairway. The fourth fairway, Margie told me later, of the Kona Country Club. There were trees of various sizes and shapes along the edges of the fairway all in shadow. Some were tall and mushroom shaped, others short and fanlike, and still others tall poplar shaped. The fairway itself was dotted with dark, rocky outcroppings, and a couple of sand traps surrounded the green. It looked like a tough hole.

A solid line of trees bordered a road on the other side of the fairway and then another line of trees and then a green space up to the Kona Country Club clubhouse, gaily lit and elegant looking in the night. Still further on were the rooftops of a condo complex that hugged other fairways. These were decorated with palms here and there between the houses and condos for a tropical effect. Beyond that were more golf course fairways and finally the ocean. I'm not sure if I could really hear it or just thought

I could hear it 'cause I knew it was there, but I was pretty sure I could hear the surf.

Margie pointed out a large building off to the left near the ocean that was eerily dark.

"That's the Kona Key," she said. "They just closed it and I'm sad because they used to have a Polynesian show and you could hear the drums and music and singing. I hope someone buys it and renovates it soon. I don't want to watch it fall into disrepair."

"That would be pretty expensive real estate to leave undeveloped," I said, as if I knew what I was talking about.

"Yes it would, but you don't know Kona. Things around here don't always make a lot of sense. There are just too many different sides on too many issues," Margie sounded discouraged.

It seemed likely there was something tangible behind that tone, but I was either too tired or too stupid to pick up on it then, and besides, Margie was already on to another topic.

"There's Kona up the shore. You can just see the lights. And the cruise ship. Looks like it's leaving."

I looked and saw the lights of Kona and its small harbor. A cruise ship was indeed steaming away in the night.

"What's the next port of call after this?" I asked.

"I don't really know," Margie said. "I don't pay much attention to them. I've never been on a cruise and I don't think I'd like to go on one. I think if I was on a boat I'd always want to be on shore." Margie turned away and I heard her pouring drinks. I watched the view.

"Here you go," Margie returned beside me and pushed a tall skinny glass at me. It looked innocent enough, but it was a big glass.

"Go ahead," Margie encouraged.

"What's in it?" I asked.

"Just taste it!" Margie said.

I took a sip. Smooth. A little sweet, but not too sweet. I nodded my approval. It tasted pretty tame and I said so. "This thing have any booze in it?" I held it up as if I'd be able to tell.

"Yes it does and you'd better be careful, Joe," Margie cautioned. "They have a way of sneaking up on you. Long Islands are not what they seem to be."

Margie clinked her glass with mine. "To Kona!" she said.

"To Kona," I echoed and we both took a drink.

Margie put her glass on the table. "Try the pupus," Margie ordered and then turned and headed indoors. "I'm going to put on something more comfortable. Try the hammock. It's wonderful. But be careful. I can hardly get out of that thing sometimes."

After I picked up a cracker with cheese from the pupu platter and watched Margie disappear inside, I spotted the hammock she'd warned me about. It was a huge one, printed like a flag in red, white and blue stripes. I moved tentatively toward it. Tentative not because I was afraid of hammocks. Tentative because I was wondering what Margie was going to appear in that was 'more comfortable'? Should I run away? What could be more comfortable than what she had on? I, of course, had nothing to put on. Damn airlines!

I know a lot of men – maybe even most men – might have read something into what Margie had said, but it was clear to me from everything she'd said up to this point that she was happily married. She talked about Jack in positive terms, even though she did admit he was a workaholic. And as for me, I was happily married as well. At least I wanted to be. Which was the whole point of the vacation.

45

Added to the top of those two things, the truth of it was that Margie was out of my league. It's good to know your limits. I know mine. So I assumed she was just going to get her bathrobe on or something equally harmless.

I ambled over to the hammock at last. I like hammocks, and they seem to like me. I looked for a place to set down my glass while I got in, but there wasn't one so I raised my glass, said 'cheers' to my wayward wife, and finished my drink in two large gulps. Then I set the glass on the ground and eased myself into the big boy.

Margie wasn't kidding. It swallowed me up completely. From 'inside' the hammock all I could see were the sides of the hammock, the stars above, and the outline of two palm fronds against the night sky.

It was very cozy and I closed my eyes to rest for just a second; I felt suddenly warm and fuzzy – the effects of the Long Island – and I said quietly into the night: "Jillian, you should be here. This is really nice."

Au Naturale

The next thing I remember, I was squinting against the sunlight, and it took me a long moment to remember where the hell I was.

Had I slept outside all night in this thing? Evidently I had because when I looked up, I saw the same view as the night before, except the palm fronds were now bright green and framed against a turquoise sky with cotton ball clouds.

I rolled my tongue around my mouth and smacked my lips. Toothpaste and mouthwash were in order I decided, and I started to extract myself from the hammock. It was then that I heard the sound of someone swimming.

Slowly, and with some difficulty, I managed to roll out of the hammock to a sitting position. I sat there rubbing the sleep from my eyes with both hands, then looked over at the pool and saw Margie swimming laps. I like to swim and the thought occurred to me that I should go and shower and put on my swimsuit and join her. But then I remembered that my luggage was lost, and so was my wife, and I was lucky I still had my wallet. I growled and glanced again at Margie cutting bladelike through the water.

And it was then that I noticed something wasn't quite right. I felt my brain twirling, trying to register what it was that was odd; but since I was still half-asleep and was only hitting on two cylinders – my brain is not a V8 but it does have four cylinders when it's working hard.

I rubbed my eyes again and the world got clearer. The swimming sound stopped suddenly and I looked toward the pool again. *Focus... focus.*

"Good morning sleepy head," Margie sang with almost painful cheerfulness.

I'm not a morning person. At least not after I've slept in my clothes. And I do need my coffee.

I was about to respond with something clever and snotty, like 'so's your old man,' when the last cobweb cleared and those two other cylinders kicked in and Margie's image came into sharp focus.

It couldn't be!

But it was.

Margie at the far end of the pool with one arm up on the lip of pool to hold herself there and she was smiling just as casual and natural as could be except for one teensy weensy thing: she was completely naked!

What the $#&@? My brain nearly exploded.

I bowed my head quickly and pretended to rub my eyes again as my dumb ass brain recalled for me: 'She did say she was going to put on something more comfortable.'

"How do you feel," Margie called in that same cheery voice.

"Fine. Just fine," I squeaked out, wondering what I was supposed to do.

"I'm afraid there's bad news on the luggage," Margie said.

I was pretending to examine my toes and was grateful to have something else to think about other than that my wife's best friend being there in the pool without a stitch of clothing on. It was a lot to think about. I focused on a crack in the lanai two feet in front of me.

"Lost?" I could have guessed that last night.

"Worse," Margie said.

I tried to think what could possibly be worse.

"Worse?" I squeaked out still watching the crack intently.

"Blue," Margie said cryptically.

Okay, I had it figured out. This was one of those really, really realistic dreams you have when you drink too much and wake up in a strange place. You know them. They seem genuine but can't possibly be real. Obviously I was still asleep. My subconscious was diddling away and I'd wake up in Chicago with Jillian and...

But I knew that wasn't true. I *was* awake. I don't dream in color, and Hawaii in the daylight is a Technicolor production.

"They brought your bag by taxi, but I sent it back. It was covered with blue." Margie's additional information did nothing for me.

I couldn't think what was next so I started with: "I don't..."

"That blue stuff they use in toilets?" Margie said.

I was still confused. "Toilets?"

"I'm afraid so," Margie said. "It must have leaked all over your suitcase. Anyway, the guest room is straight back and to the right if you want to freshen up. I'd show you but I have twenty laps to go... unless you want me to..."

From the corner of my eye I saw that Margie had turned and was about to push herself out of the pool. I jumped from the hammock and bolted for the house. "That's not necessary, Margie. Finish your swim. I can find the way."

"I'll get some of Jack's things for you when I'm done," Margie called. You're about the same size. Towels are next to the shower."

I hurried unsteadily through the living room shaking my head and muttering in my most disapproving manner: "Naked! Naked as a jay bird!"

I spotted Magoo lying on the best chair in the living room. He looked up and growled at me. I growled back. "Sure, take her side," I snapped.

When I found the guest room I was still shaking my head in disbelief, but with a few walls between me and the crazy lady in the pool, I started to calm down.

The guest room was exceptional. It was larger than any hotel accommodation: king size bed, an armchair, a bookshelf. I noticed that most of the books had self-help titles by Dyer, Dr. Phil, and that Indian guy. I wondered briefly if there were any dealing with flirtatious blondes. Probably not.

I headed straightaway through the bedroom for the guest bath. It too was palatial. There were the customary double sinks, a big tub and a shower stall with seven, count them, seven shower heads including a huge 'rain shower' head. The stall itself was designed for two. Actually I think it was big enough for four if you were all good friends. I don't have any friends that are that friendly.

I started the shower, stripped to my birthday best, and stepped into luxury. Soap and shampoo provided.

The warm water perked me up and had me whistling in no time. My brain had all but forgotten Margie, nude in the pool until...

"Want me to get your back?"

Guess who? I recognized the voice instantly, but my exact reaction to Margie's appearance was swift and silly. I believe my exact verbal response was "Ack!" And I remember my exact physical response was to cross my legs and cover my man parts with my hands. Like I said: swift and silly and pretty much useless.

I looked in the direction of the voice. There was Margie. She was stark naked and sipping a cup of coffee!

"Sorry," Margie apologized. "I didn't mean to startle you." It was an admission of guilt I guess, but not for intruding on my shower but rather for startling me. She didn't bother to look away as I stood there uncomfortably. In fact she stared at me intently for several seconds with one of those bemused looks that people get on their face when they're no longer actually looking at something but have turned their focus inward. And it was at this point that she asked aloud to me and the universe in general: "Why on earth do you suppose men have nipples?"

Once again, she didn't appear to expect an answer, and in any event I was still speechless and befuddled and wondering what the heck was going on.

Then, without another word Margie pivoted sharply and left the bathroom. I waited a moment, anticipating her return, but finally breathed a sigh of relief and dropped my 'cover-the-family-jewels' stance as I heard her calling from the bedroom.

"I put some shorts and shirts on the bed and I found some underwear still in the package. There are some new swim trunks, too. Jack is such a clothes horse! Wear what you want. People walk around Kona in nothing but swimwear day and night." There was a pause, then she added: "I better go dry my hair and put on makeup. I must look a fright."

I took the opportunity of Margie's departure to grab a towel and wrap it around me and left the shower. I cocked my head till I heard footsteps then thanked the Lord above. And I was just starting to relax when I heard a small sharp scream and a loud thud. Then silence. The clock ticked. Something was wrong.

"Are you okay?" I called as I ran into the guest room where I found Margie sitting on the tile floor rubbing an ankle. She looked up at me.

51

"I slipped." Margie said, stating the obvious.

She tried to stand. It was a no-go.

"Oh, Joe, I don't think I can put any weight on it. Can you carry me?"

'Carry you?' my brain shrieked. *'You're naked! And I'm naked under this silly towel. Of course I can't carry you!'*

I cast a panicked glance around the room searching urgently for some way – something – to carry her with without actually picking her up. A forklift would work. Unfortunately, few bedrooms come equipped with forklifts.

It didn't take long for me to realize that I had no other choice than to do as she asked. So with great reluctance and a huge helping of apprehension, I went over and bent down and picked Margie up.

She was incredibly light and I swear I did my best not to look at her nearly perfect champagne glass breasts which were right there, just inches from my face. I started for the living room and tried to picture my mother. Why my mother? Think about it. I was carrying a gorgeous naked woman in my arms. If I hadn't tried to picture my mother, things might have gotten *very* uncomfortable.

"Just put me out by the pool," Margie directed, her arms tight around my neck and her head resting on my shoulder.

How much can one man endure? I tried to picture my grandmother.

"You should lie down," I said as I started across the living room toward the master bedroom. "I'll call a doctor."

"Don't be silly, Joe. I'll be fine in a minute, just put me out in the sun."

I stopped. "Are you sure?"

"Yes, yes. I'm sure," Margie urged.

I corrected course and started for the pool, eager to deposit her somewhere, anywhere and quickly so that I could get back to my room and find some clothes.

Of course this was not in the cards, for just as I started toward the pool my towel slipped off!

"Good grief,' I cried, stumbling slightly over it.

"What's wrong?" Margie asked, unaware of what had transpired. "Am I too heavy?"

"No, you're... I just..." I certainly didn't want to tell her what had happened. It wasn't that I was concerned she would see my manhood. She'd already done that. It just seemed totally weird that I was nude and she was nude and that neither one of us knew the other one at all.

But that quickly became the least of the trouble because as soon as I stepped outside, I had a new, more demanding predicament to deal with.

There by the pool, interrupted from his task of sweeping leaves from the surface with a large net, was a well-tanned, well-muscled, blonde young man with a huge grin on his face.

I stopped dead. Margie hadn't seen him yet.

"What's the matt..." she started, then noticed 'Pool Boy' and after a brief pause gave him a grin and a little wave.

"Aloha, Nicky," she said calmly and adjusted herself so as to hide some things from view. Then with just the slightest hint of embarrassment in her voice she added: "Joe, this is Nicky. He takes care of the pool. Nicky, this is Joe."

Nicky, still showing all of his perfectly orthodonticized teeth, nodded at me. I nodded back, with less than a full smile on my lips. I thought it was inappropriate that he kept smiling like that, but I suppose...

Margie then said the first logical thing she'd said all day. "Maybe you should take me to the bedroom," she whispered softly.

I responded by turning quickly around and heading toward Margie's bedroom; Margie waved goodbye to Nicky over my shoulder.

Don't Leave Me Here

Several minutes later from the phone in the guest room wearing someone else's underwear, shorts, and shirt, I related the events since my arrival to Jillian who I pictured in L.A. surrounded by 'normal' people, if there are normal people in L.A.

I wasn't getting the support I expected.

"She was completely naked!" I reiterated for the umpteenth time.

Jillian's voice came back calm and cool. "She's always been a free spirit."

"Doesn't it bother you that she's walking around in front of me completely naked?" Surely this wasn't in the vacation brochure.

"Did she make a pass at you?" Jillian asked.

"Of course not," I admitted. "That's not the point. The point is..."

"So what are you complaining about? She's got a great body."

Well that was true, but Jillian was missing the point. She appeared to have a total lack of concern or interest in my dilemma, which convinced me she wanted me to hang up so she could get on with her work. My mouth worked a moment, but nothing came out.

"Well? Jillian repeated.

Finally, I managed to say calmly: "I'm not complaining, Jillian. It's just... People shouldn't walk around naked when they have house guests. You've got to say something to her."

Jillian laughed. It wasn't a fun laugh; it was that laugh she uses when she thinks I'm stupid.

"What would I say?" Jillian chided. "Margie please don't walk around naked in front of my stodgy insecure husband?" She paused. "If it bothers you, Joe, say something. If you knew Margie, you'd realize it means nothing. That's just the way she is. She's very self-confident about her body." Another pause. "I'll bet she didn't even realize she was naked."

This was the wrong thing to say and it got me going. "She didn't realize she was naked?" My voice cracked on the last syllable. Surely Jillian had stretched the realm of possibility. "Are you serious? How could she not know she wasn't wearing clothes?"

Margie yelled from the living room: "Hey, in there. I've got lunch. By the pool."

Jillian heard her. "Go have lunch, Joe. Let it go and have lunch."

"So you're not going to say anything?" I was angry and astonished.

"No, I'm not," Jillian said flatly and then said goodbye and hung up. I stood for a moment with the receiver in my hand. She hadn't even told me when she was going to be finished in L.A.

I hung up the phone and slunk hopelessly toward the living room, hoping that Margie would at least dress for lunch. And as it turned out, Margie did dress for lunch. At least if you consider an infinitesimally small lemon yellow bikini top and a brightly colored wraparound dressed. It was progress, I suppose.

"What did Jillian have to say?" Margie asked.

I pulled out a chair and sat down across the table from her. I felt that keeping a table between us was a good plan.

The table was set with brightly colored plates and placemats in the shape of palm leaves. Lunch itself was fresh fruit, small sandwiches – turkey – ice tea – real ice tea, not the Long Island kind – and taro chips. My kind'a food. Margie was having a salad.

I reached for a sandwich. "Not much," I said. That at least was certainly true.

"Everything going okay in L.A.?" Margie passed the bowl of chips. I took a handful.

"Just fine," I lied, helping myself to a couple of slices of papaya. I had no idea how things were going in L.A.

"Those trunks look good on you," Margie said, referring to the pair I'd borrowed from Jack. They fit okay, but I didn't especially like them, they had this big floral print. I'm conservative in my dress. My swimsuits are navy and black.

"I called the airlines about your luggage; they're going to issue a check. I hope it covers whatever they wrecked."

"Mostly old clothes," I said, "Not a big loss. I might even make a profit. Still, I'd like to have my own stuff. Not that I don't appreciate..."

"Oh, I understand," Margie said, batting the air. "Men are sooooooo territorial. When I told Jack I loaned you his swimsuit, he said: 'tell him to keep it.' Why are men like that?"

It was a rhetorical question with no answer required, so I stuffed my face quietly.

"Jillian and I used to share everything, " Margie said.

I thought that wouldn't be likely anymore since Jillian was a few sizes larger. Had Jillian grown that much? Had Margie shrunk? I chalked it up to the difference in styles back then when things were baggy and loose.

Margie said her ankle was fine and she was going to take Magoo to the vet and see if he had one of those 'chips' and to check him out and she'd drop me off in Kona and I could do some shopping. She'd called Sheila and chewed her out and Sheila promised to find an acceptable condo in short order. By the end of the day at the latest.

A half hour later we were in the car, retracing our trip of the previous night in the same positions, except this time Margie wasn't wearing a big floppy hat so she could drive with both hands.

Margie dropped me off in 'downtown' Kona and promised to pick me up in an hour. I did my shopping: socks, underwear, a new pair of sandals, tennis shoes, a navy swimsuit, a couple of t-shirts, one of those Hawaiian print shirts, a pair of khaki shorts and a tan golf shirt with an alligator over the left breast. I know that doesn't sound like much, but I figured it would be enough to last till Jillian came back. It's not that I can't pick out my own clothes, it's just that she has a better eye than me. At least that's what she says.

I frittered away the remaining half hour – men are far more efficient at shopping than women – strolling through Kona and having an iced coffee on the seawall. I arrived back at the designated pickup spot and thirty-seven minutes later Margie pulled up. She didn't explain her tardiness but she *was* agitated by her experience at the vets.

Yes Magoo did have a chip in his neck and his real name was – are you ready? – 'Lord Becket.' I kid you not. Well Lord Becket's owner, a Mrs. Stephen Grumage of L.A., was contacted by Margie who found her to be a nasty woman who said she would under no circumstances accept delivery of the 'Lord' if Margie managed to get him on a plane and suggested that Margie should take him down to the volcano and drop him in, at which point Margie said she called the woman something which Margie would not repeat for me and got hung up on. So Margie called the woman back just so she could hang up on her.

"Some people," concluded Margie, "should be barred from owning pets."

"So, what now? I asked. "About Magoo, I mean?"

58

"I'm keeping him," Margie said with decisiveness and cooed at him and gave the little cur a scratch under his chin. I dropped my bags in the back seat.

"What about Jack's allergies?" I asked.

"Jack will have to deal with them," Margie said bluntly and parked Magoo on my lap. And with that we took off for home.

It was after two when we got back so I took a nap – spending money always tires me out – and when I awoke I felt much better. I had my own clothes, my own room, and I'd decided I was going to have a talk with Margie about appropriate and inappropriate behavior. So I made my way to the living room, but I didn't spot Margie. I did find Magoo there, chewing on a slipper which he probably wasn't supposed to have, but Margie wasn't around so rather than risk a dog bite I just left him to it. I headed for the back door to see if she was out there. Nope. I went back in and then heard water running. More specifically, the sound of a shower.

I followed the noise, which led me to Margie's bedroom. I paused just outside the door. *Should I?*

It was my thinking at that point that there was no better way to impress upon Margie the need for privacy than an object lesson. I certainly had a right to intrude on her shower. After all, she'd intruded on mine. Still I hesitated.

'Go ahead,' that little voice in my head nagged. 'She's got it coming. Besides, she'd got nice hooters.'

'It's not about nice hooters,' I scolded. 'It's the principle of the thing.'

'Sure it is.' the little voice mocked me.

Despite what the little voice said about hooters I knew they weren't what drove me through Margie's bedroom and into the master bath, but it's hard to remember that in retrospect.

I hesitated just before I got to the bathroom doorway. On the far side of the room was a big full-length mirror, steamed over so you couldn't see clearly, but I could see a figure moving about in the shower stall and I heard humming. I think it was Brahms's, but I'm not much on classical music, so it's just a guess. I paused, screwed up my nerve, stepped into the bathroom, pivoted toward the shower stall and said casually: "Want me to get your ba....?" The 'ck' lodging just at my larnyx.

'Why is that?' you ask. Simple. It wasn't Margie in the shower. It was a tall, leggy brunette with hooters the size of casabas shampooing a mountain of thick dark hair!

She must have heard me because she paused in her task, squinted toward me, and teased provocatively in a voice that dripped with sexuality. "Hey, Pete, why don't you join me." Then she resumed shampooing.

Since I wasn't Pete, and she wasn't Margie and she obviously had soap in her eyes and thought I was someone else, I took the opportunity to make a run for it.

But as I turned around I found my way obstructed by a fellow with glasses who was a bit taller than me and had a receding hairline, and a very prominent jaw. He had a pleasant looking face but at the moment he wasn't looking at me pleasantly. My brain told me that this was Pete and I opened my mouth to try to explain, but...

I recall seeing a fist the size of a dinner plate appear suddenly in front of me and then everything went black.

Meet the Neighbors

The ceiling fan swirled high above as I opened my eyes. Margie was leaning over me, looking anxious. Behind her were the couple I'd met earlier in the bathroom: the busty brunette from the shower, who now was sporting a pair of glasses that might have been fashioned from pop bottle bottoms – which explained her confusion about who she was sharing the bathroom with – and the guy who I assumed was Pete and who *had* been invited into the shower and was the guy who had hit me and was responsible for the sharp pain emanating from my nose.

Thankfully they both looked concerned and not angry.

"Sorry," Pete muttered "Margie didn't mention houseguests so I thought you were a prowler or something."

I tried to sit up; Margie pushed me down.

"Stay put. You've got a nose bleed. Here, see if this helps." Margie placed a large ice bag over my face that obscured my view. It felt heavenly.

"Amanda doesn't think it's broken," Margie said.

I assumed Amanda was the brunette and even though I didn't know if she had any medical qualifications I was encouraged.

Obviously I owed everyone an explanation and an apology and so I did my best to clarify why I'd done what I had and apologized for how it turned out.

Pete and Amanda were good sports about it and although Margie taunted me with "see what happens when you try to teach people a lesson," we all managed to share a laugh.

Margie explained that Pete and Amanda were neighbors and Amanda was her best friend and that I'd probably be seeing a lot of them during my visit, adding: "Of course you've already seen all there is to see of Amanda," which drew another round of laughter.

We chatted a bit and I found out that Pete and Amanda, like most residents of Hawaii, were transplants – Montana – had no children or pets, liked to spend time in Vegas, and collected classic cars. Pete owned his own helicopter and he invited me for a ride whenever I was up to it. I thanked him and didn't mention that I'd never go up in his helicopter because I was scared shitless of large commercial planes and helicopters were just rocks that stayed aloft by God only knows how.

I found out that Amanda and Margie had been friends 'forever' which sounded unrealistic unless they had known each other in many previous lives.

I was silently irked by the fact that during all this Pete was holding Magoo and stroking him gently and the damn dog seemed to enjoy it. *What was it with that dog?*

Amanda and Pete excused themselves abruptly after Pete announced he'd spotted the plumber's truck go by.

"The reason I was in Margie's shower," Amanda explained, "was because Pete *fixed* our hot water heater this morning."

Margie informed me after they'd left that Pete was always trying to fix things and when he did try you could be certain that professional help would eventually be needed.

"He's got a good heart," Margie concluded, "but bad hands."

I spent an hour lying on the couch with the ice bag on my face, which Margie was kind enough to keep refilled. No one had mothered me so closely since I was ten. It was kind of nice.

Eventually, I got tired of being lazy and made my way to the guest room where I washed the dried blood off my face and changed my t-shirt. I was just thinking that I could use a snack when I heard tapping on the bedroom door.

"Sheila phoned," Margie called softly. "She's got another condo for you. I'll take you down as soon as you're ready."

I closed my eyes and put my hands together to thank the man upstairs – assuming he is a man. But let's not get into that.

***

An hour later I was leaning on the railing at my very own condo watching the surf crash on the rocks only feet away. Margie was next to me.

"You like?" she asked cautiously.

"Are you kidding? It's wonderful. Can I afford it?"

"Same price as the other one. Sheila's way of making amends." Margie turned and headed indoors. "I'll put the groceries away for you. Just get comfy with your new digs."

We had stopped at the grocery store on the way down. Actually grocery shopping may be a stretch since most of the cart was filled with liquor, snacks, and stuff that Margie insisted would kill me before I was fifty.

I know it sounds like she's a nag about eating, but it doesn't really come off that way. She just has strong opinions on the issue and makes her viewpoint known. I'm just glad she isn't a teetotaler.

Anyway, I did what she said and threw myself into a big director's chair and put my feet up on a small trunk. Magoo curled up in the sun.

"Wait till I tell Jillian," I called loud enough for Margie to hear. "She better get her ass here now."

Then I remembered something that had occurred to me earlier but which I hadn't taken any action on.

"I still don't have a car. You'll have to drive me out to the airport so I can rent one."

Margie appeared on the lanai and handed me a scotch with ice and a water chaser. "I wasn't sure how you like your scotch. This is how Jack takes it."

I thanked her and poured a bit of water into the scotch. "Where's yours?" I asked. Margie disappeared and returned with a tall glass filled with clear liquid.

"Gin and tonic," she responded to my unasked question as to the nature of the liquid. She raised her glass to mine. We clinked and drank.

"A car..." Margie paused and pondered. "I think that as long as Jack is away you might as well use his. It's dumb to rent one..."

"I don't know..." I started.

"Don't be silly," Margie reiterated. You can ride home with me and drive Jack's car back. It's not like wearing his underwear is it?"

I conceded it wasn't, and admitted to driving lots of people's cars.

"Then that's settled," Margie said. "Though I'm sure you'll have to fill the tank. Jack never puts gas in anything. I can't tell you how many times he's run out of gas and I've had to rescue him."

Margie jumped up suddenly and rushed to the railing, which sent Magoo into a yipping frenzy. "Look, a whale!" She pointed out to sea.

I rushed over and followed her finger and saw the big curve of the whale's back as it swam through the water. It seemed incredibly close to shore.

"Do they come in this close often?" I asked.

"All the time," Margie said. "This is one of the best places I know to watch them. The land drops away very quickly so out where that whale is it's a long way to the bottom."

The whale showed its tail, dove and disappeared. Margie turned. "Well, we should probably go back to my place so you can get the car before you drink too much and can't drive."

"Okay," I agreed. "But you've got to let me buy you dinner someplace nice to repay you for all you've done."

"You mean for the embarrassment and the nosebleed?" Margie winked at me.

"At the very least," I laughed. Besides, I have to celebrate this great condo and I hate to celebrate or eat alone."

Margie agreed to go to dinner and she also agreed that she too hated to eat alone so we made a pact right then and there that until at least one of our wayward spouses reappeared we had standing invitations with one another for lunch and dinner at least. I was reluctant to agree to breakfast since I'd just laid in some thick bacon, eggs, and sausage at my place and I knew Margie wasn't going to have that at her house. And then too, Margie swims nude in the morning before breakfast. Not that that's a bad thing, just... Oh, never mind.

***

Going out to dinner might have been a mistake. Then again, it might have been my salvation. Why? Well, we didn't know it at the time but while we were making dinner plans, there were a couple of people up at Margie's house talking about me. And they weren't real happy with one another. In fact, one of them was *really* unhappy and he had a gun. But we didn't know any of that so we went to dinner. Ignorance *is* bliss, isn't it.

Dinner Out

"I was thinking we should go to Huggo's," Margie said after I locked the door to my condo and we headed toward the car, Magoo tucked under her arm.

I remembered Margie's endorsement from the night before. "Sounds great. Am I dressed okay?" I had no idea what the dress code in Kona was and all I was wearing was the new Hawaiian print shirt a pair of khaki shorts and some sandals. Margie herself was very casual in a sleeveless, yellow scoop-necked top and navy shorts with lots of pockets and gold buttons and clasps. She was wearing flip flops.

"This is Kona," Margie chuckled. "You're dressed fine. I've got a sweater in the car. I know you think that's silly but after you live on the island a while, you get chilled. Especially at night."

Margie stopped walking and squinted at me. "You're nose looks fine."

I wiggled it like a bunny. "Feels okay, too."

Margie pulled Magoo up to her face. "Are you hungry for some din din?"

Magoo tried to lick her face and wagged his stub of a tail as hard and fast as a curling broom.

"You're taking him with?" I was doubtful Kona was so laid back as to allow dogs in restaurants.

"Sure. Why not?" Margie said as though my concern was unwarranted. "I'm not sure he can be trusted alone at home. I caught him chewing on Jack's favorite sandals, so I guess I'll have to get him a crate or something."

I was going to suggest she just drop him off at the local dog pound but thought better of it. We could leave the little mutt in the car once the maître'd had informed Margie that dogs were not allowed.

66

Magoo sat on my lap unhappily for the short ride into town and we found Huggo's just where we'd left it. It was very crowded out front so I voiced my opinion that maybe we wouldn't get in.

Margie laughed at me and said she knew a secret password. Then she pulled into the parking lot and stopped behind two cars. I expected she'd pull out again and find a real spot, but she turned off the ignition and started to get out.

"You can't park here," I said. "You're blocking these people."

Margie looked at the cars she was blocking, shrugged, dropped her car keys in her purse and made her way around the car to pick Magoo off my lap. She held him up to her face. "Would you like a nice juicy steak?" she cooed, letting him lick her several times before tucking him under her arm. "Come on," she scolded.

I had made no attempt to exit the car. "But…" I waved at the cars we were blocking.

"Don't be such a worry wart, Joe. Lighten up! It's not a problem."

I didn't accept her assessment of the situation but assumed that later we'd be claiming Margie's T-bird from wherever they tow things in Kona.

Once I was out of the car and had joined Margie, she slipped her arm in mine as if we were old friends rather than two people who'd known each other for just about twenty four hours.

I felt a tinge of regret. Jillian had stopped doing such things ages ago. Why was that? And why couldn't I answer that question?

"Do they allow dogs in restaurants here?" I asked casually. "I mean unless it's a service dog." I wondered briefly if Margie was going to pretend to be blind.

"I don't know," Margie eyed me suspiciously. "I've never taken a dog to dinner before," she said mischievously.

"We could put him in the car," I suggested.

Margie laughed. "Don't be such a worrier. Relax, Joe." She pulled me tight – sort of a sideways hug. "You're on vacation. What you need is another Long Island."

After the night before, I was wary of Long Islands. "Maybe I'll try something tamer, like a double martini," I said.

As we approached the crowd outside Huggo's I felt my stomach tighten. Why was that? Damn it, Joe, I said to myself. Relax. Go with the flow. I took a deep breath of luxuriant island air and forced myself to relax. It's not easy for me to relax though. I'm not sure why. It's probably my mother's fault.

Huggo's was a hopping place. Music, conversations, a big, happy throng. Margie pushed past the line outside, ruffling a few feathers judging by the looks we got, and I felt my muscles tense again, but release was nearly instantaneous for as soon as we entered the place a chorus of voices shouted excitedly: "Margie!"

Margie left my arm and the maître'd gave Margie a big hug. Margie hugged him back and introduced me to Skip. Skip winked at me. I pretended I didn't notice because I wasn't sure why he was winking unless he was winking that 'you sly dog' wink because here I was with a very attractive woman who I probably had no right being with or...
"Margie's my favorite patron," Skip interrupted my deliberation and he guided us to an ocean side table for four with a Reserved sign on it. I was stunned that he hadn't mentioned the furry critter Margie was toting. Perhaps *he* was blind.

He held Margie's chair and offered menus. "The special tonight is fresh ono, Margie."

Margie squealed with delight and thanked him as he slipped away.

"If you like fish, Joe, you have got to try the ono. It's to die for." Margie dropped Magoo on the chair next to her and set her menu down on her plate. Evidently she's decided to go with the ono. I opened my menu and read. I don't like to make hasty decisions.

Magoo, for his part sat in his chair happy as a clam just to be near Margie.

Sandy, our beverage waitress, came over and commented on how cute Magoo was and scratched his head.

Margie took charge. "I'll have the usual and Joe will have a Long Island. He definitely needs a Long Island."

I was about to object, but then just surrendered. They were tasty and I'd have this one with food so it'd be okay. At least that's what I told myself.

Sandy nodded and started to leave, but Margie added: "And a bone, if you have one back there."

Sandy smiled and disappeared. Almost at once another waiter brought water and bread.

"So what do you think?" Margie asked me. I assume that she meant what did I think of Huggo's, since I think a lot of things and at the very moment she asked that question I'd been thinking that Margie must be chilled because her nipples were poking very hard against her top.

I looked around and nodded approvingly. "Nice place." What's not to like? It was trendy, the food smelled wonderful, and if our reception was any indication, we were going to get the royal treatment when it came to service. The weather was perfect, seventy-five, seventy-six tops. There was a light breeze blowing. Waves washed gently against the rocky shore not a dozen feet from us. There were no bugs. I didn't have to get up for work tomorrow. Drinks were on their way. We had arguably the best table in the restaurant. What could I possibly complain about?

Margie smiled and lifted her glass of ice water. "I'm glad you approve. A toast?"

"Shouldn't we wait for the real stuff?" I said.

Margie continued undeterred. "To Kona," she clinked my glass with her's. She took a sip. I took a sip. I put down my water and returned to my menu.

Our drinks appeared, as did a large bone for Magoo. They were brought by Sissy, a young waitress who could have been a throwback to any flower child of the sixties. She knew Margie of course – did everyone know Margie? – and she complemented her on her purse and fawned over the new 'puppy.' Margie wisely withheld the story of how the puppy had come to her.

Sissy left and I stared a moment at my drink. It was a big glass.

"Go ahead," Margie encouraged.

"I'm going to pace myself after last night," I told her. "I'll be driving later and don't wish to see the inside of your local jail."

Margie chuckled and sipped her cosmo.

I continued to peruse the menu. Sissy reappeared and stood ready to take our order.

"Everything looks great, but I do like fish and I think I'll trust Margie on the ono." I looked at Margie and asked: "Should we start with some calamari?"

Margie made a yuck face. "Go ahead, I'm not into fried stuff."

I ordered the calamari and the ono. "Make it two," Margie said. "And a filet mignon for my friend here,"

Margie said, patting Magoo. "No seasoning please and I think he'll take it quite rare."

Sissy slipped away and Skip reappeared looking glum.

"Margie, there's a problem" he said and looked down at Magoo in the chair. "There's been a complaint about the dog." He paused and you could tell he didn't want to say the last part 'cause he wouldn't look at Margie when he said it. "I'm afraid you're going to have to put him in the car."

Margie looked up at Skip, then at Magoo. "Who complained?" she asked, and stretched her neck to look around at who might have done it. I followed her lead.

"Margie, I'd rather not..." Skip started.

But Margie had already identified the culprit. He was easy to spot because he was looking right at us only three tables back. He was a beefy guy, at least fifty pounds overweight, and balding. He was with his wife who had her back to us. Short hair, stylishly cut. They were both well dressed. People with money. Lawyer, I guessed.

Margie stood and dropped her napkin. "I'll be right back, Joe." She squeezed past Skip.

Skip gave me a desperate look. "Is she always this difficult?"

"I really can't say," I answered. "We're only recently engaged."

Skip looked surprised but had other things to do so he turned and walked quickly away, hoping, I suspect, to avoid stray bullets. I opened my menu and pretended to read, but it was only a ruse. I'd noticed that if I held the menu up high enough I could see the dining room through a mirror that seemed appropriately placed for my benefit.

As Margie approached the lawyer's table, I saw the man's face tighten. Yup, he was the complainer. He looked up at Margie with an unfriendly scowl. I was

71

certain it was a lost cause and that Magoo was headed for the car.

I could only see Margie's back, but I knew she was talking because her hands were moving. She always talks with her hands, which adds to my angst when she drives.

I saw the man glance quickly in my direction, then back at Margie. His face relaxed a bit. What *was* she saying? The wife turned and I saw her profile. Attractive. She said something to Margie who had also turned a bit and I saw Margie press her hand to her chest and laugh at whatever it was the wife said. Then Margie said something and they all laughed hard. Margie leaned over, took the wife's wrist, and shook her head seriously. What *was* she saying?

The wife turned and looked my way. My eyes darted back to the menu, even though I didn't think they could see me through the mirror from so far away.

When I had the nerve to look up again, Margie was smiling and skipping back to our table; Mr. and Mrs. Complainer toasted something or other.

Margie arrived and sat down with great panache, patted Magoo on the head, picked up her napkin and straightened it on her lap. She took a sip of her cosmo and looked out at the ocean. She totally ignored me.

Somehow she had managed to quell the wrath of Mr. and Mrs. Complainant, and clearly she was not going to tell me what had happened unless I pulled it out of her.

I pretended not to care, but I'm no good at that. I caved after thirty seconds. "Okay, what did you say to them?"

Margie gave me a sly smile. "Nothing really. It's fine," Margie patted Magoo again and looked again at the ocean.

She was enjoying not telling me. I tried again. "Okay, you win. What did you say to them that made them change their minds?"

72

Margie took another sip of her cosmo and let it trickle down her throat. She looked at me closely, as if she were trying to decide whether she would tell me. She must have decided I'd suffered enough because she smiled, leaned over the table and said in a whisper: "I told them you'd bet me $500 dollars that I couldn't take a dog to dinner and get away with it."

"You what?" I gaped.

"I told them, you had..." Margie started.

"I heard you. Are you telling me they bought that? That's all it took?"

Margie leaned back a little, put her elbows on the table. She folded her hands and rested her chin on them. She smiled at me. It was a very pouty and provocative pose.

"Well, I didn't put it exactly that way. I told them you're my husband and that you've always been such a know-it-all that you drive me crazy, and I said I'd buy them dinner with my winnings." Margie made a sniggering sound.

"So, *I'm* buying them dinner," I said. I looked up at the mirror to see them order another round of drinks.

"No, I'm buying them dinner, Joe" Margie patted my hand. "Dinner's on me. But really," she added. "Jillian never mentioned how serious you are."

I was about to protest that I wasn't always serious but our waiter appeared with our food, including Magoo's steak which was cut bite-size and served on a paper plate for obvious reasons. I let her comment go and for the next ten minutes Margie and I ate quietly, discussing only the quality of the food, the exotic atmosphere, and the absence of our spouses.

It was during one of the quieter moments in the meal that I happened to look up and saw a man sitting at the bar who turned away as soon as I glanced at him. This in itself isn't odd since people had been going out of their way to check out Margie all evening. What was odd was that the guy looked vaguely familiar to me.

I mentioned it to Margie. "I think I know that guy at the bar, but I can't figure out where in the world I know him from."

Margie turned to look. "The big guy?" she asked.

"No, the guy next to him."

Margie turned back. "I saw him looking over here before. Maybe he's thinking the same thing as you. You should go say hi."

"Why would I do that?"

"Don't you want to know where you know him from?" Margie seemed genuinely amazed at my lack of curiosity. "You want me to…"

"No I don't want you to… Just leave it alone."

Margie eyed me. "I'd go say hi."

"I'm not you."

"Maybe he was on the plane with you," Margie said and fed Magoo another piece of steak.

"Maybe. Or maybe he looks like someone else I know," I said.

"Well, it's going to bug you for hours and hours," Margie said with certainty.

"No it isn't. I've already forgotten it." I caught movement in my 'rear view' mirror. "Don't look now," I said. "But here come The Complainers."

The Complainers stopped by the table on their way out, and were actually awfully nice and quite cheery – I assume they'd ordered wine with their meal in addition to the drinks – though I really hadn't been paying attention. They even patted Magoo on the head – Magoo let both of them do so without a snarl or a snap which of course upset me since he still growled whenever I tried the same. And as a final salute, Mr. Complainer shot me with a finger-gun and said: "Better luck next time, son."

Our waitress came over and cleared the dinner plates and I begged off on a second Long Island and skipped dessert, despite Margie's encouragement. Where would I put it?

Margie took out her credit card. I took out mine. We argued briefly about who would pay. Thankfully, she was insistent and I put mine away. I'm not cheap, but I *was* on a budget.

Skip came over to ask how the meal was and we raved. He thanked us, told us to have a nice evening and started off. Margie called after him and said we need a check.

Skip returned, looking surprised. "But didn't they tell you?" he asked.

Margie and I exchanged looks.

"The couple that complained about the dog?" Skip said. "They bought you dinner."

You could have knocked me over with the a feather!

Later as we approached Margie's car, which was still parked exactly where she had parked it and did not appear to have been slashed, keyed, or otherwise vetted for poor parking manners, Margie lectured me.

"I don't understand why you're so surprised, Joe? People are nice if you give them a chance."

"Or if you lie well enough," I countered.

Margie shot me a look. Actually I was beginning to think of it as 'that' look. It showed disapproval, but of a maternal sense. Nothing mean about it, just a 'pick up your room or they'll be no dessert after dinner' look.

As we drove out of the parking lot, I watched Margie. Who was this woman? One moment she's a provocative vamp swimming nude and prancing around naked, upsetting my sense of decorum and making me nervous.

The next moment she's tending my wounds and displaying the maternal character of a mother hen. Then later she's using her feminine charms and wiles to get her way and solve life's little problems. It was all very confusing. Very confusing. She was not at all like Jillian. Not like Jillian at all.

An Unwelcome Guest

As we pulled slowly into the driveway back at Margie's she seemed distracted.

"What's the matter?" I asked, sensing her hesitation.

"I don't remember leaving the light on in the kitchen," she said.

"You probably didn't notice; it was light when you left," I said logically.

"I'm sure I turned it off." Margie stopped the car. She hesitated a moment then continued in a whisper. "I've got a funny feeling, Joe."

The hairs on the back of my neck rose. "You think someone's inside?" My voice too was just a whisper. I wanted to say: "you know if you leave your whole place open, you're sure to attract problems," but I didn't.

Suddenly Margie brightened and gave a nervous chuckle. "Oh, I'm sure it's nothing. Maybe Amanda came over for something." And with that Margie pulled into her usual parking spot, shut off the car, and came around to gather Magoo, who, as usual, leapt into her arms to get away from the mean, ugly, man he was forced to ride with.

I climbed out and we met at the door. Again Margie paused.

"Margie, if you think there's something wrong, we should go next door and call..."

Margie laughed lightly. "Don't go getting all melodramatic, Joe. This is Kona, not New York!"

That may be, I thought, but to err on the side of caution I said: "Let me go first."

It's not that I'm brave or anything. It just seemed the manly thing to do. I do think of myself as manly – though I may be alone in that regard.

"Okay," Margie agreed quickly, which convinced me that although she said she didn't think anything was wrong, deep down she might have a different feeling.

Margie unlocked the door and I pushed it open.

Yes, I know that's crazy. She leaves the whole front of the house wide open, but she locks the back door. Go figure!

I slipped into the darkened entry and cocked my head. Nothing. A block of light spilling from the kitchen onto the floor of the upper landing. Margie came up behind me, holding Magoo tight.

"I don't hear anything," I whispered.

Margie tiptoed past me and dropped Magoo on the floor where he, Magoo, let out a low, nearly inaudible growl.

"That can't be good," Margie whispered. "Come this way."

Margie took my hand and we tiptoed silently toward the kitchen doorway.

Margie peeked inside and then let out a big sigh. "No one's here," she said happily.

She seemed to think that that was that; I wasn't so sure.

"Let me look around a bit," I said and headed back to the living room and flipped on the lights.

Margie followed me and turned on more lights.

"See," she said, sweeping the air with her arm dramatically likes those models on the game shows that indicate the prize you might win. "Everything's fine. Magoo's not growling and I don't see anything out of place. It was probably just Amanda."

Although I was coming around to her way of thinking, I continued my stroll through the house until Margie came and found me.

"Let's go check outside," Margie said. "The stranglers always hide in the bushes."

Margie took my arm and I let her guide me through the house, but when we got to the living room she suggested she stop and make drinks while I go outside and look for the bad guys.

"I think we're both a little on edge," she said by way of apology, as if either one of us needed an excuse to drink.

I agreed with her but told her to make mine weak because I had to drive back to my condo. So I buried my hands in my pockets and stepped out into the night. The air was crystal clear and a sliver of moon immediately caught my attention, its features sharper than I could ever recall.

I thought if we were going to sit out by the pool we should have some light, but nothing harsh to dampen the moonlight. I decided the underwater pool lights would be just the ticket so I searched near the door and found a bank of switches that appeared promising and I tried my luck. The first switch lit the fake tiki torches surrounding the pool. Okay. That was nice. The second switch lit the path lights that ran along the bushes. That too added to the ambiance. I hit the third switch and, bingo, the underwater lights came on.

It was unfortunate, however, that their illumination didn't accomplish the objective I'd hoped for. Not in the least. What they *did* illuminate was quite shocking and left me staring at the pool trying to comprehend what exactly I was looking at.

And while my mind was grinding away, Margie appeared next to me with our drinks, an ice tea for her, and a scotch for me.

"Here you go," she said looking up at the sky. "Isn't it a beautiful evening?"

I didn't respond. I couldn't. My eyes were glued to that thing in the pool, but I took my drink mechanically.

"Here's to our safe and sound arrival back home." Margie clinked her glass against mine. Finally she noticed I wasn't paying attention. "What's wrong, Joe?" she queried.

"Margie," I said, in a voice that was broken and shaky. "I don't know how to tell you this, but..."

I turned to see her looking at me expectantly.

"What is it? Joe. Spit it out. "

I took her chin and turned her head so that it was pointed at the pool. Her eyes stayed on me at first, then they followed to see what I wanted her to see. Two ticks of the clock passed by.

"What the..." Margie began. Then she must have let her glass tip because she spilled her drink on my foot. "What the hell is that?"

Of course her question was purely rhetorical. Anyone could see *what* it was. It was a body – a man's body – a dead man's body, floating face up in the pool!

Margie ran to the bank of switches and turned on the big lights. Detail emerged.

The dead man was wearing a nice black and gold Hawaiian shirt and tan slacks and penny loafers, and his eyes were open to the heavens above. There was a bullet hole in his forehead and the water in the pool was the color of pink lemonade. I'm guessing from the blood.

Magoo finally noticed something odd and moved to the edge of the pool where he was growling menacingly. Yorkies can't really growl menacingly, but they think they can, so I'm helping him out.

"Who's that?" Margie asked.

I looked at her. "How the hell should I know? Don't *you* know?" I inquired. Not that I really expected her to know.

80

Margie looked at me as if I'd just let one go.

"Of course I don't know! Why..." Margie looked back at the pool. "Do you think he's dead?"

I rolled my eyes; I tried not to but it just happened. "Yes, Margie. I'm pretty sure he's dead. You see that hole between his eyes and that red stuff in the water. I'm pretty sure that's a bullet hole and the red stuff is blood."

"Eeewee," Margie squirmed and shuddered. "What should we do?"

"I think we should call the police," I said calmly.

"Are you sure?" Margie asked.

I wondered what other options she might be considering, but I persisted. "Yes, Margie, I'm pretty sure that when you find a dead body floating in your pool you have to phone it in."

I started indoors; Margie continued to stare at the pool and sip her drink, which she'd already spilled, of course, but didn't seem to notice it wasn't there.

I heard her say softly as I headed for the phone: "What am I going to tell Jack?"

The Cops

In a matter of minutes, the place was crawling with cops and I was out in the yard giving what little information I had to the lead on the case, Detective Lo.

The detective had a pleasant face and was dressed in a big aloha shirt and tan slacks. I took him to be a native Hawaiian since he was built like the pro wrestler. In case you didn't know, Hawaiian's tend to be very imposing physically.

I was pretty certain he was a no-nonsense kind of guy, not that I was planning to give anyone any nonsense.

He was questioning me first since technically *I* had discovered the body and he took notes as we talked. I explained how we'd come home from dinner and felt that maybe someone had been there and explained how we'd searched the house and then come out by the pool and found the body. I concluded with: "And that's when we called you."

"You didn't touch the body?" Lo asked.

"No! Why would I…"

"Did you find a gun?"

My face went blank. "It didn't occur to me to look."

"And you say you've never seen this man before?"

"No! Where would I…"

"And Mrs. Geanosa, she didn't look surprised or nothing?"

"Of course she looked surprised! There was a body in her pool!" I thought I knew where that question came from so I quickly added: "She had nothing to do with it detective. She was with me all day."

"So you are her alibi?"

I didn't like the way his questions were going. "What are you insinuating?"

82

"I'm not insinuating anything, Mr. Thomas. There's been a murder and the body is in Mrs. Geanosa's pool. I have to assume there's some connection between the murder victim and the location. Do you own a gun?"

"No," I snapped. "And if I did, the airlines would have lost it!"

He looked at me and waited.

"The airlines lost my luggage. I'm sorry. My vacation is not going well," I said.

Detective Lo lowered his pen and nodded toward the corpse that was being wheeled from the yard on a gurney.

"Neither is his, Mr. Thomas. Do you have anything to add to your statement?"

I thought a moment. "No," I said, "only that I'm certain Mrs. Geanosa had nothing to do with this."

"You already indicated that." Detective Lo stared at me. Finally he pulled a calling card from his pocket.

"If you think of anything, call me. Even if it's something you don't think is important."

I turned the card over in my hand nervously. I'd never had a cop's calling card before. It seemed ominous that I had one now. "I will, detective," I said softly and pocketed his card.

One the of the uniformed officers walked by just then and the detective told him to check the freezer, which made me wish I hadn't mentioned it. Not that I thought there was anything to it, only that the detective *did* think there was something to it.

The detective turned to leave, then turned back.

"Mr. Thomas," he said flatly. "Don't try to leave the island."

He turned again and left me standing outside pondering what exactly *that* meant while he went to talk to Margie in the living room.

I was too far away to hear their conversation, but I could see Margie got a little agitated with the detective near the end of the interview, and when he was done with Margie he motioned for me to join them.

"This whole house is a crime scene," he told us. "You can't stay here tonight. You'll have to find a hotel or…"

"I've got friends across the street that will be happy to put us up, detective," Margie said curtly. "Can I get a few…"

"No. I'm sorry, Mrs. Geanosa, but until the crime unit has been through everything, the answer is no."

"Can we at least get my husband's car. Mr. Thomas has a condo…"

"Again, Mrs. Geanosa, until we are done the answer is no."

"So we're just left with the clothes on our backs?" I asked.

"I'm afraid that's the way it is," detective Lo said.

"Come on Joe, I'm sure you can stay at Amanda and Pete's too." Margie started for the door. "Can I at least take the damn dog!"

Detective Lo said nothing. He'd already turned his attention to one of the patrolmen.

Margie scooped up Magoo, who I'm sure was glad to be away from all the feet milling about, and we made our way up the drive toward Amanda and Pete's.

We encountered Amanda at the top of Margie's drive, being held at bay behind tape that announced this was a 'crime scene.' She was all over Margie to tell what had happened and Margie was only too eager to oblige.

So while they blabbed a million miles an hour, I tagged after them feeling a bit left out.

84

I did make a mental note to write in my journal: 'Vacation. Day Two. Discovered murder victim; became a murder suspect.'

Amanda and Pete's Place

The Sogol house – that's Amanda and Pete Sogol who you met earlier – was every bit as nice as Margie's place, though it looked a bit more lived-in. By which I mean it was a little messy.

There were a few plates that hadn't made it to the dishwasher and some socks that hadn't made it to the laundry room and a large pile of newspapers that hadn't been recycled.

They were impressive papers: New York Times, Wall Street Journal, Washington Post, and Barron's to name a few. Pete hadn't impressed me as a serious reader when we met, but neither had Amanda. So I had to wait to discover who the owner was. If you'll pardon my obvious chauvinism, I felt that Amanda was just too busty to be brainy but I eventually discovered my error. Amanda's brain I found was even more impressive than her physical attributes.

We gathered in the living room – where Magoo seemed to prefer Pete's socks over Amanda's – and we were drinking hard liquor. Yes, I know we're drinking too much but under the circumstances, can you blame us?

Despite my objection, I was wearing one of Pete's clean robes. It was a little too big for me, but beggars can't be choosers, and I remember thinking that there was a good chance I would never again wear clothes that were my own.

"I felt like a criminal!" Margie said after she'd told Pete what had happened with the detective. "He kept asking me if I knew who it was and I kept repeating that of course I didn't know who it was. Why would I know who it was? I can't imagine who... Or why? What on earth was he doing in my pool?"

I tried to calm Margie down. "Relax. Once they realize there's no connection between you and the victim they'll back off. I think they suspect me too. That detective said as much."

"Why would they suspect you?" Amanda asked.

"Because I was there. I'll bet there's some statistic or something that says '9 out of 10 times the perp reports the murder.'"

"The 'perp'?" Pete was obviously not up on detective show slang.

"The perpetrator, Pete. The *killer*," Margie said with emphasis. "I'll bet you're right, Joe. I'm going to call my attorney right now." Margie got up. "Where's the phone, Amanda?"

Amanda gave Margie a pained expression and pointed. "The kitchen? We haven't moved it in years."

"Oh, that's right," Margie made for the kitchen.

"It's awfully late, Margie," I called. It wasn't that I was worried about the attorney. I was just stating the fact in case someone wanted to say 'time for bed.' It was 4 a. m. in Chicago and I was still on Midwest time.

"For what we pay him he should stay up all night," Margie countered.

Now that I was alone with Amanda and Pete I thanked them for taking us in and we spent the time until Margie returned sharing views on how odd it was to find a murder victim in a pool and which detective shows we liked best.

Margie returned and stood looking at the three of us with her hands on her hips till Amanda asked: "Well?"

"Joe was right! They do suspect us. Frank says we should have called him immediately. We shouldn't have said anything!"

Margie continued as she found a chair. "And he says if they contact us again, we're to say nothing. Nothing at all until he sees us."

"Just clam up?" I asked.

"Exactly!" Margie said.

"But won't we look guilty?" I asked. I didn't want to look guilty.

"Frank says we already do," Margie said. "He says that eight out of ten times it is the perp who calls it in!"

I didn't like that, even if it did prove I was right.

Amanda shook her head. "They should teach you this stuff in grammar school."

I noticed that Amanda did most of the talking in the Sogol house. Pete, it appeared, was a man of few words, which is okay with me. I'm not criticizing, it's just an observation.

Amanda suggested we stay with them for a couple of days. "Until you find out what direction this thing is going."

Margie poo pooed her idea. "Don't be silly, Amanda. They'll be done at my house in a few hours and ... Oh! The pool. The blood!"

"They can get that out," I said confidently. "It's probably already out. Chlorine kills damn near anything." I yawned and stretched uncontrollably. "Right now, I think I've got to sleep. I'm dead." Yes I know it was a poor choice of words under the circumstances but that's what I said.

"You're right, Joe," Margie said. "What we need is a good night's sleep. We won't worry about a thing until tomorrow. The police will ask around and find we had nothing to do..."

Margie's spiel was interrupted by a knock at the door. Since it was late, we all looked at one another, puzzled.

88

Pete got up and opened the door. Two uniformed cops stood outside.

"Mr. Thomas? Mr. Joseph Thomas?" the taller of the two asked.

Pete stepped aside and pointed at me; I got up and came forward.

"I'm Joe Thomas," I confessed.

The cops stepped inside.

"We've been sent to bring you in for further questioning."

"Now?" I asked suspiciously.

"Now," the taller cop said convincingly.

"And if I refuse?" I asked bravely.

"We'll place you under arrest and bring you in anyway."

Margie was on her feet and rushed toward the door. "Don't say a word, Joe! Not a word! I'm calling Frank."

The Prime Suspect

Frank Bonza, Margie's attorney, was a distinguished-looking gentleman who I pegged to be in his late 50's. He had a full head of salt and pepper hair and that ruddy look of a man who is still physically active. He was also as tan as that movie star all the comedians joke about – I think it's George Hamilton but I could be wrong. I'd told him everything there was to tell about me and Margie and Jillian and the circumstances with the dead guy in the pool. He knew all about Jack of course since he was Jack's attorney too.

He listened attentively and quizzed me now and then, and when things finally came to an end, he told me not to worry. There wasn't going to be a problem. I was pleased to hear this and felt confident that in a little while I'd be out of this place and back at Amanda and Pete's where I might get some shuteye.

He filled me in as to what was about to happen during the interrogation and that I should wait after each of the detective's questions in case he – Frank – wanted to object. And under no circumstances was I to elaborate. Simple yes and no answers were the best.

When Detective Lo joined us, Frank took the lead.

"Okay, detective, I've spoken with my client and we're ready to answer your questions. But keep it civil, Lo. I'm in no mood for any of your heavy-handed tactics."

"Yeah, yeah," the detective growled and turned to me.

"Why did you tell me you'd never seen the deceased before, Mr. Thomas?"

"I didn't recognize him," I said honestly. "As I told Mr. Bonza, I'd all but forgotten the incident at the airport."

"You expect me to believe you never saw the deceased before you ran into him at the airport in Honolulu?"

"That's right. Never," I said.

"As far as he can remember," Frank added.

"As far as I can remember," I echoed. I thought that was a smart move because I'm terrible with faces and the dead guy could have been in the seat next to me on the airplane for all I know.

"Okay, tell me what happened," Detective Lo said, his voice tinged with cynicism.

"You already know. Your detective saw the whole thing. That's why I'm here."

"I'm interested in your version."

"Go ahead, Joe," Frank encouraged me and gave me a pat on the back.

"Well... We ..."

"We who?" Lo interrupted.

"Jillian, my wife, and I. We were in the airport in Honolulu and there were these... I guess you'd call them greeters. You know the girls in hula skirts. They were walking around putting leis on people and I thought it would make a good picture. I just got a new camera and was on the lookout for opportunities to use it. So I took a picture of them and suddenly from out of nowhere this guy comes at me and demands my film. He says I don't have the right to take his picture. He makes a big scene and security comes running. Anyway, he's very adamant. I tell him that I think I have the right to take a photo of anyone in a public place, but to placate him I showed him my camera and explained it was digital and I deleted the photo. He seemed okay with that and walked away. And that's it."

Detective Lo squinted at me. "That's it? You didn't perhaps run into him again and your argument escalate...?"

"No! Absolutely not! I didn't see him again until he was dead in the pool."

Frank took over. "Detective, Mr. Thomas' alibi is air tight. He has spent the entire time since he's been on the island with Mrs. Geanosa. I think you need to move on with your investigation." Frank started to rise. "Let's go, Joe."

I stood up.

"Not so fast," the detective barked.

Frank sat down and I followed suit.

"You're wasting your time, detective," Frank said.

"What's your relationship with Mrs. Geanosa?" the detective asked gruffly.

"Why, she's my wife's oldest and dearest friend," I started. "They went to..."

"Come, come, Mr. Thomas. We're all adults here," Lo interrupted. "You can...."

Frank stepped in again. "What are you driving at detective?"

"Just that your client isn't being honest. I have a witness who saw Mr. Thomas carry Mrs. Geanosa, naked, to her bedroom this very afternoon!"

Frank looked at me impatiently. I'd sort of skated over that part of the story with him. I felt a trickle of sweat run down my back. It seemed this thing was taking a very nasty turn. I pictured myself in jailhouse dungarees. I imagined a guy named 'Tug' looking at me lovingly.

"It's not like that," I stammered woefully. "Let me explain..."

New Day; New Worries

I opened my eyes slowly and watched the fan swirling above and reviewed the previous day's events. Today will be better, I told myself. At least that was my thought at the time.

There was a crick in my back from sleeping on the sofa. It wasn't the most comfortable night's rest I'd had, but at least I wasn't in jail.

Although I didn't know what it was, the fact of the matter was that there *was* a very close connection between the dead guy in Margie's pool and me, but at the present time I had no idea what that connection was and since ignorance is bliss as I said before, I was for all practical purposes blissful. And ignorant.

I rolled into a sitting position and rubbed the sleep from my eyes. Across the living room, Magoo – who was snoozing on a big, cushy footstool – opened one eye and glared at me. I glared back.

I smelled coffee and heard muffled voices in the distance so I stood up and followed the scents and sounds to the Sogol kitchen where I found Margie and Amanda. They were still in their bathrobes and although they both had messy hair and pillow creases on their faces, they looked charming. Each was holding a coffee mug the size of an NFL helmet.

They were in the middle of a heated argument concerning the advantages of investing in derivatives versus long and short option sales, which I found intriguing. That kind of chatter never happened at my house. I know nothing of such things, so I waited patiently and listened. Finally, Margie acknowledged my presence and asked what I thought.

Since anything I might say on the subject would be babble, I delivered my standard investment line: "I generally buy high and sell low."

The ladies looked at me a bit sorrowfully. Generally it brings a chuckle, or at least a smile.

"Could I have a cup of coffee?" I asked and pulled the robe I'd been forced to borrow from Pete tight around me. There *was* a chill in the air.

Amanda went to the cupboard and got another helmet-sized mug and poured the dark liquor of life into it. She handed it to me and I drank deeply.

"You sleep okay?" she asked thoughtfully.

I nodded affirmatively. I had in fact slept soundly once I returned from the police station.

"I've got a bit of a crick in my back," I acknowledged, "but otherwise I'm fine. Where's Pete?" The ladies smiled and chuckled.

"Asleep," Amanda answered. "If he doesn't get his twelve hours he's a grouch."

I didn't have a follow-up to that, so the conversation turned to breakfast, which I admit to being a big fan of. Amanda swung into action and began pulling together the ingredients for what I consider a perfect breakfast, e.g., eggs, bacon and toast.

Margie scoffed at us and said that we would be sorry for our eating habits when we were old. She refused to even think of eating such rot and went and found a banana and sliced it up and rummaged around and discovered some old yogurt to top it off. I grimaced.

While the 'good' breakfast came together, we again reviewed the events of the night before.

"You know I was thinking," Amanda said as she put bread in the toaster. "How did detective Lo know about your encounter with that man in Honolulu, Joe? Someone must have told him."

"Didn't I tell you? It was one of his policemen. Evidently he was in the airport for some reason and saw everything that happened. I'm glad I didn't try to deny anything. I'd be eating cold porridge for sure."

"But what was he doing in Honolulu?" Amanda asked.

"Frank asked that question, but Lo wouldn't say," I answered.

"That sounds suspicious," Margie cut in. "I think we need to find out what he was doing there and we need to find out the name of the murder victim and everything we can about him. Maybe then we can figure out what he was doing at my house. It doesn't make sense. Why on earth would anyone follow someone just because he took their picture?"

"And why would someone kill him for doing that?" Amanda said emphatically.

"That is a puzzle." Margie turned to me. "What was he doing when you took his picture?"

"I don't know. Nothing I guess. Just talking to some guy I think. And I wasn't taking *his* picture, I was shooting the hula girls. I just remember noticing the other guy when I showed him the picture I'd taken. It was only this big." I indicated with thumb and forefinger that the camera display was just two inches square.

Margie perked up. "Was it 'That Guy' at the restaurant, Joe? The guy you thought you knew?"

"Hum," I hummed. I hadn't thought of that. "I suppose it could have been. He did look familiar, but... If he was at the restaurant he couldn't have been at your house committing murder."

Margie pouted. "You may be right. But there might have been time for both. He might have come to the restaurant after the murder. Still, I think it's important to find out who 'That Guy' is. Don't you agree Amanda?"

"Definitely," Amanda said and turned the bacon. "But I'm sure you're right and that the guy the murder victim was talking to was the killer, whether or not it's the same guy you saw at the restaurant or not."

"What makes you so sure about that?" Margie wanted to know.

"Well," Amanda said. "If the two men were talking about something that they didn't want anyone to know about– which we already know is true because the victim confronted Joe about the picture – and they were having some sort of argument or maybe they were plotting something or... Anyway, maybe the other guy – the guy who wasn't in your pool – took the opportunity allowed by the altercation with Joe to cover up a murder and make Joe the suspect." Amanda started to butter the toast. "If you follow my logic."

I did not follow her logic. Nor, based on the look on her face, did Margie.

Amanda noticed our confusion. "Think about it," she said and sliced the toast.

Okay, I thought about it and after a bit I had sorted it out. I think. Amanda had to say it again for Margie before she said she understood. It's not that I was quicker than Margie, it's just that it wasn't easy to follow.

Amanda served breakfast at the kitchen island and I dug in with gusto.

"You know," I said with a mouthful of egg. "I don't think getting involved in this whole thing is a good idea. Let the police take care of it. That's what they're good at."

Margie made a face. "Yeah right. And that's why you're their prime suspect? Don't you want to clear your name?"

"It's not really such an important name," I said glumly. "And I'm sure the police would take a dim view of us getting involved with their investigation. I'll bet Frank and Jack would tell you the same thing; I know Jillian would."

"Oh, poo," Margie plucked a piece of bacon from my plate and tossed it to Magoo who came over, looked at it, growled, and walked away. Was it me or the bacon? I'd never heard of a dog who didn't like bacon, so I suspected it was me.

Amanda dropped a bit of toast and Magoo gobbled it down.

"We're not really trying to find out who killed the guy, just who the victim is and why he was at my place," Margie picked up the bacon and offered it to me. I love bacon, but not from the floor. I declined; she tossed it in the sink.

"I called Jack this morning. The police already contacted him. He hasn't a clue who the guy in the pool was or why he was at our place. I have to say though," Margie paused, "he didn't seem all that alarmed about the murder. I asked him if he was coming home and he just said 'why?' He said we were making a mountain out of a mole hill."

Margie looked at her coffee reflectively and took a sip. "Honestly, Jack can be so insensitive sometimes." She paused again. "But I suppose he's right. What can we do?"

"I'll look on the Internet after breakfast," Amanda said. "The newspaper had a name in it. What was it? Lou something."

"Lou Krauthammer," Margie said. "I remember because it was such an odd name. Why would anyone keep a name like that?'"

No one had an opinion on that subject.

Amanda and Margie spent the remainder of breakfast speculating about Lou. I stayed out of it as best I could unless one or the other asked me point blank to agree or add something and then I gave as little information as possible. I didn't want to solve the murder, I just wanted my wife to return from L.A. and finish our vacation. Or start it, as the case may be.

The dishes were already in the dishwasher when Pete shuffled into the kitchen looking hungry so Amanda started breakfast preparation all over.

I requested permission to take a shower and Margie told me to use 'hers.' It wasn't actually hers but since she'd been given the guest room she had taken ownership.

I hesitated. There must have been something in my hesitancy to indicate apprehension about using 'Margie's' shower because the ladies promised not to intrude on me, so I made my way to the shower in the guest room. It was a nice shower but not as big as the one in Margie's place. It did have a frosted glass door which gave me some comfort.

As I showered and wondered about getting a shave and brushing my teeth, someone must have read my mind because I found a fresh toothbrush, a tube of toothpaste and a razor sitting by the sink when I got out of the shower. These were accompanied by a little note that said: 'For Joe's use.' I don't know who delivered them but I was glad to have 'em.

I shaved and brushed and did those other morning things that polite people don't talk about and eventually appeared in the living room where I found Margie and Amanda still in their robes on the couch talking and drinking coffee. Pete was asleep in a big recliner.

"The police are done at my place," Margie announced. "We can go home and you can get Jack's car. Won't it be nice to get back into our own things?"

"Yes," I agreed. "Of course it would be nicer if I actually had my old things, but at least I've got clothes that don't belong to someone else. Have you talked to Jillian? I tried to reach her from the bedroom, but she didn't pick up."

"No," Margie said. "Jack didn't answer either but it's early there. Let's go to my place and find out what's what."

Back at Margie's we went our separate ways. Margie went to change and I, since what few clothes I had were down at my condo, made my way outside to sit in the sun. I was a free man and figured I'd better take advantage of it.

Twenty minutes later, Margie joined me wearing a short powder-blue top and some sort of flowered wraparound thingy. She eyed the pool suspiciously. The color was gone, but I wouldn't have gone in.

"I'm going to have the pool guy empty it and clean it and bleach it and... Would you like some lemonade?"

I did in fact want some lemonade, so Margie headed for the kitchen while I pondered what the day might hold for me and I was just thinking how upset I was that Jillian had made no effort to call when I heard the phone ring inside and a moment later Margie yelled that it was Jillian.

Since I wanted a private conversation with my wayward wife, I took the phone into the guest room.

Of course Jillian was unapologetic about not calling sooner, even after I'd explained the events of the previous day. She wasn't all that shocked about things because the police had called her late last night. And she didn't even seem all that shocked that I was the frontrunner for being the perpetrator. Of course she already knew about Margie being naked and all that.

I tried to make her understand how serious the situation was. "That detective has me pegged as a philandering killer," I complained. "He's got me in his crosshairs and he's ready to fire. I'm worried. I saw Shawshank Redemption."

"I'm sure the detective..." Jillian started.

"When are you coming?" I barked. "I want an answer now."

"Joe, I don't know when I can get away. Things have gotten..."

"Are you ever coming?"

"Of course I am. Two more days. Promise. Just two more days."

I thought that was too long but I had no leverage. I did make her promise on her mother's grave, even though her mother is still very much alive, and then she said she had to run and that was the end of it.

When I rejoined Margie by the pool, she had added a white visor to her ensemble and a pair of heart-shaped sunglasses. She was sipping lemonade through a red straw.

"You don't look very happy, Joe. What'd Jillian say?"

I repeated her lack of concern and the two day thing.

"Well then we'll just have to have fun together. There are lots of things for us to do. How about lunch?"

I looked at my wrist where I generally wear a watch but it wasn't there because it was in lost luggage heaven. It couldn't have been later than ten thirty and we'd only just finished breakfast.

"Not now, silly," Margie shook her head. "I know a great place up at the north end of the island at Kawaiihae. They have the best pizza and loads of other stuff. Let's go there. We'll stop along the way and shop. I think you need more than one pair of shorts."

I agreed that I did need more than one pair of shorts and as I didn't have any other plans, I accepted Margie's proposal to lunch with the caveat that Magoo stay home. Margie didn't like that idea since he was still new but she offered to take him to Amanda's, which satisfied me.

In no time at all we were Kawaiihae bound.

As this was my first trip outside Kona since my arrival, Margie again provided a running commentary concerning everything there was to see along the way and a history about those things she knew about. I already told you Margie babbles as fast as she drives so I'll save you the long version and cut to the chase.

As we passed the small boat harbor just north of town, Margie lamented Jack's absence.

"It's too bad Jack's not here. He's got a big cabin cruiser. Did you know that? What a toy. He likes to fish. Do you fish? Anyway we keep it there. I could take you out but I'm not a very good skipper. The last time Jack let me drive I hit a sailboat and we got sued. I do have keys to the boat though if you want to try."

"I think I'll wait for Jack," I said quickly. I could drive a speedboat, but a cabin cruiser sounded a bit much and I certainly wasn't going to get lost at sea with Margie.

Margie pointed out that the land from the small boat harbor up to the commercial harbor outside the town of Kawaihae was considered a 'lava desert' since it had been formed by various eruptions of three volcanoes: Mauna Loa, which means 'long mountain', Mauna Kea, which means 'high mountain,' and Hualalai, which means... Margie didn't know.

Anyway, this lava desert is relatively flat, rocky and not very scenic, unless you find acres and acres of lava dotted with scrub brush and an occasional donkey scenic. The airport is located here, which is a good location for anything that needs long flat runways.

According to Margie, the desert defines the weather for this particular area. It is dry, hot and sunny virtually all the time. Of course such perfect weather did not go unnoticed by hotel and condo and golf-course developers who knew they could build fantastic upscale places along the coast – on the small pocket beaches that survived the lava flows – put in football-field sized pools, lush gardens, and all sorts of glamorous golf courses, tennis courts, shopping malls and even an occasional lake, and charge a fortune.

These *gold coast* resorts are on your left as you head north. You can't see much from the road since the highway steers clear of the ocean by about a quarter mile, but you get glimpses of them and the lush greenery around them. Margie pointed out the 'Four Seasons Hualalai' as we passed, with "rooms so expensive no one can afford them." There was also a development there with homes "so expensive no one can afford them."

A little further on, Margie informed me was a destination resort area called Waikoloa or something like that, which according to Margie is actually a cluster of resort hotels, condos and private homes at some bay I can't spell or pronounce. Margie claimed 'The Hilton Waikoloa' was almost as fantastical as a Disney theme park with water taxis and light rail to take you to your room.

"It has a dolphin pool where you can swim with the dolphins and a swimming pool that goes on forever. Of course there's a waterslide and falls at the far end."

Margie felt it was a bit much, but it was a fun place to visit and have lunch or just stroll around. But we'd save that for another day.

I noticed a helicopter take off from a small heliport on the right side of the road and said a prayer for the occupants. I don't generally pray for other people but for helicopter passengers, bungee cord jumpers, zip line travelers and other extreme sport enthusiasts I make an exception.

Unfortunately, Margie noticed the chopper too and although she was in the middle of telling me something or other about the Mauna Lani resort up ahead, she hit the brakes hard and made a right so fast I had a flashback to the Mad Mouse carnival ride I threw up on when I was eight.

"A helicopter tour!" Margie shrieked. "That's it! You'll get to see the whole island and the volcano and ..."

Margie yammered away, while I began to sweat and hyperventilate. I did not want to go on a helicopter ride.

But Margie had already made her way to a parking spot. "I made reservations for you and Jillian for tomorrow, but we're here now, so let's see if there's space. You'll love it, Joe! There's no better way to see the island." Margie shut off the engine and was out of the car before she turned and looked at me. "What's the matter, Joe? You look pale. I'm sorry I hit the brakes so hard. Did I..." She paused. "You're not afraid to fly are you? I heard you telling Pete you'd go up with him."

Of course I'm afraid to fly! And even more so in a helicopter. Who in their right mind isn't? Had I really told Pete I would go up with him? What possible reason did I have for saying that? I know I'm a blockhead, but...

I saw that Margie was waiting patiently for an answer so I dug in my bag of dumb excuses and came up with the only one that sprang into my feeble mind, which was currently filled with terror.

"Of course not!" I said with false bravado. "But I already told Pete I'd go with him and we don't have a reservation today and..."

103

"Oh, reservation smeservation," Margie wisecracked and reached in the car for her purse. "Come on, let's at least see if they've got room. Pete won't mind. You can go with him too. He's a great pilot but Amanda says he's a terrible tour guide. He says things like: 'that's the volcano' and 'that's South Point.' He's got no zing. No zip."

Before I could think of another excuse, Margie was half way to the booking office.

Yes, I had let Jillian talk me into the idea of a helicopter tour, but that was months ago and I was certain I could come up with an excuse before it actually happened. There was no way I was going to go up in a helicopter! For God's sake, those things are just lead weights with whirligigs on top.

I opened the car door and climbed out slowly; Margie was backpedaling toward the booking shack and waved for me to catch up, which I wasn't about to do since the smell of aviation fuel already had me queasy and my knees were starting to knock. *'Think,'* I thought. *'Think. There's got to be a reasonable way out of this without looking like a big ass sissy chicken. Perhaps I could have a seizure. Or a heart attack. Or maybe someone could hit me with a car.'*

I looked over at a big blue helicopter sitting on the landing pad. There were three people around it; one of whom was certainly was the pilot. Unfortunately, none of them were over the age of twelve. Okay, that's a slight exaggeration. But not much.

"They've got room on the next flight!" Margie leaned out the door of the booking office and called to me. "Come on!"

I suppose you're wondering why I couldn't just tell Margie I was afraid to go up? It's simple. I'm a guy. Guys don't admit their fears, especially to women.

And so it was that five minutes later I was standing outside with the other morons who were going to risk their lives on the same flight with me, and I was arguing with Margie.

"I just assumed you were going along," I repeated.

"Don't be ridiculous," Margie scoffed. "You've gotta be nuts to ride in one of those things. Pete's been after me for years. I keep telling him 'those things are just lead weights with whirligigs on top.'"

I peered closely at Margie. Could she read minds?

Margie took note of my scrutiny. "What?" she asked warily.

"Nothing," I responded. Had she really been able to read my mind she wouldn't have had to ask 'what.'

I looked again at the chopper. Was I going to do this? Really? Just because I couldn't let Margie know I was a chicken I was going to suffer the pangs of fear and horror. I knew I wouldn't see anything. My eyes would be closed the whole time...

Margie pushed at me gently. "There. They're starting to board. I'll go shop while you're gone and pick you up right here. We'll do lunch." Margie smiled and turned to leave. "Have fun. You'll love it."

'No I won't,' I wanted to cry, but it was too late.

I watched Margie for a moment and wondered how awful it would be if I ran after her and confessed my fears. It would be dreadful, of course, and no real man could do it. So I turned and started shuffling along toward the waiting chopper with the other victims; I recited the Lord's Prayer under my breath and cursed myself for being male and having more testosterone than common sense.

***

If the fear of taking a ride in a helicopter had my undies in a bunch, I would have been doubly horrified had I

105

known that at that very moment a short distance away, a much calmer individual was watching me intently through a pair of binoculars and was on his cell phone relaying my whereabouts to his partner in crime.

"Yeah, I know it was supposed to be tomorrow but he's there now. What do you want me to do?" the caller asked.

He listened attentively for a moment. "Yeah, I can get a hold of him. He should be able to get into position before it arrives. They fly the same route every damn day."

The caller listened briefly again and then hung up. He punched digits on his cell phone and waited. "It's me. I need you to do that thing we talked about *today*. Yeah, I know it was supposed to be tomorrow, but it's today! Can you do it or not?" There was a pause. "Okay. Good. Get in position and I'll call back with the registration numbers once it's in the air."

The caller hung up and trained his binoculars on the heliport and waited.

How Prayer Works

It was sundown and I was in the living room at Margie's enjoying pupus and drinks with Amanda and Pete. The TV was on.

"Shush," Amanda hissed and Pete and I stopped discussing the latest football scandal and focused our attention on the tube.

"Here it is!" Margie turned up the volume.

The news anchor – a forty-something, seasoned newscaster with bushy eyebrows and a full head of hair looked seriously into the camera. Above him and to his left was an insert of a helicopter in the air.

"Tragedy was narrowly averted today when a missile was launched at a Big Island helicopter by what police are describing as a crazed pothead," he said. "The Blue Angel helicopter was on a routine flight over the north end of the Big Island, where steep, virtually inaccessible, canyons and thick vegetation make an ideal location for the island's estimated 200 illegal pot growers. According to pilot Trace Neidermeier, an Iraq war vet, there was a puff of smoke from the ground and..."

There was a cut to a close-up of Trace with a microphone in his face. Trace was well tanned and had that square jaw that made him look rugged. Unfortunately he had a Wilford Brimley mustache that needed a trim badly.

"I didn't really have time to think," Trace said, looking cool and collected. "As soon as I saw the smoke, my combat experience took over and I let the chopper drop about 200 feet in a free-fall. Of course the passengers nearly (bleep) in their pants, but it missed us by a mile. Everyone's okay. Crazy pot heads."

Amanda sucked air and looked at Margie then at me then turned her attention back to the TV anchor.

"The missile eventually landed on the Parker Ranch where it destroyed one all-terrain vehicle and spooked a herd of cattle. No injuries to our bovine friends have been reported. Police have asked the army to bring..."

Margie dropped the volume.

"That was Joe's flight?" Amanda asked. "I can't believe it."

"Yup," Margie said. "If he hadn't given up his seat to that guy from Austin, he'd have been on that thing!"

You see, I did find a way out of my dilemma at the heliport by surrendering my seat to a guy who was on his last day of vacation and desperately wanted to go on the helicopter tour. I could have made a profit on the ticket, but being the warm, sensitive guy I am, I didn't. The guy I gave my seat up to was very appreciative at the time, but I suspect he's cursing me at the moment.

"Did you tell Jillian?" Amanda asked.

"I did," I answered. "She was underwhelmed. Acted as though things like that happen every day."

"Imagine," Margie said with eerie inflection. "If you'd been on that flight and if that missile hadn't missed? You'd be..." Margie stopped and stared blankly.

"Dead!" Amanda finished. "But he didn't get on the helicopter and he's not dead and nobody was hurt. So let's go someplace for dinner and celebrate."

"How about that French place?" Margie suggested.

Pete, who hadn't said boo up to this point gave his opinion of that suggestion. "Too expensive. Let's go have fish and chips at the small boat harbor ..."

"Yuck," Amanda spit. "I hate that place."

The decision making continued in that manner for a bit without any resolution until it was interrupted by a knock at the door. Amanda went to answer and came back looking perplexed.

"It's for you, Joe."

"For me?" How could it be for me? Everyone I knew on the island was right there in front of me! Who on earth *could* it be?

I Didn't Do Anything

It was the same cast of characters as before in the same drab, dreary interrogation room: Frank and I on one side of the table, Detective Lo on the other side. No one looked happy. I was the unhappy, nervous guy.

Frank and I had already gone over things together so Frank took the lead again.

"Detective, this is obviously just a coincidence. No one is trying to kill Mr. Thomas. The helicopter got too close…"

"I don't believe in coincidence, Mr. Bonza." The detective turned to me: "Who wants you dead Mr. Thomas?"

I squirmed as much from the heat of the room as the question. "No one, detective. No one. I'm a 38-year-old middle manager. I haven't fired anyone in five years. I don't gamble, smoke, or play around."

"What about your wife? What about Mr. Geanosa?" Lo eyed me suspiciously.

"Why would either of them want me dead?"

"'Cause you're playing around with Mrs. Geanosa?" he suggested.

"Detective, please," Frank said, coming to my defense. "Now you're trying to implicate Mrs. Thomas *and* Mr. Geanosa? I spoke with them earlier. They are both in L.A. working. Mr. Thomas has told his wife all about his 'encounter' with Mrs. Geanosa. She is not upset. She sounded amused actually. As for Mr. Geanosa, he's quite aware that his wife is a flirt. If you're concerned that they are somehow involved why not interview them yourself."

Lo snorted and took a new track: "What about insurance?"

"Life insurance?" I scoffed. "I only have a modest policy. Believe me; I'm worth more alive than dead."

Frank added: "Do you think Mrs. Thomas fired a missile at the helicopter? You've been watching too much television detective." He paused. "Detective, last night you tried to blame Mr. Thomas for killing someone he had just met. Now you're suggesting that someone is trying to kill him? Are you going to charge him with kidnapping the Lindbergh Baby?"

Lo leaned back in his chair and looked hard at me. "He's too young for that," he said disagreeably.

The way he said it made me wonder if he meant it.

We continued the Q and A for a while longer. I answered as best I could. My answers were: "I don't know, I haven't a clue, and search me." Not a lot of variety, but then I *was* clueless. Finally the detective grew weary and the interview ended exactly like the last one.

"Don't try to leave the island, Mr. Thomas." Lo turned to Frank. "Get him outta here."

Margie had also been called to the station, though I'm not sure why, and so, while Margie got grilled, I found a bench by the front door of the station and pondered my fate. *Was* someone trying to kill me? *Why* would anyone want to kill me? I had no answers to either questions of course.

Margie filled me in after the fact that the detective covered the same territory with her that he had with me, hoping, I'm sure, that he'd get different answers and catch us with the goods. Of course we didn't have any goods with which to get caught.

"But you didn't go on the helicopter ride?" Lo asked her.

Margie shook her head exasperatedly. "Didn't Joe tell you anything?"

Lo leaned forward: "I'd like to hear it from you, Mrs. Geanosa."

"Oh, I get it. You're trying to find a hole in our stories aren't you? Well, we don't have one because we're both…"

"Please, Mrs. Geanosa, just answer the question."

Margie gave a virtually duplicate explanation of the events of the morning and how she'd gone shopping.

"I went shopping and bought this really pretty yellow and black polka dot sundress and some yellow sandals and a pair of sea shell earrings and this matching bracelet." Margie held up her wrist to show it off. "Cute huh? And later, *after* I picked Joe up, we had lunch at that little place with the mermaid out front and I had the most scrumptious salad with bean sprouts and…"

"Mrs. Geanosa," Lo moaned. "Please. I'm not interested in what you bought or what you ate, I just want to know if you were with Mr. Thomas all this time."

"Yes. Of course I was. I mean most of the time. He had to wait for me at the heliport of course."

"So how long was it from the time you parted till you reconnected?"

"About two hours."

"And you remember that because…?"

"That's how long it takes for the helicopter tour! Jeez, didn't Joe tell you anything?"

Frank waded in. "Detective, you've now heard virtually identical stories from both of my clients. Is there anything else?"

Detective Lo looked cross and stared at Margie for a long moment. Margie smiled back. Actually she claimed it was a smirk, but she's so darn cute her smirks look like smiles.

"No. That'll do for now," the detective finished.

What Next?

We returned from the police station to find Amanda and Pete reading out by Margie's pool. Amanda had a tome the size of the Oxford dictionary. I would tell you the title but it was in French and I don't read French. Apparently Amanda does read French. I assume she also speaks it.

It gave me comfort to find that Pete was reading something less challenging, to wit: one of those Manga books. You know the ones that are so popular in Japan. This one was in English and although the title wasn't all that provocative, 'Girl at Large,' the cover showed a scantily clad young woman being dragged off by her blue hair into some Technicolor forest by a monster with six arms and two heads. The young woman was amply endowed and something about her reminded me of those women I'd seen on the Vargas cards I'd found years earlier in my uncle's sock drawer. I made a mental note to ask if I could read it when he was done.

Amanda put down her book; Pete continued to read.

"So, what happened?" Amanda asked.

Margie revved up the old verbal Gatling gun and delivered a detailed narrative of her interrogation under the glare of Detective Lo's spotlight. She made it sound so dramatic I was sorry I'd missed it. I suspect, however, she embellished it some. I don' t think there were any thumbscrews involved. Margie tends toward the melodramatic in case you hadn't noticed.

I made my way to the liquor cabinet and found a bottle of Dewar's and poured myself two fingers of it and brought it out to the pool just as Margie was finishing up and adding: "Joe could probably tell you more."

Amanda looked up at me. I played dumb — which I find easy to do for some reason.

"You didn't ask anyone else if they wanted a drink?" Margie appeared to be annoyed with me for some reason.

"Would you like a drink?" I offered apologetically.

"Yes I would, I'll have a Long Island. Amanda?"

"Sounds good to me," Amanda said.

I didn't move. "I don't know how to make those," I said honestly.

Margie mumbled something that sounded like 'lame ass' and got up and started indoors. "Pete what do you want?"

"I'd prefer a beer," Pete announced.

"Then go get a beer," Amanda ordered.

"Don't be silly, Amanda. Joe, can get him a beer." Margie said it very politely though I could sense she was starting to think I was a sluggard.

"Where do you keep the…" I started.

"In the refrigerator!" Margie snapped. "In the kitchen."

Since I *did* know where the kitchen was, I started off.

"And bring some ice in the ice bucket," Margie said.

"Where's the ice bucket?" I asked.

Margie growled and rushed past me. "Never mind, I'll get it. Just go out by the pool …" she didn't finish the sentence, but I heard her mumbling under her breath. "Just like Jack. They're all alike. All alike."

I believe she was referring to men, but I'm not certain.

I sat down across from Pete and realized that although I'd only managed to down one finger of scotch so far I was beginning to feel the effects. It then occurred to me that it was getting dark and I was starving.

Although Margie had enjoyed the little place where we'd had lunch, I'd been less than thrilled with it and

114

consequently ordered what I considered to be the safest thing on the menu: a cheeseburger and fries.

Unfortunately, the chef's idea of a cheeseburger was not my idea of a cheeseburger – I think the meat was some sort of brown tofu – and the fries were not golden brown strips of Idaho potatoes but fat little squares of what Margie told me was fried taro. Needless to say, I dieted.

"Is anyone else hungry?" I asked as Margie arrived with a server holding ice teas, Pete's beer, and the ice bucket. She also arrived with a 'look' for me.

I tried to salvage my reputation by offering to do something I do exceedingly well. "I'll order pizza!"

Pete thought that was a great idea, but Margie and Amanda both dissed it. There was some discussion of Chinese, but Pete vetoed that. Eventually it was decided we'd go out and have dinner at some hotel whose name I don't remember because I'd finished off all three fingers of scotch and was wondering whether I could walk and talk without embarrassing myself. Yes, I should check out the Betty Ford Clinic, but not till the vacation's over please.

Margie insisted on taking Magoo with us. She said he'd been alone too much and I was to the point I didn't care. Pete and Amanda said we'll never get in with a dog, and I countered with a wry "don't bet on it."

The restaurant at the hotel whose name I can't remember was very nice and we managed, because of Amanda's connections, to get a table right by the water and a blind eye to the fact that we had a pooch with us. Magoo was on his best behavior and sat patiently with Margie in a big oversize chair and took tidbits of bread from Margie and kept a low profile.

Amanda began the dinner conversation. "You know, Margie, I was up most of last night trying to find something on that guy in your pool."

"And...?" Margie asked expectantly. "What did you find?"

"Nothing! Absolutely nothing!" Amanda seemed totally amazed with the discovery.

"I'm not surprised," Margie shook her head sadly. "You're always touting the Internet as the all knowing all seeing answer to everything, and here it is no help at all."

Amanda gave Margie the stink eye. She obviously took a dim view of Margie's assessment of the wise and powerful WWW.

"That's not the point at all," Amanda said and tossed a crumb of bread at Magoo who caught it like a left fielder and waited for more.

"Oh?" Margie said. "Then what *is* the point."

Pete, being a very practical person, was paying no attention to the ladies. "I'm thinking of getting the T-bone, Joe, what are you getting?"

"That sounds good to me," I answered. "How're the fries here?"

"Those thick kind."

"That's it then," I'll have the T-bone." As I said this, I realized the table had fallen silent and I glanced over to find Margie and Amanda looking at me as if I'd been talking in church. I shrugged and they turned away.

"The point is," Amanda continued now that Pete and I had been properly chastised, "that's nearly impossible! The Internet has gotten to the point where if you can't find someone on some site or another they probably don't exist! Even fictional characters leave a trail."

Margie was about to reply with something or other in disagreement but our waitress came at that moment to take our order. This put Margie off track.

After the waitress left, Margie was on to a new topic.

"You didn't say anything about my new dress, Amanda. What do you think?" She was wearing the polka dot dress she'd bought earlier.

"Very nice," Amanda said. "And the sandals are just adorable. But I'm trying to make a point here."

Margie's expression indicated she was unaware there had been a disconnect from the original conversation.

"My point is," Amanda plowed ahead, "if there's no information on the guy, he's using an alias or something! The question then becomes: Why is he using an alias? Surely the police know the name is an alias. Why are they using it to identify him in the paper without saying that it's an alias?"

Something had distracted Margie again.

"Is that Carol and Tom from up the block?" she asked.

Amanda turned to look. "Yes it is. Now…"

"That's a bad color on her. Brunettes should never wear brown. There's no contrast."

"Margie!" Amanda raised her voice. "Will you please focus?"

There was some eye-fluttering and brow wrinkling, but finally Margie made it back on track.

"So what's the next step if the all knowing, all seeing Internet has failed you." Margie continued her disparagement of the web.

Pete, as I've said, was paying no interest to this conversation. I think it was because there was an attractive young blonde with one of those strapless tops that men are always watching and thinking: What holds that up? And hoping: Maybe it will fall down.

I on the other hand had been paying attention to the conversation and reiterated my caution as to not getting involved and that the police would take a dim view of it.

"Why should they have all the fun!" Margie said with a tinge of annoyance when she paused to pay attention to me.

"Fun?" I was perplexed. "Since when is murder fun?"

"I told you nothing exciting ever happens around here and now we've got the inside track on a real murder. I think it's kismet. And I think it's fun."

"I agree," Amanda said, putting in her two cents.

I was about to say something important, but the drinks arrived at that moment and they were followed shortly by salads and then the main course and between the drinking and eating most of the conversation drifted toward whether or not we liked our selection and whether or not it was tasty and whether or not someone could have a bite.

We were back at Margie's before the topic returned to the dead guy in Margie's pool, and since it was late the only important decision that got made was that tomorrow they would figure out how to proceed.

I stayed out of it and assumed that once Amanda and Margie discovered they couldn't find any information on the dead guy, they'd give it up. Of course I didn't know Margie and Amanda very well. And I didn't have a clue as to what was going to happen in my life. I never do.

And if you've been paying attention I had had way too many drinks to drive myself back to my condo, so I had another sleepover at Margie's.

I think I'm paying too much for my condo. What do you think?

Where's Jillian?

The next morning I was awakened by a phone call from Jillian who was thrilled to tell me that the project she'd been called back to L.A. for was being picked up for a follow-on.

"That's really exciting," I said with no enthusiasm. I was concentrating more on the pounding in my head from excessive alcohol consumption. "But need I remind you that you're supposed to be here on vacation with me?" The fact that she seemed insensitive to this had me rather disappointed.

"I know," Jillian said with what I felt was feigned empathy. There was a long pause. "I've got it!" Jillian crowed. "Why don't you fly here? I'll still have to work, but we can have dinner together and we'll be together, and…"

I stopped her. "Jillian. As you may recall, I have been told that I cannot leave the island. I'm under investigation by the police. For murder!" I tried to keep my voice level but I'm afraid my frustration came through.

Jillian admitted she'd forgotten about that, and sort of apologized, but she made it clear that she was not going to leave her job and fly back to Kona. "That would be the same as quitting, Joe. And you know how much I love this job."

I was about to launch into a philosophical treatise on love, but thought better of it. I told her I understood and she once again promised that in a few days she'd be right here with me. And no I wasn't *that* gullible but I pretended to be. And by the time we hung up and I made my way out to the pool, where Margie was properly clothed in a bathrobe, I was beginning to think that nobody cared about me at all.

Margie noted my long face and made me tell her the whole story.

"I don't even try with Jack anymore," she sympathized. "You've got to learn to roll with the punches."

Before I could tell Margie that I thought I was quite good at rolling with punches, Amanda burst through the front door as though a ghost was chasing her.

"Guess what?" she said breathlessly, her breasts heaving under her clingy top, and continued before either Margie or I could guess or wish her a good morning. "I just got off the phone with Daisy…"

"Who's Daisy?" I asked and received a dirty look for interrupting.

"She's a friend of ours from the gym," Margie explained hastily.

"And Margie's lesbian lover," Amanda said with a wink.

I perked up. Here was something new.

"She is *not* my 'lesbian lover!'" Margie barked. "And don't go telling Joe that. He doesn't know you're kidding." She stuck her tongue out at Amanda.

"She's a computer wizard," Margie added. "The police use her all the time to help with cyber crimes. And for the record I'm not the least bit interested in her sexually. I'm a very happy heterosexual female." Margie said with indignation.

"She's really cute," Amanda said playfully. "Maybe if you gave it a try."

"Get to the point, Amanda." Margie's patience had worn thin.

I was wondering if there was any truth in Amanda's ribbing, but had no way to find out.

"Okay. Okay," Amanda caved. "Anyway I was talking to Daisy this morning and she let it slip that the brother of our murder victim is coming today to claim the body!"

"Really?"

"Really."

"Did you get his name?"

"She wouldn't tell me that, but I'm sure it's not Krauthammer. She said he's arriving on the five o'clock flight from Phoenix."

Margie looked at her watch. It was morning, why check the time now?

There was a pregnant pause in the conversation and I'm pretty sure I could hear wheels grinding inside Margie's head – it turned out to be the pump for the pool.

"We've got to meet him when he lands," Margie said finally.

I shook my head back and forth. "I don't think the police are going to like that," I cautioned. "I would assume they'll meet him and want to talk to him."

"So?" Margie bristled. "We'll just be there to see what he looks like. Maybe get a clue. Maybe he'll want to talk to the people who found his brother's body."

"Yes. Good idea, Margie," Amanda agreed.

I cleared my throat. "Don't forget, I'm still the prime suspect. Do you really think he'll want to meet me?"

Margie and Amanda looked at one another.

"But you didn't do it. We'll tell him that." Margie seemed certain he'd want to meet me.

I decided to shut up. If they wanted to spend their afternoon out at the airport wasting time, that was up to them. I had decided I was going to go to my condo and sit out on the lanai and read a book and look for whales.

At least that was *my* plan, and I did make it back to my condo and I did see a whale and I started a book, but when four o'clock came I found myself sitting in the back of Amanda's Highlander headed to the airport. They had nearly badgered me to death to come along. Why they didn't badger Pete I don't know.

"Tell me again why I'm here?" I asked.

"Because you're the one who found the body. If he wants to talk to anyone it'll be you," Amanda responded with certain logic.

"But I already told you that I'm sure the police aren't going to let us talk to him. They're still investigating the murder. In fact…"

"Oh, lighten up, Joe," Margie scoffed. "And stop trying to direct traffic all the time. Maybe the police have asked all their questions already. Maybe he'll be there all alone. Let's just take it one minute at a time."

"If the police aren't there to meet him how will we know who he is?" I asked. I too know some logic.

My question struck a nerve because I got the same answer from them both: "Shut up, Joe. They're brothers; we'll know!"

So I shut my trap for the remainder of the trip, vaguely peeved that my logic had been so abruptly discarded and wondered how that book I was reading would end.

We arrived at the airport with time to spare and Margie was quick to point out that there was no one there who looked like they represented the police.

I responded with a blistering: "We'll see."

The plane landed and passengers began trickling through the arrival gate. Amanda thought the second man through looked a lot like our victim. Except for the same receding hairline, I disagreed. Margie's choice was a man whose only resemblance to the murder victim was that he had big hands and big feet. I told her she was nuts.

All told there were six men who came through the gate that Margie or Amanda thought looked enough like our murder victim to be his brother. Luckily they all had checked luggage so they were in the luggage corral waiting for it while the ladies decided who to jump on first.

"What's the plan, Margie? Amanda asked finally.

I thought they might have considered earlier how they were going to approach a perfect stranger and ask: "Are you the brother of the guy who got murdered a couple of days ago?" But obviously they had not.

So while Margie and Amanda debated the best technique for approaching the men they'd selected as possible kin of the late Lou Krauthammer, I stood around with my hands in my pockets and watched the more attractive ladies in the crowd. Hey, it's what men do when they're doing nothing.

My eyes were drawn to a well-tailored woman traveling with a much older gentleman. 'Trophy wife,' I determined, since they seemed much too cozy to be dad and daughter. And as I watched them pass through the crowd, my eye was suddenly drawn to someone sitting over in the smoking section who looked extremely familiar to me.

I walked over to Margie and Amanda. "Ladies," I said without taking my eyes off the smoker. "I think I've found the brother."

"Where?" Margie said.

They both turned toward me. I nodded in the direction of the smoker.

Their eyes followed my nod, then there was a combined intake of breath.

"Holy cow," Amanda swore.

We were now looking at a man holding onto a small carryon and smoking calmly and looking around casually. He was the spitting image of the man we'd found two days earlier floating in Margie's pool. A *twin* brother, I was certain, unless of course you believe in reincarnation.

"What'll we say?" Margie asked.

I knew an old trick that had worked many times over the years. "Watch a master," I said smartly and left Amanda and Margie glued to their spot.

'Smoker Twin' noticed me as I got close and he looked up as though he were anticipating my arrival.

"Lou?" I said. "Is that you?"

Smoker Twin gave a little start and then said apprehensively: "Lou's my brother. I'm Norman, we're twins."

He stood and I offered my hand. "Wow, you sure are. It's Davenport isn't it?"

"Stanton," Norman corrected with no ill will.

I shook my head. "Of course, I'm sorry." I paused. "I haven't seen Lou in years, how's he doing?"

"He's dead," Norman said bluntly. "Murdered."

I had been understudy in the senior play so I was quick to fall back on my old high school thespian training.

I let my mouth fall open. "What...what happened?" I sputtered convincingly.

Norman was about to respond when the familiar bass voice of Detective Lo accosted me.

"Mr. Thomas, I'll have to ask you to step away. Mr. Stanton, I'm Detective Lo, we spoke on the phone. Could you come with me?"

The detective pushed past me and gathered Norman around the shoulder and ushered him toward a squad car waiting at the curb. Norman looked over his shoulder uncertainly at me. I waved.

Margie and Amanda ran to join me. "What did he say?" they chorused.

"Did you find out anything?" Amanda added.

I shared what little I'd discovered with them; a first and last name.

"It's not much," Margie pouted.

But Amanda was more positive. "At least we have a real name. I'll check it on the Internet."

Margie opened her mouth, stuck her finger in it and feigned gagging. "I'll check it on the Internet," she said mockingly. "You know what you can do with the stupid…"

"Ladies, ladies," I intervened, glad to be out of the investigating business for a while at least. "Let's go have a drink; you're much too involved in all this. The Internet can wait."

There was cold silence for a moment, then Margie opened with "Huggo's" and Amanda countered with "Jake's," those being two watering holes that I'd already been to or heard of.

Like two two-year olds, they continued their argument all the way back to the car and didn't stop quarrelling about where we should go till we got back to Kona where I suggested we have a drink at Don the Beachcomber's. I'd been reading about it in the travel book Jillian brought and it sounded like fun.

Since I was the guest, common sense prevailed and that's where we landed. After the first drink, Amanda and Margie made peace and we ordered pupus and had a second drink and waited for the sunset.

Margie explained that it's a tradition in Kona for lovers to kiss just as the sun sets and since neither Jillian nor Jack were available, she suggested we should make the best of it. Amanda said she didn't want to be left out, so I was the envy of all the guys in the place – and a few of the girls as well – when I got kisses from both ladies once the last ray of sunlight dipped below the horizon.

Margie was the better kisser and her lipstick flavor of the day was peppermint. I preferred bubblegum.

Hello Norman

Pete joined us when we got back to Margie's and we ordered pizzas. Margie wanted to BBQ some fresh fish, but Pete wouldn't hear of it, so when the doorbell rang a half hour later we assumed it was the food and were very surprised – and a little disappointed – when Margie returned with Norman.

Norman got introduced all around and after a little awkwardness and an apology for my having misled him about knowing his brother, we settled down to the purpose of his visit, which was to see where his brother's murder had occurred and try to figure out what had happened. As he said, "the police don't seem to have much."

He asked a lot of detailed questions about where we were when we found the body and what time it was and we even had to go out by the pool and stand as we were standing when we did find the body. He was very thorough in his questioning, even more so than Detective Lo, and I asked him if he had police training but he just laughed and said "only traffic court."

I was beginning to wonder if Detective Lo had mentioned my possible involvement in the murder and moments later it became clear he had because Norman asked about my altercation with Lou at the airport in Honolulu.

I told him the story and he listened attentively and when I finished he said: "Yeah, Lou always was a hothead."

So now it was my turn to ask if he thought Lou would have followed me to continue the fight.

"Naw, I can't see that," Norman scoffed. "You did what he wanted. What would he be mad about?"

I agreed.

"So why do you think he came here?" Margie asked.

"Don't know," Norman said thoughtfully. "You don't know him. Joe here doesn't know him. I don't suppose your husband knows him." He paused at this point while Margie shook her head in the negative. "It's a mystery," he finished. "Heck, I didn't even know he was going to Hawaii," Norman concluded.

The doorbell rang again and this time it was the pizza. We invited Norman to join us but he declined, so we said our goodbyes and he promised to let us know if he got any new information and we promised to let him know if we got any new information and we exchanged phone numbers and we showed him out.

"Seems like a nice guy," Pete said after he'd gone.

We all agreed with Pete except I made the caveat that he didn't seem all that broken up about seeing where his brother had died and we agreed that maybe he could have choked up a bit. But Pete suggested that maybe they weren't that close and so we let it go and turned our attention to the pizza.

Margie ate a tofu salad— yuck! She said it was delicious but I didn't believe her. Magoo got crusts and at least one slice of Pete's pepperoni. I don't believe in giving dogs people food so he got nothing from me. Besides, he doesn't even like me.

After dinner, Amanda and Pete went home and I headed for my condo. The idea of being alone was bittersweet. On the one hand, I would be away from Margie. On the other hand, I would be away from Margie. I know that sounds dumb, but the fact of the matter was that Margie was starting to grow on me. Quirky can be fun or at least interesting, and Jillian was nowhere in sight.

I arrived at my condo and climbed out of the car and opened the door and turned on the lights. At least I tried to turn on the lights. The switch didn't work. I found my way inside and tried another switch. Same result. I managed to find the phone and discovered there was no dial tone. Had I had my luggage, I would have had a flashlight to check the fuse box, but as you know I didn't have my luggage.

I went outside and found darkness. Yes I should have noticed earlier, but I'm not all that observant. I spotted some people standing around and went and had a talk with them. No power for two hours and management was making no promises.

Unlike these folks who were stuck without lights, I had an alternate place to stay, so I got back in Jack's Volvo and headed back to Margie's. I ran out of gas two blocks shy of her place. I cursed Jack for never filling up his tank and myself for not looking at the gas gauge.

Margie answered the door with about a pound of face cream on her kisser and was amused by my predicament but not surprised.

"We do have sporadic outages all the time," she said, and added: "You know where the guest room is."

I thanked her for the umpteenth time and found the guestroom and made myself comfortable. I wasn't all that sleepy and would have watched TV, but since Margie didn't allow TVs in the bedrooms and I didn't want to watch in the living room, I read a book I found on the nightstand called 'Six Months in the Sandwich Islands' which I thought at first was a cookbook but discovered was a memoir about a woman's experiences in old Hawaii – which were commonly called the Sandwich Islands back then – in the 1890's.

I could hear Margie walking around for a while, then she must have called it a night. It was well past eleven when I finally turned out the lights and pulled my pillow close. I used to have a wife for that purpose, but she wasn't there so the pillow had to do.

I was almost asleep when I heard something. Now I know I hadn't been around that long, but there *was* a noise and it didn't seem to belong. I let it go at first because I figured Magoo would bark or something. Every dog I've ever known barks at strange noises, so the fact that he didn't bark gave me comfort. Still, there was that sound.

Unable to put it aside, I slipped quietly out of bed and listened. The noise seemed to be coming from outside by the pool, so I crept out of my room and into the living room.

There was very little light. Margie had turned off most of the outdoor lighting and the sky was overcast so there was no moon. The only real illumination came from those funky lights that ran along the bushes and their glow was dim at best.

My eyes adjusted slowly to the dark, and I stood a moment halfway through the living room and watched.

There! Something moved. Near the bushes I could see the shadow of a person, hunched over and moving slowly along, occasionally blocking one of those lights.

Okay, Joe, what do we do now?

I hadn't thought about what I was going to do when I got out of bed. I guess I just assumed I'd discover a paper cup blowing around the yard or something. The idea that it was a prowler was more speculation than concern.

What was he doing out there?

I don't know why I assumed it was a man. Probably because you don't hear about many female prowlers.

It was at this point that I caught sight of something else moving and turned to see Magoo, low to the ground, stalking cat-like toward the intruder. I could barely hear a low snarl.

What's he up to?

I watched Magoo creep forward slowly and cautiously. Then, when he reached the edge of the living room, the little guy sprang up and ran outside, yapping and snarling as ferociously as if he was a real dog.

The startled intruder stood up, gave a yelp and dashed headlong through the bushes onto the golf course. Magoo stayed inside the yard and continued to snarl and yap at the spot where the prowler had made his escape.

Light flooded the living room and I turned to find Margie pulling on her robe. "What the hell...?" she started, looking at me as if I was the cause of the commotion.

"Magoo just chased away a prowler," I said cheerfully.

"An intruder?" Margie said. "What did he want?"

Yes, I did think this was an odd question and although I immediately thought of a blistering response I didn't want to lose squatters rights so I didn't use it. I just said: "I think we should call the cops."

I'm sure it was after two a.m. when Detective Lo and the uniforms left. He'd arrived a few minutes after the first patrol car and asked us a whole bunch of questions that were just a rehash of questions he'd asked us earlier and had nothing really to do with the intruder. And because neither Margie nor I knew a damn thing, we had few answers. He seemed particularly unhappy that we couldn't tell him the answer to the question: "What was he looking for?"

I gave him a "hell if I know." Margie gave him a "search me." Of course he didn't take her literally, but I think some of the uniforms were hoping he'd delegate the job.

The hubbub awakened Amanda – Pete could sleep through firefights in Iraq and thus was immune to measly sirens – who came to offer comfort and stand around half dressed and getting in everyone's way and distracting the police officers who were already distracted by Margie.

The police eventually left and even though it was very late, or very early, depending on how you looked at it, I lost my desire to sleep temporarily so the three of us sat around the kitchen island and drank coffee. If there'd been donuts or cookies or anything sweet at all in the house, Amanda and I would have had that too, but Margie doesn't buy that sort of stuff. The best she had to offer was yogurt or fruit. We declined vigorously.

"Who do you think it was?" Amanda asked for the fifth time.

"I can't image," Margie said for the fifth time.

"I don't think it was a burglar," I said. "It was like he was looking for something out by the bushes. He didn't make an effort to come inside even though the doors were open." I turned to Margie. "You've really got to start closing those things at night. Anybody can just waltz right in and..."

"That's what Detective Lo said," Margie said irritably. "Do you close yours, Amanda?"

"No," Amanda offered. "But then I haven't had anyone murdered in my pool or poking around my yard at midnight."

Margie made a face. It was supposed to be a 'yeah, yeah, I've heard that all before' face, but because her hair was all messy and her face was still covered in face cream, it made us laugh.

"What's so funny?" Margie wanted to know.

Amanda ignored her and pressed on. "I should have checked out the Stanton brothers on the Internet. I wonder if it was Norman that was here."

"Why would Norman come back? And what could he be looking for?" Margie asked the question, but I was thinking the same thing.

"Maybe something was missing off his brothers' body. A ring or something," Amanda suggested. "Anyway, how should I know. It's just a guess. Either of you got a better one?"

We shook our heads.

"I'd better get home," Amanda said finally. "Pete'll wake up and think I left him."

Her comment surprised me. I didn't know Pete and Amanda that well. They seemed to get along marvelously, but like I said I'm new to the village. "Does he worry about that a lot?" I asked.

"He should be so lucky," Amanda chuckled. "See you in the morning…make that afternoon," and she left us alone.

Margie picked up Magoo, praised him for his bravery, gave him a piece of bread and then headed for her room. I finished my coffee and headed to bed and fell asleep almost as soon as my head hit the pillow.

***

While I slept and dreamt of having sex with my wayward wife, the intruder was arriving back at his place. He picked up the cell phone he'd bought the day before in Honolulu – one of those cash only phones – and made a call concerning me and Lou what's his name. I probably wouldn't have enjoyed my imaginary roll in the hay if I'd known that, but I didn't know anything so I had a very good imaginary time thank you.

Beach Day

The next morning I had just finished showering and was wrapped safely in my bathrobe when Margie appeared at my bathroom doorway and announced with her customary enthusiasm: "Beach day!"

I looked at her lifelessly. She was all smiles.

"I don't think I'm up for the beach, Margie." I was feeling sorry for myself because imaginary sex is not all that great the morning after. "Why don't you go with Amanda and Pete, I was sort of thinking of heading back to my condo..."

"Oh, don't be a poop," Margie teased and turned to leave, then popped back in and said: "It's on the calendar."

The reference had no context for me so I stared at her and waited for an explanation.

"I told you, I made a calendar of things to do when you and Jillian came and today is beach day." She looked at me as if that made perfect sense and that to disagree would be mad.

"I don't know," I said again and reached for the shaving cream. The truth was I didn't *really* feel like being alone.

"What's to know?" Margie said. "I'll get the beach stuff together and we'll stop at your place for your swimsuit and whatever else you need." Then she was gone.

I shaved and put on underwear and checked myself in the mirror. 'Tourist' white. I sucked in my gut and turned sideways. "Not bad," I said approvingly, then let go of my stomach and winced. "You need a gym."

I pulled on yesterday's pants and t-shirt to hide my hideousness and headed for the living room.

Margie was already there, dressed in a lime green string bikini that contained less material than a wash cloth.

133

Thankfully she was wearing a sun-yellow cover-up. It was see-through, of course, and so it didn't really cover anything. Why it should be called a cover-up I have no idea.

I was speechless. Maybe in time I'd learn to accept that Margie's clothes were more appropriate for soft-core porn than for a thirty-something housewife. In the meantime... Well, in the meantime I'd just have to adjust to being overwhelmed.

Although I tried to make my face reflect my disapproval, Margie beamed at me as bubbly as ever. "Surf's up!" she sang and proceeded to inform me that Amada and Pete had a prior engagement and would not be going with us, which was a disappointment to me since I'd been hoping to use Pete as a buffer between Margie and me. The one good piece of news was that Magoo was staying home. Dogs are not allowed on the beach.

Margie had rescued the Volvo from up the street with a container of gas she kept in the garage for such "emergencies" and we loaded it with every conceivable piece of beach gear you could imagine, including a cooler the size of a loveseat. I tried to sneak a peek inside it, but Margie playfully slapped my hand and teased that "you'll see later."

The drive to Hapuna Beach was just as dizzying as my other rides with Margie. She talked nonstop about this, that, and the other. I'll save you the specifics of her barrage since any knowledgeable travel book will cover the same topics in two or three hundred pages. I did learn two important facts however. Amanda and Pete were independently wealthy and therefore did not work – at least not in the conventional sense. And two, Margie did not like driving Jack's car.

When we arrived at Hapuna Beach, I found it was exactly as Margie had advertised it: a long crescent of pure golden sand glittering gemlike in the sun with the deep cobalt blue Pacific Ocean for contrast. It looked very inviting.

I found the path down to the beach was steep and especially so since we were burdened with a picnic basket, that cooler (with wheels that worked great until we hit the sand), grass mats, beach towels, beach chairs, an umbrella, a day bag and two large coolie hats.

I informed Margie I would not wear a coolie hat since I thought the term offensive and as a general rule I looked dopey in any hat other than a Chicago Bulls baseball cap, which was with everything else I owned in the Bermuda Triangle. Despite my objection Margie insisted on bringing them and insisted they would be needed to prevent sunburn. She said she had heard them referred to as 'conical Asian' hats, a term that she hoped I would be able to live with. I said that that was a better name but I still wasn't going to wear one.

It was still relatively early so there wasn't much of a crowd on the beach. A pair of darkly tanned young men played Frisbee at the water's edge and a few dozen bathers frolicked in the waves. Of course there were many bathing beauties lying on the beach catching the early rays. None of them really deserved to be called beauties however. Some were more whale-like in form.

"Isn't it magnificent?" Margie bubbled as if she'd never seen the place before.

"Lovely," I said without passion. "Where to?"

Margie pointed over where the rocks ran down to the surf, cutting the beach almost in half.

"Jack and I go over there." She started to lead the way. "You've got to be careful of the riptide here, Joe," she cautioned. "It can be very dangerous. Are you a good swimmer?"

I took offense at the suggestion I was anything but a good swimmer and threw back my shoulders – at least as much as I could considering I was burdened like a gold miner's burro – and thrust out my chest for emphasis. "Captain of the Roseland high school varsity swim team," I bragged. "I worked my way through college as a lifeguard and have been credited with saving six people, give or take one or two."

Margie looked at me with admiration. "Well I won't worry about you then. But don't get too cocky. Lots of good swimmers get in trouble with these rip tides."

I told her I'd be careful and we made it to the bottom of the hill and past a lifeguard tower. Margie waved at the occupant.

"Aloha, Marshall."

Marshall, who was blonde, well muscled and tan as the proverbial beach boy, looked down and grinned at her and gave me a look that said to me 'what are *you* doing with her?' But then maybe I was reading too much into it.

"Nice suit, Margie," he said warmly.

Margie did a little twirl. "Mahalo," Margie sang, then under her breath she said to me: "Marshall's been a lifeguard for ages. He's a little old for the job if you ask me. But..." She let it go.

We trudged through the sand till we arrived at a spot where Margie suddenly and unceremoniously dropped her load. I followed suit.

Margie then picked up the beach umbrella and began to screw it into the sand. I tried to help, but Margie shooed me off, so I just stood back and observed. She had good technique and a few minutes later our beach camp was complete. Margie kicked off her sandals and removed her cover-up.

As I said, it wasn't much of a cover-up but I think everyone on the beach watched her take it off. I removed my t-shirt self-consciously; I'm certain no one watched that.

"You know, Joe," Margie started as she sat down on her grass mat and began to dig in the day bag for something or other, "Jillian needs a real vacation. You have to get her away from that job."

Margie found the tanning lotion she was looking for and began applying it liberally to her face and neck and arms and legs as best she could reach.

"I try," I said and seated myself comfortably on a straw mat and tried not to watch Margie spread the lotion over every inch of her exposed skin. I'm not a strong man, however, so I was powerless to turn away and felt guilty because I couldn't.

"She really loves her job," I said. "She's always excited about going to work, especially when she's got work in L.A. When I go out of town on business for a week, I come home exhausted. When Jillian comes home it's like she's *been* on vacation."

"Well it's good that she likes her job. Still…" Margie passed me the lotion and laid down on her stomach. "Do my back, please?" It wasn't so much a request as an order.

I was thinking of Jillian's face the last time she'd come home from a business trip and how energized she'd looked while I mindlessly squeezed lotion into the palm of my hand. I was about to apply the lotion to Margie's back but stopped abruptly. *Should I be doing this?*

"Don't be stingy with it," Margie said.

I looked at the lotion in my hand. It was too late to stop now, and there really wasn't anything wrong with what I was going to do but... as soon as my hand touched Margie's back I felt a current run up my arm.

What was that?

I shook the reaction off and applied the lotion gently, self-consciously, reluctantly.

"That feels sooooo good," Margie cooed.

I know what you're thinking. 'What's wrong with this guy? He *should* be enjoying this.' Well I wasn't. The truth of it was, it was torture. I felt like a child molester. Not that I know what a child molester feels like, only that I felt very, very uncomfortable with what I was doing. *'You're not doing anything wrong, It's just tanning lotion.'* My brain said. But it felt wrong in some way and naughty too and I was getting... Never mind what I was getting.

I finished finally and Margie sat up quickly and took the tanning lotion.

"Okay, your turn. On your stomach buster," Margie ordered. "I don't want Jillian kvetching that I didn't take care of you."

There was no escape from it, at least not that I could think of, so I lowered myself onto my stomach and waited for Margie to start rubbing lotion all over me. I thought I was prepared, but I wasn't, because as soon as I laid down Margie surprised the hell out of me by throwing her leg over my back and sitting down right on my ass!

Of course she weighed nothing, but...

I'm pretty sure you can guess what my physical reaction to this was, so I'll spare you the details. I am, after all, a very normal warm blooded male with normal reactions to normal everyday stimuli and... Oh forget it. What I'm trying to say is that I was unable to control my reaction and although it *wasn't* an unpleasant reaction, it *was* discomforting under the circumstances.

Margie drizzled lotion on my back and began to apply it in slow soothing circles. I was in agony. Or was that ecstasy?

"My goodness, Joe, your muscles are tight as fists," she said. "Relax. I'm not going to hurt you."

It occurred to me that while she may not physically injure me, I might be psychologically scarred forever and I perhaps I should object. But I didn't want to hurt Margie's feelings. At least that's what I told myself.

"Isn't that better?" Margie hummed and pushed her small palms hard against my back.

"Yeah... yes," I mumbled, unsure of how much more I could take.

Suddenly Margie stopped her rub down. "Oh, oh, look who's here," she said with disgust.

I turned my head and saw Detective Lo making his way toward us through the sand.

"What's he doing here?" Margie kept her voice low.

I hoped at this point that Margie might have the good sense to dismount me, but she didn't and I braced myself for the encounter.

The detective arrived and I looked up at his surprisingly cheery face framed by a cloudless sky. *What's he smiling about?*

"Aloha, Mr. Thomas, Mrs. Geanosa" he said agreeably. If he'd been wearing a hat, I'm sure he would have tipped it. "It's nice to see you two enjoying yourselves."

The smile held. I couldn't read it. It might have been genuine. It also might have been insincere.

"I spoke with Mr. Geanosa in L.A. He was unable to identify the man in your pool."

"Well of course he was," Margie huffed. "Why should he be able to? We don't travel in circles where people are murdered."

Margie's response was pretty shrill so I thought I should take charge. "Did you figure out what he was doing there?" I asked.

"Not specifically. He's from New Jersey and he's got a long record with the authorities there. Seems he goes in for blackmail." Lo stood quietly letting that information sink in.

"Well no one is blackmailing me." I responded with a tinge of guilt. "I haven't done anything to be blackmailed for." Of course as I said this I was thinking that carrying Margie naked to her bedroom and lying on the beach with her on top of me might be cause for blackmail in some circles.

"I wasn't suggesting..." the detective started.

"Oh, sure you were!" Margie broke in. "Anyway, what are you doing here? You're not supposed to question us without our attorney."

"I wasn't questioning you. I'm just having a day at the beach with my family." The detective turned and pointed to a pleasant looking woman and three children fifty yards away.

Margie made a harrumphing noise and the detective turned to leave. "Have a pleasant beach day. Aloha." He started to walk away then stopped and turned back.

"Oh, Mr. Thomas. I've been meaning to ask you. When will Mrs. Thomas be joining you? I hope she's not ill."

The detective didn't wait for an answer. He just turned again and headed toward his family.

I watched him go a while then said to Margie: "You know what he's thinking over there, don't you? He's thinking we're doing something wrong."

"Well we're not," Margie said stiffly and began massaging me again. "We're not doing anything wrong."

"Of course we're not," I agreed. "But he thinks we are. And we're still suspects."

"Don't let him get to you, Joe," Margie stopped her massage. "How about an ice cold beverage. I brought ice tea, water, and guava juice.

Margie leaned over and opened the ice chest and began to dig in it. She pulled out a bottle and opened it. "Try the guava juice. You'll love it. Now roll over and I'll do your front."

You've got to be kidding? Roll over? Now? The prospect put me in a panic. *Like I was going to do that on a public beach. Not without a hat I wasn't!*

I took the bottle of guava juice from Margie and stayed on my stomach.

"Not just now, Margie" I said casually. "I think I'll just lie on my stomach in the sun a while."

Margie slid off me and plopped on her mat. "Okey doke, but let me know when you want more."

More? I thought. I don't think I can take any more.

Walking Margie Home

Despite the lotion, the beach umbrella, the coolie hat (which I did wear because the sun was more intense than I could ever imagine) and other efforts to mollify the sun god, I was crispy by the time we headed home. Margie made a stop at the local grocery store and picked up a bottle of vinegar, which she claimed was absolutely the best astringent for sunburn. She also picked up dinner fixings, since she reasoned rightly that I wouldn't want to go out for dinner if I was feeling toasty.

Back at my condo Margie bathed me thoroughly – no she did not give me a bath, I meant it figuratively not literally – in vinegar and then set about making dinner, which she informed me was going to be a surprise.

She sent me out on the lanai with a scotch and orders to enjoy the view.

I smelled like a fresh spinach salad, but had to admit the vinegar worked marvelously at reducing the sting of the sunburn.

Twenty minutes later, Margie joined me with a second scotch and a glass of white wine for herself and then hurried away and returned a moment later with two dinner plates, utensils and the appropriate condiments. She disappeared again and returned with our dinner, which was fresh Wahoo (which they call Ono in Hawaii) with a tangy pesto sauce, a salad of locally grown field greens, lightly dressed with vinaigrette, and sticky rice covered with a ginger-based cream sauce. The only reason I know any of this is because Margie told me what it was. I just call everything 'food.'

It was fantastic.

"Where did you learn to cook like this?" I asked between bites.

"I don't know," Margie said looking off at the ocean for a moment. "I'm sort of a natural I guess."

Well natural or trained at Le Cordon Bleu, I was delighted with every bit of my meal and we spent our dinner time eating and discussing food – the good the bad and the ugly of it. I admitted to burning water and confessed that Jillian's idea of a gourmet meal was dinner reservations.

Margie informed me that Jillian had regularly burned popcorn in the microwave in college and she pondered why so many people cooked with microwaves and little else. There is no answer for that of course. But how did they cook before microwaves? Now *that's* a mystery.

For dessert, Margie served Ben and Jerry's Cherry Garcia ice cream, which is one of my favorites and one of hers as well. We followed dessert with another round of drinks and watched the sun set, which tonight, because of a cloudy horizon was not so spectacular. I'm not complaining. Just noting. And yes I did get another kiss. Strawberry.

Sunset was followed by another round of drinks and a serious discussion on the next day's adventure. I realized half-way through Margie's dissertation extolling the thrill of shopping and resort prowling – which is what was on the calendar for tomorrow – that I was no longer as intimidated by her amazing looks as before and that I was having quite a good time with her.

You've no doubt already figured out that I was becoming infatuated with Margie (do people still use that word?). Still, I wasn't consciously aware of it. I thought I was crazy in love with Jillian, who you can probably tell doesn't seem all that crazy about me. But I didn't want to think that, so I was, as they say, clueless.

I don't think Margie did anything to lead me on. She's a natural born cook and a natural born flirt, but an innocent flirt and if there was any subtext to our relationship, it was mine. She seemed very happy with Jack.

Anyway I told Margie that I was more interested in going snorkeling or scuba diving than shopping, but she reminded me that you can't scuba dive within 24 hours of drinking heavily – something we had already done – and that if I really wanted to do something on the water we should book a reservation to snorkel with the Manta Rays at night.

I thought that was a great idea and we had a drink on it.

Now if you're keeping track you may have noticed that we'd had quite a bit to drink and so when Margie suggested that she best be off, I nixed the idea.

"You've had way too much to drink, Margie," I said sternly. "And so have I."

"I know," she slurred. "I should call a taxi."

"Don't be silly," I said. "There are two bedrooms. You can stay the night here. I've spent plenty of time at your place. Now I can reciprocate." No I wasn't thinking anything dirty. It was an innocent suggestion. Cross my heart and hope to die.

"What about Magoo? I can't leave him alone," Margie said. "He's been alone all day."

I'd forgotten about the little mongrel. It probably would have been unkind to leave him alone all night, especially since he was still getting to know his way around Margie's. And he might take it out on her by eating a sofa or at least a rug.

"Maybe Amanda and Pete could go over…"

"Of course! Amanda can give me a ride," Margie sang. "Where's the phone?" Margie got up and staggered into the condo. A moment later I heard: "Well, what did you do that for? Okay, forget it."

Margie returned and plopped in her seat and giggled. I waited for her to say something. Margie looked at me blankly.

"Well?" I asked finally.

"Well what?" Then she remembered. "They had too much wine with dinner."

Margie rose suddenly. "I think I'll just walk! It's a nice evening and it'll sober me up." She stood and began to leave.

"You can't walk," I protested. "Let me call a taxi."

Margie shook her head. "Nope. I've decided. I'll walk. It's not that far if I cut across the golf course." She headed indoors. I got up and followed, realizing as I did so that I was quite woozy.

"I can't let you do that," I said firmly.

Margie turned and looked me in the eye. "You're not my mother," she said sternly, then giggled. "You don't look anything like her." She sniggered again and picked up her purse and started for the door.

"Margie," I pleaded. "Be reasonable."

She was determined to walk, however, and short of tying her down I couldn't think of any way to stop her from leaving.

"Okay," I said, "then I'll go with you."

Margie stopped and turned at the door. "Okey doke. I'll buy you a drink when we get there."

She waited for me to find my sandals and after I locked the condo we went off into the darkness. I let Margie take the lead since I was unsure of the best route.

It was a beautiful evening as we crossed the parking lot and made our way through a gap in the bushes and spilled out onto a fairway of the golf course. Margie immediately kicked off her flip-flops.

"Take off your sandals, Joe. The grass feels wonderful." She did a little twirl.

I was reluctant to do that. Not because I'm up tight – which I am – but because I didn't think it was an especially smart thing to do. There are crawly things after all.

"I don't think that's a good idea," I shared.

"Oh, poo," Margie teased. "It feels so cool and luxurious." She did another little twirl and fell over.

I rushed over, but she'd already righted herself and sat on the ground giggling. "I fell over."

"Yes you did," I said and held out my hand to help her up. She took my hand with both of her hers, but instead of pulling herself up, she pulled me down and I toppled over and fell next to her.

Margie laughed uproariously. "You fell over," she said, laughing so hard she snorted and then laughed harder still because she'd snorted.

Of course I laughed too. It was pretty funny.

We sat together on the cool grass till Margie laid down and stared up at the sky. I followed her lead and laid down next to her. It was quiet and warm and the closeness to the earth scented the air.

"I haven't done this in ages," I said, looking up at the first stars. "Why is that? When did I forget to just look up?"

The moonless sky sparkled.

"When I was a kid back in Chicago my friends and I would go sledding at night and when we got tired of climbing the hill and sliding down we'd lay on our backs and look up at the stars and try to name the constellations. I don't think I've done it since then."

"It's stupid," Margie said. "We should do this *all* the time."

I agreed with her and for the next few minutes we just lay there watching the sky darken and fill with stars.

Suddenly I heard a sound. I couldn't place it at first, but it seemed very familiar.

Margie must have heard it too for she sat up quickly, grabbed her flip flops, and jumped to her feet. "Run, Joe!" she yelled, and began sprinting up the fairway.

I got to my feet and took off after her. I recalled the noise now, but there was no escape. A second later the first sprinkler hit us and a second later we got hit from all sides. In no time at all we were thoroughly drenched and laughing and running and slipping and falling and getting up and running again.

We didn't find safety till we made it to the roadway that separated one fairway from another. Soaking wet, and for the most part sober, we stopped long enough for Margie to put on her flip flops and then we trudged cold and wet to Margie's where I dried off and was given a fresh pair of pajamas and a robe that Margie assured me Jack had never worn and we joined up again out by the pool for a drink and watched the stars from our safe haven.

Magoo had been pretty good, though Margie decided she should not leave him alone until he stopped eating her underwear. I didn't say so at the time, but it occurred to me that she could achieve the same results if she stopped leaving her underwear on the floor. Right?

We called it a night when the moon rose and vanquished the starlight.

***

It must have been a few hours later when I awoke. It wasn't anywhere near morning and I'm generally a sound sleeper so I was wondering what might have awakened me.

I remembered our intruder and listened attentively for telltale sounds of his return, but all was quiet. I decided a trip to the bathroom might help me get back to sleep and after that I thought, 'what the heck, why don't you just check things out in the yard.'

I tiptoed through the living room and stepped outside. It was chilly and the clouds had rolled in so there were no stars; it was very dark. I listened. Nothing. I was about to go back to my room when I glanced at the pool. What's that, I thought?

There was something in the pool. No not another murder victim. It was small and lacked definition. A palm frond? I walked over to the bank of lights and flipped on the one for the underwater lights so I could see what it was.

It was Magoo! He was just laying on the surface, motionless. "Oh my God!" I shouted and dove in without thinking and grabbed hold of him as I surfaced, then swam to the edge of the pool and dropped him onto the pool skirt. I pushed myself out of the pool and knelt next to him.

Margie was up and running through the living room. "What's the matter?" she yelled breathlessly.

"It's Magoo. He's drowned," I told her and tried to figure out if you could give mouth to mouth to a dog.

"Oh, no," Margie knelt next to us and stroked Magoo lightly. "What can we do?"

I had no idea, but I knew I had to try something. I put my ear to his chest. His heart was still beating; that was something. And he was breathing a little, but I heard a gurgling noise so I knew we needed to get the water out of his lungs.

I picked him up by his back legs and held him upside down.

"Pat his back lightly," I told Margie. She did as I said and a small amount of water spilled from Magoo's mouth.

I laid the little guy back down. He moved one hind leg.

"He's coming around!" Margie shouted.

I put my ear to his chest again. No gurgle. That was good.

The little guy began to move his legs and a second later he rolled onto his stomach and then on his feet. He threw up twice and took a step forward.

Margie stood up and took off her robe. "Here, wrap him in this."

Without thinking, I reached out to pick up Magoo to put him in Margie's robe, but that was a mistake because before you could say 'Thanks for saving my life,' he bit me! On the finger!

I gave a yelp and he let up. Margie threw the robe over him and gathered him up. "He's not very grateful is he?" she offered. "Is it bleeding?"

I looked. There were tooth marks but no blood. "Naw. It's okay. But we better get him to a vet to check him out."

Margie agreed with me and an hour and a half later after waking the vet and waking Amanda – who refused to drive us but gave us her car keys (you might recall both of Margie's cars were at my condo) – we were back from the vets with "one lucky dog" who hit the floor running toward his food dish, which Margie filled.

The veterinarian applauded my actions and said I'd done the right thing. Margie also applauded my actions and hugged me so hard I thought my ribs would crack. She kissed me too. At least someone was grateful.

We made our way to our respective bedrooms and I fell asleep almost immediately. It was late and it had been a long day-night. Sometime later, however, I woke and felt a presence creeping onto my bed.

149

Margie?

I didn't know what to do, so I pretended to be asleep. A moment later was taken aback when Magoo started to lick my face – yes I would have preferred it was Margie but ... well you know.

I opened my eyes and reached out and patted his head. It was too dark to see if his tail wagged or not, but I figured it did.

Then I watched the little mutt settle onto the pillow next to me. I smiled. All was right with the world again. I was happy that my efforts had been fully acknowledged, that was until I realized the little beggar had gas.

Jillian's a Pill

In the morning, I called Jillian who didn't think my story of what had happened the night before with Margie was at all amusing or my life-saving efforts with Magoo were interesting. She thought it was mundane and we returned to our conversation of why she was in L.A. and when she might return to our vacation. Promises were made but I had no confidence they would be kept and after a breakfast of coffee and fruit and some toast — which I shared with my new friend – Margie and I walked back to my condo so she could pick up her car and I could have a bacon sandwich.

We agreed to meet up again at noon and go shopping and resort hopping, my only alternative being to stew at the condo which I was reluctant to do because I'm just not good at stewing and I really did need more clothes.

When Margie came to pick me up, Amanda and Pete were with her, so the prospect of having a guy to talk to lifted my spirits and made me hopeful that the day would go better than anticipated.

We had a great lunch at a little place whose name I can't recall and then went shopping. At least Margie and Amanda went shopping. I spent about twenty minutes picking up four pair of shorts, six t-shirts, three vintage Hawaiian shirts, pajamas, a robe and slippers. After that Pete and I sat outside the shops and discussed all matter of important sports topics and the sorry state of the economy.

And since I had the opportunity, I asked Pete a question that had been on my mind for some time. "What's Jack like?"

I really didn't know diddly squat about him. I'd seen pictures of him around Margie's place, so I knew he was handsome and had muscles in places I don't. But other than the bits and pieces Margie offered, I hadn't a clue. Besides I wanted a guy's perspective.

Pete pondered my question a while – actually, he may have just wanted to finish ogling the attractive Asian woman who passed by – and replied in what I'd come to recognize was Pete's crisp, clear style: "He's okay."

Obviously I was going to have to dig.

"You don't sound like a fan," I offered. "Don't you like him?"

Pete's brain worked a bit. "He's kind of cold," Pete said. "Frankly I don't know what Margie sees in the guy."

"Opposites attract," I suggested lamely.

"I suppose," Pete said. "But he's always trying to control things," he added after a while. " Margie's not someone anyone can control."

"Yeah," I said. "She does have a strong will. Do they ever fight? Margie talks about him like he's a saint or something. I don't think my wife talks about me that way."

Pete looked at me sideways. "That's too bad. You're a nice guy. I told Amanda the other night it's too bad you don't live on the island."

I accepted his compliment but before I could say thanks, Pete continued. "Jack and I never connected. I always felt he was talking down to me. I get the impression he thinks he's better than other people."

"Does Amanda share your opinion of him?" I asked.

"She puts up with him 'cause she and Margie are like sisters. I've never heard her say anything negative but I don't think she's a big fan."

I was digesting this information and was about to ask a follow-up question when the ladies appeared and forced us off our comfortable bench and on to bigger and better things – or so they said.

152

We hit a few resorts, including that one that was like Disneyland, and a couple of places that smelled of old money – lots of old money – and Pete and I ogled the beautiful golf courses that were everywhere. But since we mostly watch golf on TV, we didn't talk about actually going golfing.

By late afternoon I was exhausted and suggested that dinnertime was approaching and insisted on treating everyone – unless, of course, they wanted to go someplace fancy. I got an undeserved laugh.

Five minutes later we were in the car, which was now crowded with packages, two of which were mine – the rest were Margie's and Amanda's – and the conversation centered on where we might have a fun dinner.

Since I hadn't a clue as to where we might eat, I just listened as various venues were tossed out and shot down. Pete liked meat. Margie, as you know, is a vegetarian. She wanted someplace on the water. Amanda said she'd agree to just about anything. I agreed with Amanda, so long as there *was* meat on the menu.

We finally settled on a place in Kona across from the harbor that had Mexican food and we found a table on the upper level with a view of Kailua Bay.

Once we got seated Margie reminded me that if we were going scuba diving in the morning, we couldn't drink. I was in need of a drink – shopping does that to me – but I did want to scuba so I ordered pop. I got the details from Margie as to where I was to meet Bobby – our guide.

"You have to be at the pool at 7:30 a.m. I know it's early, but you have to get instructions in the pool before you can go in the ocean." Margie stopped and returned a wave from a young man climbing into his car down on the street. "Bobby's boat is at Keauhou Bay. You know where that is?"

153

"Sure," I said. "It's right next to my condo where I sometimes sleep."

Margie made a smug face and continued. "I'll meet you at ten. Since you were a lifeguard, Bobby said it shouldn't take long to get you used to the equipment. I'll bring Jack's scuba gear. You've got your own mask and flippers, so you should be set. Are there any questions?"

"Nope," I said. But I think you'll make a great mom someday."

Margie missed my sarcasm and thanked me for the compliment, then picked up her ice tea and took a sip. With characteristic enthusiasm she remarked: "Isn't this place great?"

I tried to talk Pete and Amanda into coming with us on our adventure, but they didn't scuba and didn't want to learn and besides they wanted to drink Margaritas.

We ate and the drinkers drank and we watched as the cruise ship sailed into port. Margie explained they – the cruise ship passengers – wouldn't come ashore till morning and it was a good thing "'cause they'd stink up the place."

I took it Margie didn't like tourists but she defended her jab by explaining they made it hard to get a table anywhere when they came ashore.

I was enjoying my chimichangas and rice and refried beans but wishing I could wash them down with a cold Dos Equis, when I spotted 'That Guy' again. The one I'd seen at the bar at Huggo's. He was seated at the bar here and he *was* having a margarita.

"There he is again," I said to Margie, who turned to look. Amanda and Pete turned to look too. Luckily 'That Guy' wasn't looking our way. It might have been uncomfortable.

"I told you before, Joe. Go over and say hi and figure out where you've seen him," Margie dove back into her fish tacos.

Amanda agreed with Margie. Pete took my side. "Do you really care where you've seen him?" he said practically.

Since I didn't care, I said so, and returned to my meal, but I watched the guy every now and again and noticed he glanced at our table at least a half dozen times. Of course that wasn't any more often than any of the other guys at the bar. Margie and Amanda drew attention everywhere we went.

"He's probably following you," Amanda ventured when she saw me glancing at him. "I'll bet he's with the police."

"That doesn't make sense, Amanda," Margie responded. "The first time we saw him was *before* the murder. Why would someone be following us then?"

The mention of the murder turned the topic of conversation in that direction and before I could say "stop" we were knee deep in theories about Lou Krauthammer or whatever his name was. I was weary by the time I paid the bill and we got out of there.

'That Guy' slipped out ahead of us so I couldn't check him out more closely on the way out. He *was* a slippery fella.

By now I really, really wanted a drink but I didn't have one even though Margie dropped me off alone at my condo where I'd laid in a month's supply of liquor.

Had I known what the next day would bring, I would have had at least three large tumblers of scotch and washed it down with a couple of beers, but I didn't know and no one else did either except for a couple of people who wanted me dead. Why they wanted me dead I don't know. But they did.

Fish and Turtles and Trauma

Bobby was male – not that I was surprised – and he gave me a first-class, albeit brief, course in scuba diving. As predicted, my confidence in the water proved invaluable so I was fully prepared at ten when Margie appeared in her T-bird and pulled up at the dock.

"I hope you haven't been waiting long," Margie apologized, even though she was right on time. Today she was dressed in what I'm sure she thought was a conservative one piece swimsuit. Compared to others, it was, but it was cut high at the hips and low in front and back, and it looked as though it might have been painted on, so in her world that did pass for conservative

Bobby and I had already loaded a large Zodiac with equipment and Margie popped the trunk on her T-bird and Bobby went to give her a hand.

" You're not late, Mrs. Geanosa. No need to apologize," Bobby said, and then added: "Nice duds."

Margie struck a playful, provocative pose and flashed a smile. "Thanks, Bobby, but you always called me Margie before."

Bobby jerked his head toward me. "I didn't want Mr. Thomas to think..."

Margie batted the air. "He's used to me by now. So how'd he do in the pool?"

I fielded the question. "Bobby says I'm the best student he's had in ages." I turned to Bobby: "And you can call me Joe."

Bobby nodded and took Margie's equipment and passed it to me. "He's a natural," he said, then "hand me that tank please? The red one."

I did as directed. "What else do we need?" I asked.

"Nothing. We'll shove off as soon as the skipper gets here."

Since we would be diving close to shore, it made sense to have someone in the boat to hold it steady in the waves.

"There he comes," Margie announced. "And right on time." Margie waved. "Saulala! How are you this fine morning?"

I turned to see our skipper trudging across the parking lot with the determination of Godzilla conquering Tokyo. He was a huge Polynesian guy with wild hair and he was almost as wide as he was tall. Not fat, but built like the proverbial brick shit house.

Saulala looked miserable; he shook his head. "Don' as'," he cautioned. "I parti' wit da boyz las' nigh'. Don' mention food and I' be fine."

I got introduced and found Saulala's hand was the size of a catcher's mitt; he had a very firm handshake and managed a warm and winning smile. We all climbed in the boat and once we were seated we took off at full throttle.

It was a short trip, just out of the bay and along the shore for about ten minutes. Saulala throttled the engine back and turned the bow into the slow swells.

"That bedda," he said and massaged his temples. He must have had a really bad night.

Bobby, Margie and I pulled on our wet-suits and got into the rest of our gear.

"Okay, here's how we'll do it." Bobby said, pointing as he gave instructions. "You go first, Joe, then Margie, then me. We'll take a few minutes on the surface to check equipment, then we dive. Me first, Joe, then Margie in the rear. Make sure you watch my hand signals. Any questions?"

"Yeah," I said. "How come I've got this huge tank? I thought I was going to use Jack's."

Jack's tank, which Bobby had commandeered, was considerably smaller.

"I switched 'cause my tank is bigger. First timers always suck a lot of air. This way we can all stay down twenty to thirty minutes. Don't worry, Joe, I adjusted your belt for the added weight. In the water you won't notice a thing."

Margie, who had thought to bring a waterproof camera, stood and aimed it at me. "Smile," she ordered.

I did as I was told, then I took the camera from her and took a picture of her with Saulala and then her with Bobby and then Saulala took a picture of the three of us and ... You get the idea. We took a lot of pictures.

A minute later we rolled out of the boat and into the water where we spent about a minute on the surface adjusting equipment. Bobby gave the thumbs up and we dove – Bobby, then me and then Margie.

I had snorkeled in the Caribbean where the water is shallow for hundreds of yards, but diving in the deep open water surrounding the Big Island was both amazing and intimidating. But my initial concerns passed quickly and in no time at all we were swimming along a coral-encrusted ledge littered with an amazing assortment of colorful and breathtaking fish in all shapes and sizes.

A green sea turtle soared past me and I turned to see Margie give me a thumbs up and snap a photo. I'd like an 8 by 10 of that please.

We'd been under for only a few minutes when Bobby stopped and took out his mouthpiece and shook his head. He seemed annoyed at something and began to clear his mask. Then suddenly he doubled-over and began to spasm. Something was horribly wrong!

Margie spotted it too and reacted first; she sped by me like a torpedo and grabbed Bobby under his arms and pushed him toward the surface. An instant later I joined her and we broke through quickly to the surface.

Margie spit out her mouthpiece and shook Bobby's head. "Bobby, can you hear me?" she called, then to me: "He's not breathing!"

Margie yelled for Saulala. "Bring the boat. Get on the radio, tell them to meet us at the dock with an ambulance."

She needn't have wasted her breath. Saulala must have spotted us when we surfaced and knew there was trouble for he was already speeding toward us and as soon as he pulled alongside he reached down, grabbed Bobby's tank and yanked him into the boat in a single motion. Then he grabbed Margie's tank and did the same. I had reached the side of the boat and managed to pull myself in by then.

An instant later we were running at full throttle with Saulala on the radio relaying our problem to whomever.

Bobby was unconscious at the bottom of the boat and Margie was next to him, holding his hand and looking terrified. My lifeguard training kicked in and I quickly began CPR. I was really worried because Bobby wasn't looking too good.

***

Ten minutes later Margie and I were standing on the dock watching the ambulance pull away, its siren screaming.

Margie shivered even though she had a big towel wrapped around her, so I gave her a hug.

She looked up at me. "You were wonderful, Joe. I wouldn't..." Margie started then choked back tears. "What do you suppose...?" Margie shook her head and looked perplexed. "Do you think he was partying with Saulala?"

He could have been, but I hadn't a clue about that and we couldn't ask Bobby or Saulala; Saulala had gone in the ambulance too.

"I better get you home," I said, and we picked up the scuba gear and headed for our cars. "We could both use a drink."

A half hour later Margie and I were by her pool, not talking, just staring. You know the way people do when something earth shattering has happened and you don't know what to say or do. I finished the last of my scotch and struggled to my feet. "Another one?"

"Sure. Hit me," Margie said. "I'm going to call the hospital while you make 'em."

We staggered inside together. We'd only had the one drink, but mine had been a triple and Margie's had been a tall Long Island and both were on empty stomachs... Well you know how it is.

I headed for the bar. Margie to the telephone.

As I refilled the glasses I listened to Margie's conversation.

"Yes. Hello. I'm calling about Bobby Douglas. Can you give me any news? We were with him when he..."

I looked over and saw Margie's face light up.

"That's wonderful," she sang. "Mahalo. Thank you very much."

Margie hung up the phone, ran to me, wrapped her arms around me and gave me a big hug. I almost spilled the drinks.

"He's going to be fine! A full recovery!" Margie continued to hold me for a very long time, then she let up and took her drink. She knocked her glass against mine. "To Joe, my hero!" she took a big swallow.

I started to protest that I'd done little but she'd have none of that.

"Just wait till I tell Jillian what a ... and Jack! I've got to tell Jack too."

Margie was suddenly all lit up and ran back to the phone and began punching buttons. I made my way outside and slid into the lounge chair and tipped back my glass. Gosh it was nice to be noticed.

Amanda showed up about then and asked why I was drunk in the middle of the day and I had to fill her in. All she could say was: "And that's why I don't go scuba diving."

The Lindbergh Kidnapper

We were in the interrogation room again. Frank and Detective Lo sat across from each other, and I sat off to the side. The detective looked angry. Frank looked annoyed. I tried hard to look invisible.

"We're not going over it again detective," Frank said flatly. "Both Mrs. Geanosa and Mr. Thomas have given you statements. Neither one of them has a motive to hurt Bobby Douglas."

Frank pushed back in his chair and stood up. "As to why Mr. Douglas changed tanks with Mr. Thomas, if you don't believe my clients' stories, check with Mr. Douglas. What you should be doing detective is trying to find out where the bad tank of air came from..." he stabbed the table with his finger "so you can determine if there's any reason for whoever filled it to want to injure Mr. Geanosa, whose tank it was, or Mr. Thomas, for whom the tank was initially intended."

Frank stabbed the table again. "In any event detective, Mr. Thomas *saved* Mr. Douglas' life! Would he have done that if he wanted to kill him?"

Detective Lo sneered at Frank. "Okay, I got the statements. Don't tell me what I should and shouldn't be doing."

The detective then stood and leaned over the table and stabbed it with his finger. "Since Mr. Thomas has come to the island there has been a murder, the attempted downing of a helicopter, and now a near death by drowning. We found scratch marks on the trunk of Mrs. Geanosa's car where the tank was stored. It had obviously been jimmied open.

"All these things are connected to Mr. Thomas in one way or another. Something is going on Mr. Bonza. Where there is smoke, there's fire, and Mr. Thomas is a raging inferno."

The detective turned to me and glared. "Mr. Thomas. That tank was intended for you. Who wants you dead, and why?"

Again, I hadn't a clue. Was the tainted air really intended for me? I shrugged and tried to be invisible again.

The detective turned back to Frank and the two men glared at one another briefly.

"So we're done here?" Frank asked.

"Take 'im," Detective Lo answered and left the room briskly.

We met up with Margie in the squad room where she had been waiting patiently.

Unknown to us as we left the station, another detective named Jimmy Koi, who resembled Jackie Chan except he didn't have his money and couldn't jump over moving cars, ambled over to Detective Lo. They watched us leave.

"Want me to follow those guys around boss?"

Detective Lo looked down at Jimmy a moment. "That's not a bad idea. But just the guy for now," detective Lo said. "See how things develop." Jimmy nodded.

Frank dropped me off back at my condo, and I called Jillian to update her and to ask when she might join me. Her answer was the same as yesterday. "Just a day or two longer."

She didn't seem at all interested in what I'd been through and you might even say she seemed annoyed that I'd called so I tried some reverse psychology on her. "Aren't you afraid that Margie and I are going to get cozy being together all the time. She's a very attractive woman."

"Are you trying to make me jealous?" she asked with a hint of disbelief in her tone.

I could sense her shaking her head at my sad attempt. Of course she saw right through it. Margie was out of my league and she knew it.

"No," I lied. "But I feel neglected, and I know Margie is upset with Jack for being away."

The rest of the conversation isn't worth describing and as soon as I hung up on Jillian, Margie called and we compared notes about our respective spouses.

"Jack and Jillian are cut from the same cloth," Margie said sadly. "Work, work, work."

"Come on over to my place," Margie said finally. "We'll go see Amanda and Pete and make them entertain us."

"Do they do that?" I queried.

"Sometimes," Margie said. "Anyway, I don't want to sit around here."

I drove up to Margie's and didn't notice that someone was following me. Why should I notice? I hadn't done anything. And when I got to Margie's we went and pestered Amanda and Pete until sunset and made them give us dinner and drinks.

Yes we were drinking way too much, but can you really blame us? The good news was that since we were at Amanda and Pete's we had steak for dinner. Margie had salad. I think she's part bunny. No, not the Playboy kind, although I'm sure she could easily qualify.

After the after-dinner drinks, Margie and I and Magoo stumbled back to Margie's. No one was sober enough to give me a ride home and Margie wouldn't hear of me taking a taxi, so it was back to our respective rooms where we tucked ourselves in, and slept. Boring, huh?

I had a sex dream about Margie, but I'll not provide details. I'll just state for the record that it occurred and let you make up your own scenario.

I know I said this before, but it bears repeating: I think I'm paying way too much for my condo.

The Run Down

I woke the next morning without the hangover I'd expected and showered and shaved and started toward the living room, but stopped to read a small handwritten note taped to the door jamb of my bedroom: 'Beware! Nude swimmer!!' The i was dotted with a little heart and there was a smiley face after the second exclamation point.

Margie's writing style seemed to fit her and I cautiously made my way through the living room to the kitchen. I could hear Margie in the pool, but kept my eyes straight ahead. Yes, thank you, I am a gentleman. I already felt guilty about the dream so I didn't need any ogling to make me feel guiltier. After all, if Jillian were here it would be a moot point.

In the kitchen I found coffee and poured myself a mug. I found the local newspaper on the island, West Hawaii Today, and pulled up a stool to read and drink. I was still reading when Margie appeared across the island dripping water everywhere. She was 'dressed' but in an extremely short white terrycloth robe that said 'HIS' on it.

I pointed out to her that she was wearing Jack's robe and she gave me an odd look and then said: "Nope, this one's mine."

For a moment I was confused, then it clicked. Of course. It made perfect sense if you understood Margie and I was beginning to. Which kind of scared me.

"Cute," I said approvingly and Margie smiled brightly, pleased, I believe, that I was intelligent enough to figure it out by myself. Then she shooed me outside in the sun by the pool and promised to bring breakfast after she'd changed.

By the time I'd finished the sports page she joined me 'dressed' in a strappy little sundress that was the same color as the flecks of gold in her eyes. I'm pretty sure she wasn't wearing underwear. Don't ask me *why* I thought that. It has something to do with VPLs. Ask your mother.

She carried a tray with her, which held the proper breakfast apparatus and breakfast itself, which consisted of fruit – sliced and whole – yogurt, and some sort of whole grain cereal, and tofu milk. Blah!

She saw that I was disappointed with her offering but didn't apologize. She said something to the effect that if I couldn't handle eating healthy food I should go down the street and beg from Amanda and Pete who ate bacon and other meats and butter fried eggs and cinnamon rolls and were going to die a horrible death from heart disease or colon cancer whereas she, Margie, would still be spry and healthy. Actually I didn't hear the latter part of Margie's rant. 'Cinnamon rolls' caught my attention straightaway.

Over breakfast – I ate fruit – we discussed the day's options. Margie had it on her calendar that we were going to Hilo, but said that that wouldn't be any fun with just the two of us and Pete and Amanda didn't like it there so we had to come up with something else. Hilo, just so you know, is the largest city on the island and the county seat. It is on the east side of the island, which is the rainy side, and because of this is very lush and beautiful, like a rain forest. There, that's all I remember from the tour guide.

We pondered our options. Actually Margie did the most pondering, I was still thinking about cinnamon rolls until Margie sat up straight and announced with delight: "You haven't been on your helicopter ride!"

I nearly spit my papaya across the room! The *last* thing I wanted to do was go on a helicopter ride. I quickly dug in my brain for any other activity we might engage in and then I remembered biking.

Back in Chicago, when there isn't snow on the ground or freezing rain, or some other weather fiasco, I do a fair amount of biking, and when I found out I was going to Hawaii I looked up things to do and one of them was to bike the Ironman route.

The Ironman route is 112 miles, which is further than I wanted to bike at any time anywhere, but I figured there was an 'easy' 26-miles somewhere in there that I could handle.

So rather than squash Margie's helicopter enthusiasm – she wasn't going to go, we already knew that – I commented that I hadn't had a lick of exercise since I'd come to the island and proposed a bike ride.

As it turned out, Margie was a big biking enthusiast but rather than jump on board she looked me hard in the eye and asked: "Are you in good enough shape?"

I took that as an insult. Not that my pale flesh and spare tire didn't lend itself to that assumption.

"I'm not a total couch potato," I responded defensively. "I get plenty of exercise and...."

Margie didn't let me finish. She apologized and said she thought the idea was fine and we hashed out the details; Margie suggested we bike from Kona to Hapuna Beach, which was about 40 miles.

"There are lots of places to stop short if you can't handle it." Margie eyed me again with that look of skepticism she'd shown when I first proposed the bike ride. "We'll get Amanda to pick us up and drive us home."

She glanced at her watch. "We'd better get cracking. We don't want to be on the road after noon. That gives us about three hours. Can you keep up that pace? Thirteen miles an hour?"

Again I was offended. "No problem," I said confidently and rose from my chair. "Perhaps we can do a round trip?" I paused and looked at Margie who looked as if she were going to say something negative, but didn't. "Where can I rent a bike?"

"Not necessary," Margie said flatly. "You can use Jack's."

She then headed for the phone where she called Amanda and after that we went out to the garage where Margie pulled down her bike and then Jack's – both of which were those super light weight models that Lance Armstrong uses.

According to Margie, Jack was *not* a biking enthusiast. She'd tried to get him into the sport but failed. I was a bit reluctant to use Jack's bike because of the bad air incident but Margie assured me I was nuts and checked out the tires and chain and everything, then she went inside to change.

Five minutes later she returned in a shocking pink cycling jersey and black pants with shocking pink trim. Both appeared to have been sprayed on and then shrunk with a hairdryer. I could see her bellybutton quite clearly. You didn't need an imagination to think how she looked nude – of course I'd already seen her nude so.... Let's change the subject.

My only wardrobe change was from sandals to tennis shoes, which I'd been smart enough to bring in the car in case of an emergency. What kind of emergency? I don't know. For some reason they were in the car. In my shorts, t-shirt and tennis shoes, I looked like a nerd going for a ride compared to Margie, who looked like a pro. Now that I think about it, Jillian had once told me that that was exactly how I looked.

We had a short argument about my wearing Jack's biking shoes which was resolved when they came up too small. Margie insisted I wear his helmet even if it was snug. I relented. I'm very safety conscious, though I'm not sure there is anything in my head worth protecting.

And so at just after 8:45 a.m. on a lovely Kona morning we set out. Slowly at first so I could adapt to the equipment.

I let Margie take the lead and set the pace, a decision I regretted straightaway since it put her derriere directly in front of me. Not that I'm complaining mind you it's just well...you know.

I made an effort *not* to stare and was doing pretty well at it, enjoying the other scenery, the exercise and the morning breeze flowing down from Hualalai.

We made our way down to Alii Drive and rode through Kona and then took a back road through an industrial area and eventually met up with Queen Kaahumanu highway, which is known as the Hawaiian Beltway because it runs clear around the island. Just so you know, there aren't other routes to choose from. I typically don't like riding in heavy traffic but there was no choice.

The traffic wasn't too bad heading north and the shoulder was wide; we encountered a few other bikers – all of whom were traveling faster than us (me) and all dressed like Margie in sexy clothes that showed their muscles and or figure. Since I had no muscles or figure to flaunt, I didn't feel bad about it.

They all gave us the friendly "aloha" as they zipped by, which was nice. And one of the male riders told me I had a nice view as he sped past me.

Margie kept up a good pace and before long I was huffing and puffing and falling behind. Eventually she looked back and took pity on me and adjusted her speed to match mine, which was very thoughtful of her but it did have a negative impact since we were now biking along the lava desert and the *only* thing to look at was her ... well you know.

"Margie," I said in an attempt to view less lecherous scenery. "Why don't you let me take the lead and set the pace so I don't keep falling behind."

Margie slowed and fell in next to me. "Okey dokey," she said happily. "And I'll do my best not to stare at your butt."

She could read my mind!

We cycled past the small boat harbor and past the airport where we left most of the car traffic and soon found ourselves in rolling terrain. Some of the ups where pretty long, so I dropped a few gears but kept going. There was a breeze from the mountains, which felt good, and since it wasn't a head wind, it didn't bother me.

It was at this point that Margie pulled alongside again.

"Why don't you let me take the lead. I can't take my eyes off your bum," she giggled and winked and started to pass me.

I decided to show her that I wasn't a total pansy.

"If you want the lead, you'll have to take it," I shot back, adding a gear and picking up the pace to pass her.

"You want to race, huh?" Margie called. "Okay, old man."

And so we raced. Neck and neck at first and then when we hit a good incline, I pulled ahead. I don't mean to sound sexist or anything, but physiology was on my side despite Margie's athleticism. Men have larger, more powerful leg muscles than women do and I pulled ahead slowly and relentlessly and had to listen to Margie swear at me from behind. We crested a rise and I kept going. Here my superior *weight* was a definite advantage. When I finally looked back, I had a good three hundred yards on her.

And that's when I saw it. The limo. A big white one with tinted windows moving fast; it was a foot over the shoulder line as it rocketed past Margie and nearly blew her off the road.

"Idiot," I shouted to no one, and moved as far over on the blacktop as possible. But it wasn't far enough!

I heard the limo close in behind me and then a rush of wind as it clipped me and pushed me off the pavement and onto the loose gravel.

The gravel caught my tire, and I started to lose control. The last thing I remember was a huge block of black lava dead ahead and Margie screaming from behind.

"Look out."

In the Afterlife

"Joe?" Margie voice seemed to be calling me from far away.

My eyes fluttered open and I saw her curly locks framed by the blue sky. She was looking down at me just as Miss Stone, the sexy school nurse had looked down at me when I took a header off the swing set in third grade. My head was in her lap.

I tried to sit up. Margie pushed me down.

"How do you feel?" she quizzed. "Anything broken?"

I moved my arms and legs slowly.

"Not that I can tell. How do I look?"

"Really bad," she said. "But I'm getting used to it." She smiled. "Sit up if you can."

She helped me sit up.

"Can you walk?" Margie helped me to my feet and I slowly straightened my right leg. "That hurts," I said.

"You're bleeding," Margie told me.

I looked down at my arms and legs. I had some road rash on my knees and elbows. "They're just scrapes," I said bravely. "Did you see that guy? He tried to kill me! He deliberately ran me off the road."

"I know," Margie said, her face expressing both awe and anger. "I saw the whole thing. Wait here, I've got some wet wipes in my bike pack. Oh, my. Look at your helmet."

I looked over to where my helmet lay ten feet away. It was split in two.

"That could have been your head." Margie said and rummaged in her pack. "I've got bandages and iodine too."

Margie carried the items over. She used the wet wipes to clean the scrapes, then added iodine and finally wrapped my wounds. Afterward, she stood back and admired her efforts.

"That should hold you. But we need to get you to a hospital and call the police." Margie left me and went up to the road to flag down a car.

Of course for Margie flagging down a car was like shooting fish in a barrel. The first one she waved at pulled over so fast you'd think it was making an Indy 500 pit stop.

I'd like to think it was because the driver was a good Samaritan, but I'm pretty sure it was because Margie was dressed like...well you know.

Jeff Wilson – our good Samaritan/Margie-ogler – was vacationing with his wife and ... oh you don't want the details.

He helped me into the back seat and loaded Margie's bike in the trunk of his four-door Lincoln. We left Jack's bike on the side of the road since it was wrecked anyway and planned to come back for it later.

Jeff asked what had happened and Margie started to tell him, but I cut her off and said only that I'd blown a tire and gone off the road.

Margie gave me a puzzled look but kept mum.

Jeff took us to the closest resort, which is where he and Annie, his wife, had a condo, and they let us use the phone to call Amanda and they served us cold beverages and some leftover veggies and dip while we waited.

If you want, I could fill you in on Jeff and Annie's entire life because we heard most of it. But I think you'd get bored. Not that they were boring people, only you probably don't care. I know I didn't. I will point out that I was of the opinion Jeff was going to have to explain a lot after we left because Annie – who was 30 pounds overweight – caught Jeff staring at Margie at least a dozen times. I was invisible.

Amanda showed up in due course and Jeff ogled her as well, and after thanking them profusely we were on our way home.

Margie gave Amanda the *real* scoop as to what had happened and then she asked me why I'd fibbed to Jeff and Annie.

"Why didn't you tell the truth? And why didn't you call the police from their house?" Margie looked puzzled. "Someone ran you off the road. You could've been killed."

"I didn't want to call the police because I think someone *is* trying to kill me," I said and received puzzled looks from both of them.

"Think about it," I said. "First, there was the helicopter, then the scuba tank, now the bike accident. Doesn't it *look* like someone's trying to kill me? Detective Lo thinks so. If I call the cops and tell them about the bike accident detective Lo is going to be certain I really am involved in Lou's murder somehow and that someone is trying to kill me. I don't want that."

Margie was still trying to puzzle through my logic when Amanda spoke up. "Joe, I'll admit you've had a bad run of luck," Amanda offered. "But if someone really wanted to kill you, why wouldn't they just do it. Of course the helicopter thing wasn't an *accident* per se, but why would someone take out a whole bunch of people just to kill you? And the scuba thing. Couldn't that have just been an accident? The cops haven't said what was in the tank.

"And the limo... You already said the driver almost ran Margie off the road too. Is someone trying to kill her as well? I'm thinking it was probably just a drunk."

Obviously, Amanda wasn't buying my premise.

"And *why*, Joe?" Amanda continued. "We still haven't a clue as to why? What's the motive here? Because you took that photo? The cops don't have a clue as to who killed Lou Krauthammer or whatever his name is. You're still the number one suspect, but..."

Margie jumped in. "They *could* just be coincidences, Joe. Nobody knew you were going to be on that helicopter. How could they? And if someone really did fix the scuba tank, how could they know you'd be the one using it? It was Jack's tank." Margie paused. "I think Amanda may be right."

"Well," I said with a huff. "I think I'm a target and it all started when I took that guy's picture in Honolulu. Somehow there's a connection between that incident in Honolulu, the dead guy in your pool, and the" – I counted with my fingers – "three attempts on my life!"

"It does sort of look that way, I guess," Margie waffled back to my way of thinking. "But like Amanda said, what's the motive? Taking a picture? That's silly."

"It's got to be more than that," Amanda offered.

"I'd give anything not to have erased that picture," I said. "I'll bet there's a clue in it."

At this point Amanda 'tsk, tsk, tsked' us thoroughly and shook her head sadly as if we were the class morons. "You people *have* to learn today's technology."

I looked at Amanda dully. What *was* she talking about? I turned to Margie; she looked at me blankly. We were both clueless.

"Virtually everything you do on your computer can be traced. Even after you delete it." Amanda lectured. "It's the same with digital cameras."

"Whatever do you mean?" Margie quizzed.

"Wait a minute," I said. "I remember hearing they caught some child pornographers that way. Something..."

I must have got it wrong because Amanda rolled her eyes and began to explain the technical details. I won't go into those since I'll get it wrong, but she claimed we could get the photo back. At least Daisy could.

Amanda dug in her top and pulled out her cell phone and I chided her for driving and talking – which is illegal in Hawaii – so she gave the phone to Margie who didn't seem all that happy about it, but she did manage to dial a number.

"I got her machine," she told us, then, "Daisy, this is Margie. I need you to help us recover a picture from a digital camera that someone deleted. Call me back on Amanda's cell phone as soon as you get this message."

Margie handed the phone back to Amanda, who returned it to its customary storage place in her bra. Why does she store it there? I haven't a clue and I didn't think I should ask. My nose was feeling just fine.

We picked up my (Jack's) broken bicycle on the way home and after that quiet reigned in the car until Margie had a new thought.

"The man who didn't want his picture taken must have been doing something illegal," Margie said.

"I think we know that," Amanda said condescending.

"Yes, well I guess so," Margie ignored Amanda's analysis. "Anyway after he let you erase the photo, he must have discovered, just as we have, that your digital camera might still contain the photo. So he followed us to the island and to my house where he was going to kill you and take your camera. But his 'partner' –the other guy in the photo – followed him and decided to get rid of him for some reason."

It was an interesting hypothesis, except for one thing.

"Why would he do that?" I asked.

Margie gave me a dirty look. I don't think she liked my question.

"I haven't figured that out yet. Anyway, later, the partner realized that he needed to get rid of you, since you're now the link to the dead guy." She gave me a dirty look before I could ask why again. "I don't know why, but it does seem that he's very persistent."

"What makes you think it's a man?" Amanda asked. "It could be a woman."

Margie wrinkled her nose. "I suppose. But the odds are it's a man. Men kill more than women and so far we haven't encountered any females in all this."

"That's very interesting, Margie," I said. "But where does it get us and who are we looking for?

Margie sat quiet for a moment. "I haven't a clue."

Silly Joe

We tried to refine Margie's scenario as Amanda drove to the hospital but were unable to make any sense of it. At the ER, after a long wait – I don't really think they were all that busy but they just liked having Margie and Amanda dressing the place up – I got checked out and given some antibiotics for the scrapes; otherwise I got a clean bill of health and was told to take it easy for a few days. I liked that advice.

The ER doc said that because I'd suffered a head injury, I shouldn't be alone for at least a few hours so we went back to Margie's and I took the phone and went into the guest bedroom and called Jillian and told her what had happened and that I was now convinced I was being stalked for murder.

She laughed hard for three minutes.

"Really, Joe? You have a bicycle accident and you're thinking someone's trying to kill you?"

She said it with that voice she uses when I say something stupid. She uses it more than necessary I think.

"I don't see where someone was trying to kill you. If they wanted to kill you they could have just run you over. Didn't you say they almost hit Margie too? Is someone trying to kill her as well? Joe, it was just a drunk. Or a bad driver."

I hated the fact that she had the same logical objection that Amanda had made.

"Well," I argued. "Maybe they wanted to make it *look* like an accident."

There was a pregnant pause.

"Why?" Jillian asked.

I gave the phone a dirty look, which Jillian couldn't see. I didn't have an answer of course.

"Joe, you're imagining things," Jillian said.

I didn't have a comeback, so I switched topics. "When are you coming back?"

"We had a setback. Two more days," she answered quickly. "I promise."

"That's what you always say!" I hollered.

Jillian made a 'humpf' sound and said she had to go and I thought she'd hung up but then she came back on and asked: "You're still going to the volcano aren't you?"

I'd all but forgotten about the volcano. It had been the number one thing on my list of things to see and do in Hawaii. But under the circumstances I wasn't sure I should and I shared my hesitation with Jillian. "Why do you care?" I asked coldly.

"You'd be a fool to pass it up, Joe. I know how much you wanted to go and if I remember right, Margie made reservations at the hotel there for tomorrow night." Her voice sounded encouraging; the edge was gone. Maybe she *did* care about me.

I paused. "We'll see," I said, and before I could say another word the phone went dead.

I made my way out to the pool where Amanda and Margie had a pitcher of margaritas waiting but I couldn't have one because the ER doc said I shouldn't so I just watched them and felt envious.

I shared with them what Jillian said and they agreed that they had been discussing and thinking the same thing.

"It's like those scary movies where everything *could* be connected, but really isn't," Amanda said. "We're open to more evidence, Joe, but we don't have any way of getting any till Daisy returns the call."

***

Meanwhile, at the police station, Detective Lo was reaming out his friend and fellow detective Jimmy Koi.

"You were supposed to be watching them."

"I tried to get the license number. But I had to hang back. I didn't want to follow too close. Then afterwards, I couldn't go whizzing past and chase the guy down. Mr. Thomas wasn't hurt that bad. The driver could have said it was just an accident."

"Yeah, maybe," Lo barked. "But at least we would have known who was driving. Listen. Get back out there and follow them. Stay with them this time. And don't screw up again."

Jimmy nodded. "Okay. Okay. I'll keep 'em under wraps."

***

Back at Margie's I decided the ER doc was wrong and had poured myself a margarita and was wondering if there was salsa and chips anywhere within walking distance when Margie lurched forward in her chair suddenly as if she'd been hit in the back of the head by a two by four.

"The volcano!" she crowed. "I almost forgot! We've got reservations for tomorrow night."

"I know," I said. "Jillian reminded me. But I think we should probably cancel. I'm supposed to take it easy, and..."

"Don't be silly, Joe! You're fine," Margie scoffed. "And you'll be much better by tomorrow. All you have to do is sit in the car."

I didn't dare tell her how nerve-wracking it was sitting in the car with her driving, so I didn't respond.

"I thought you were excited to see the volcano," Margie schmoozed. "Jillian told me so, and we've got the reservations, and besides, what else will we do? We can't just sit around here."

"I was planning on reading a book and staying out of harm's way," I said.

"Boring," Margie made the word sound as if it came from a foghorn. "Pete and Amanda will come with," Margie added in an effort to persuade me.

"Whoa, little lady," Amanda said. "Pete hates the volcano and I'm not crazy about it either. It's just miles and miles of black broken glass. Don't count us in."

Margie looked disappointed. "Then you can take care of Magoo."

"Fine. I'll take Magoo over lava any day," Amanda said.

Margie leaned forward and said to me as persuasively as she could: "Joe, I really think we should go. We've been having fun together all week, and the lava is flowing into the sea. This could be your only chance to see it." She continued her sales pitch. "You'll be amazed at how inspiring the place is: cinder cones, lava tubes, calderas, steam vents. And the sunsets and sunrises are positively primal."

Margie was running at full tilt now. "Did you know Kilauea is the most active volcano on the planet? The last time I was there you could see the lava at night pouring down the mountain just like it's done for millions of years! And you can smell the sulfur in the air. You know what Mark Twain said about that?"

I waited.

"He said 'The smell of sulfur is strong, but not unpleasant to a sinner.' Isn't that a hoot?

"He stayed at the same hotel where we're staying. The Volcano House. Do you know they've had a fire burning in their fireplace for over a hundred years? They even kept it going when they rebricked it. Of course the hotel's been renovated since then. I didn't mean to imply the place was old and worn down and..."

"You make it sound so warm and fuzzy," Amanda mocked. "It's really not, Joe. But Margie's right, you really should go. The hotel is nice and as Margie says, you may not get another chance."

In truth, the thought of coming all the way to Hawaii without seeing the volcano disheartened me. Still, it would have been nice if Jillian were along to share it with me.

I sipped my drink and watched Margie watching me waiting for an answer. Finally I caved. "Oh, what the hell," I said. "I'll go if no one kills me in my sleep tonight." Then a thought hit me. "We'll have our own rooms won't we?"

Margie laughed and said of course we would and Amanda called her house and Pete came over and we all had a nice meal. No steak, but good calamari and grilled tuna and salad made with bok choy which tasted like cabbage to me. Don't write; yes, I have discovered bok choy is Chinese cabbage.

After dinner I drove the T-bird back to my condo so Margie could pack up the Volvo with gear she wanted to bring on our trip and she left me with strict instructions to have breakfast early. "I'll pick you up at eight tomorrow morning. Don't oversleep!"

Back at the condo I made myself a snack and had a scotch out on the lanai and watched the moon set. It was a perfect night and I could faintly hear the Polynesian floor show at one of the hotels up the coast. It would have been nice if I wasn't alone, but I was. And while I sat there, I went over all the *coincidences* that seemed to center on my demise but decided that Jillian and Margie and Amanda were right. Nobody was trying to kill me. Why would they? Everything that had happened could be explained as an accident – except for the dead guy in the pool. And that wasn't an attempt on my life. That, too, could have been an odd coincidence. It was just the event that got the ball rolling. I've always had a tendency to be a drama queen and a worrywart and a nervous Nelly.

So after I had decided that, I was feeling better than I had in a while and finished my scotch and went inside and packed what I thought I'd need for the two days at the volcano and took a long shower and tucked myself in and tried not to be mad at my wayward wife. As I lay there in bed, I tried to picture Jillian naked, but Margie kept getting in the way. Naked. Not that that was a bad thing.

***

It was much later and I was sound asleep and probably snoring – I snore if I drink before bed – so I was completely unaware of the ninja-like figure slipping along the edge of the golf course from shadow to shadow making its way to my condo unit where it climbed quickly up the lanai and slipped over the railing noiselessly and then paused to listen and then carefully pushed opened the sliding screen door and tiptoed cautiously and noiselessly to my bedroom.

The ninja loomed over my bed a moment and watched me sleeping, then covered my mouth tight with a hand.

I woke up gasping for breath and looked up at the black image looming above me and holding me down.

"Muuumpf!" I grabbed my attacker's wrist and pushed away the hand and struggled from the bed and tried to flee, but the invader was swift and strong and a moment later I found myself in a half-nelson with my left arm bent behind me and a chokehold round my throat. Then I felt a hand cover my mouth again.

Awake now, I found a stray finger and bit hard.

"Yeoww!" The attacker screamed and let me go.

I recognized the voice instantly. "Margie?"

"You bit me!" Margie grumbled. "Why did you bite me?" I could make out her shadow shaking her injured hand.

"What are you..." I started to ask what the heck she was doing, but Margie recovered and put her other hand over my mouth softly, keeping the fingers clear of my teeth.

"Don't say a word." Margie hissed quietly.

"I can't breathe!" I complained.

"Breath through your nose and stop making so much noise," Margie hissed. "I'm going to remove my hand but you have to promise to be quiet."

She took her hand away and I took a deep breath. "What are you..." I started.

"Shush! Don't say anything until we get outside," Margie took my hand and led me out onto the lanai and then went back and closed the sliding doors. She tugged off the black hood that covered her head.

"What on earth are you....." I started again but Margie covered my mouth with her hand.

"Can't you whisper?" she whispered. "I'm trying to tell you, but you've got to keep your voice down." She removed her hand.

"Why do we have to whisper?" I whispered.

"'Cause I think your condo might be bugged."

"Bugged!?" My voice came up in surprise.

"Shush! Yes. And there's someone following me ... us." Margie said.

"Who's following us?" I asked in my best whisper.

"I don't know," Margie said. " I'm pretty sure it's either a police officer or That Guy from the restaurant. The one you said looked familiar."

"Why didn't you tell me this before?" I asked reasonably. "What's with all the melodrama?"

"I didn't want you to worry."

"And now you do?"

"No, only...."

"Did you confront the guy?"

"It's better if you don't. Then they don't know that you know."

"How do you know that?"

"I watch TV."

I was beginning to wonder if Margie had suddenly lost her mind.

"For days I've had this feeling that we were being followed," Margie said. "I kept looking around but I could never pin him down. I'm sure I saw him yesterday when we went for our bike ride and I saw him again this evening when I went out for some stuff after you left.

"Shouldn't you call Detective Lo?" I kept my voice as low as Margie's.

"No. If it's one of his men that is following us and I tell him, he'll just use someone else.

"So why did you come here now?" I asked. "Is the phone out at your house?"

"Don't be cute," Margie sneered. "They probably have my phone tapped."

"I suppose that makes sense. The cops think I'm a killer. They could be hoping I'd say something incriminating. So what did you want to tell me that you couldn't say over the phone. You know neither of us has done anything wrong. At least I haven't."

"Joe. I don't know how to say this, so I'm just going to go ahead and say it." Margie paused. "I think Jillian is trying to kill you."

I let her words sink in.

"What?" I blurted. I believe my reaction was completely understandable.

"Shush!" Margie shushed.

"Margie. I can't... Why would Jillian want to kill me?" I asked.

"I haven't figured that out. Maybe she took out a big insurance policy without you knowing about it."

"You can't do that," I said. "I tried... Never mind. I just know you can't do that."

"Maybe she's having an affair and she wants you out of the picture. To be honest, Joe, it doesn't sound like you and Jillian... Do you two even swap spit anymore?"

I thought her comment a bit personal. "That's none of your business, Margie. Yes things between us are rocky, but it was her idea to come here and try to reconnect. Anyway, if she was having an affair, she could just divorce me. She'd wind up with most of the money. What little there is. Margie, it's not logical. You've talked to her. Does she sound *that* unhappy?"

There was a long pause. "Well, no. But she's not exactly making the most of your vacation."

"Is Jack?" I argued.

"It's not *his* vacation," Margie reasoned, then after a long pause: "Okay. Okay. Maybe you've got a point. Maybe I jumped the gun. Still..."

"You're forgetting something else, Margie."

"What's that?"

"She's in L.A.," I said definitively. "Go home Margie. Get some sleep. We're still going to the volcano tomorrow aren't we?"

Margie nodded in the affirmative.

"Speaking of which, why didn't you wait and tell me then?" I asked.

"I was afraid something might happen to you tonight!"

"That's very sweet, but I think you're over thinking everything. You're letting your imagination run away with you."

"I suppose," Margie looked embarrassed.

"You've really got to go," I said.

Margie stood a moment and then said sheepishly: "Do you suppose you could give me a lift. I came on foot."

"All the way from your place?"

"I came along the golf course. I stayed in the shadows so no one would see me and ..."

"Let me get my pants," I said, not listening to the rest of her story and headed for the bedroom shaking my head in disbelief. "And Jillian thinks I'm a drama queen!"

Pele's House

Twelve hours later, after a speedy, and at times harrowing, drive through the quiet countryside and a few small towns along winding roads, we arrived at Volcanoes National Park.

We checked in at the Volcano House and then Margie guided me to the terrace out back and began to point out the major attractions.

"Over there, that's Halemaumau, the Fire Pit. It was quiet for a long time but it's been spewing smoke for a long time now with no sign of stopping. Over there. That's Kilauea Iki crater. It's not active and if you're up to it, we can hike across the caldera later on. I've got some bottled water and candy in a backpack. It's not a bad hike, but it gets hot. I suggest we do it late in the afternoon. Come on. Let's grab lunch, then we'll take the Crater Rim drive."

"Wait. Let me get a picture." I backed away from Margie.

Margie waited while I got ready. "Wait," Margie held up her hand. "Remember about recovering the photo! You don't want to write over that."

"Not a problem," I said. "That's on another memory stick safely tucked away at the condo."

"Okay. Shoot away!" Margie gave me a dazzling smile and tilted her head back a little. It was a nice pose; obviously she knew what do in front of a camera. I snapped the shutter.

"Here, let me take one of you," she ordered.

I handed Margie the camera and I smiled for her as best I could. I don't know what to do in front of a camera so most of the pictures of me look like I've just had a colonoscopy or a root canal.

At this point a Japanese tourist – at least I think he was Japanese – did a lot of pointing and gesturing to indicate that he'd take a picture of the two of us. So Margie handed him the camera and came over and put her arms around my neck and gave me a kiss on the cheek and the gentleman snapped the picture.

"That's for Jillian!" Margie laughed and went and got the camera.

The guy then gestured that *he* wanted to take a photo of us with *his* camera. We obliged him with a more traditional pose and he bowed gratefully and ran to catch up with his tour group.

"Now why do you suppose he wanted a picture of us?" Margie asked.

I looked at Margie. She was wearing a classic 'Margie' outfit that was picture perfect. I shrugged. "Who knows. Hey, what about the lava? Where's the lava?"

"The lava is coming from Pu'u O'o way over there," Margie pointed to the east but the hotel was in the way. "You can't see it from here. In fact it's a very long hike to get there. But the place to see the lava is down at the end of Chain of Craters road and I thought we'd wait and do that tomorrow. It's a long drive. Come on, I'm starved!"

We had a late lunch in the restaurant, which had a phenomenal view of the volcano. I had a cheeseburger and fries and a chocolate shake. Margie had chicken salad and tea. I picked up the tab to show I wasn't a total freeloader.

After lunch we drove to the parking lot for the Thurston Lava Tube and followed the trail through a virtual rain forest to the entrance.

I paused at the yawning mouth and the staircase that led down into it. "Are you sure it's safe?" I asked.

190

Margie hip checked me. "Are you kidding? It's ancient," Margie cried. "No lava has flowed here in hundreds, maybe thousands, of years."

I decided to trust her and we descended into the semi darkness.

"It reminds me of a subway tunnel," I said. "Look how regular the sides are."

"I know," Margie agreed. "Just think. This whole mountain is honeycombed with tubes like this. Some bigger. Some smaller. Imagine what it was like when lava was pumping through it."

"No thanks," I said firmly. "I'll just think of it as a subway tunnel."

Margie noted my anxiety. "If *this* makes you nervous, wait for the next stop."

The 'next stop' was Kilauea Iki crater, which is very near the Thurston Lava Tube. To reach the bottom of the crater, we had to traverse a switchback trail that made me dizzy, and by the time we reached the floor, four hundred feet below, I was pooped.

Margie looked back up the trail. "It's a lot harder going up when you're tired."

"Great," I moaned. "Are you sure it's okay to be here?"

The place was spooky as all get out and as far as I could tell we were the only people crazy enough to be there.

"It's fine, Joe." Margie shook her head at my concern. "Look there's a path. And there. Those people are coming back."

There were indeed other people but because of the size of the place I had mistaken them for ants.

"It looks to me as if it could start up any time," I said. "Where is it we're going exactly?"

"Over there. At the bottom of that big cinder mound is a big hole, the 'throat' they call it, where the last big

191

eruption took place. Here." Margie opened a four-color brochure. "That's what it looked like when it erupted."

The photo of the last eruption showed lava spewing high above the crater rim and a lava lake filling the place where we were standing.

"So this whole thing was filled with lava?" I wasn't sure I liked that idea.

"Imagine!" Margie said in wonder.

"Yeah. Imagine," I said uneasily.

We had been hiking only a few minutes when Margie, who was constantly looking high and low for things to bring to my attention, said very seriously. "Do you feel like you're being watched?"

"No," I said honestly. "Do you?"

Since Margie was under constant surveillance wherever she went based solely on looks, I found it odd that she should be able to discern a single pair of eyes at this particular point.

"Yes, I do." Margie looked up and scanned the crater rim. "There. Look," Margie pointed up at what I knew was an observation deck for those too lazy to hike the trail but who wanted a view of the crater. "We are being watched. From the overlook."

I looked up and she was right. There was someone up there, but you couldn't make out any details. "You think it's your 'tail?'" I teased.

"Don't mock me, Joe. And yes, I'll bet it is. Let me get the binoculars." Margie dug in her backpack and produced a pair of binoculars and pointed them upward. "Damn it. He's gone. Did you see that, as soon as I got out my binoculars, he left?"

"It could just be a coincidence," I said. "I didn't notice anyone following us before. Did you?"

"I didn't 'see' anyone following us. Still..."

Margie didn't finish her sentence and we continued our hike quietly until we reached the 'throat.'

If you've never been to the throat of a caldera, it is a very impressive thing. It's like looking into the mouth of a cave only this cave might just go all the way down to... Well, wherever it went it was a long way.

There was a big sign in front of it that said 'Danger! Go no closer!' so of course Margie walked past the sign a few feet to get a closer look.

"Margie, the sign says not to go any closer," I said hopelessly.

"I'll be careful," Margie said and took two more steps.

"I'm not going to help you if you fall in," I said sternly. "Come here and pose by the sign, I'll take your picture."

Margie did as I asked. She smiled in the first one.

"Make a face like you're scared."

Margie feigned terror.

"That's it," I said and took another picture. We repeated the process with me, then looked around for someone to take a picture of both of us, but we were alone.

An hour and a half later we stumbled back to the car and the cooler which I knew held a bottle of cold diet beverage. Margie took a juice box.

"That stuff'll kill 'ya," Margie said.

I gulped half the bottle down. "No. Dehydration will kill 'ya."

I finished the bottle. "Okay, chief. Is that enough for today! I'm exhausted. I can't remember the last time I walked so far."

Margie shook her head at me as if I'd just colored on the wall. "You are woefully out of shape, Mr. Thomas, but I guess we can quit for the day. You'll need your strength tomorrow when we walk out to see the lava. That's even farther!"

"I can hardly wait," I said discontentedly.

"Sissy boy!" Margie made her way to the driver's seat.

"Overachiever!" I climbed in the passenger side and we were off.

Two hours later we were standing in the hotel hallway in front our rooms. I was in 207, Margie across the hall in 208.

"Great dinner, Margie. Thanks. But you *have* to let me get the next one. I'm starting to feel like a gigolo."

Margie smiled. "Okay. I'll pick someplace really expensive."

I smiled and asked what time I needed to set my alarm for.

"Early, Joe. You want to see the sun rise over the volcano don't you?"

"Do I?"

"Of course you do! It's spectacular. Like watching a dragon awake. Anyway, I think five should be early enough."

"Five? I was..."

Margie gave me a distressed look.

"Okay. Okay. I can do that. I guess. But I'm bushed. I'm going to shower and go to bed and sleep like a baby. Especially after that last drink. What was it called again?"

"A Zombie, Joe. Honestly. You don't get out much do you?"

We stood for a second just looking at one another. I'm certain my view was better than hers.

"Well, goodnight," I said finally.

"Goodnight," Margie mimicked, then took a step forward and gave me a nice smack on the cheek.

I felt my face flush. "What was that for?"

"Oh, nothing," Margie said, opening the door to her room. "I just think you're wonderful, that's all." She

194

paused then added: "I hope Jillian knows that." Margie turned and closed the door.

I decided to skip the shower and take one in the morning but as I was washing up I saw Margie's lipstick on my cheek in the mirror, a perfectly shaped representation of lips, like you see on advertisements and on Valentine's cards. I stared at it. Was it cherry or bubblegum or...? I'd never know. I washed it off slowly and reluctantly.

Three hours later I was still lying in bed staring at the ceiling with the Sandman nowhere in sight. I turned to look at the lighted dial of the alarm clock. Five past midnight. I had no idea what was keeping me awake but every time I closed my eyes I saw Margie. At least she had clothes on.

Suddenly there was an urgent knock on the door and Margie whispered harshly: " Let me in." She sounded upset.

I got up and went to the door. "What's the matter?" I asked stupidly. I should have just opened the door, but I didn't.

"Just open the door, Joe. I don't want to stand in the hallway shouting."

"Just a sec," I grabbed my robe and put it on and opened the door.

Margie rushed past me and leapt onto my bed and pulled her knees up to her chest. She shivered. She was dressed in flannel pajamas with little puppy dogs on them.

"What's wrong?" I asked.

"You've got to let me sleep here tonight." Margie said.

"But..." I started to object.

"There's a bug in my room!" Margie snapped and shuddered and picked up a pillow and hugged it tight against her for protection.

That must be one hell-a-va bug.

"Well," I said, trying to remain calm. "Let's get the manager. They'll give you another room."

"That won't work," Margie shook her head hard enough to made her curls dance. "They're full. I heard the desk clerk say so earlier."

I was bewildered. "But Margie, there's just the one bed. It wouldn't look right if we shared the same room. What if Jillian or Jack found out?"

"Oh, don't be silly, Joe. It wouldn't look like anything. Jack wouldn't care. And neither would Jillian. They'd both understand. Honestly, you can be such a fuddy-duddy. It's a queen size bed." She pouted and stretched out her arms to indicate the largess of the bed and then looked at me with puppy dog eyes. "I promise to be good."

Oh yeah, what about me!

"Maybe I could stay in your room," I suggested.

"Okay," Margie said as she loosened up and slipped herself under the covers. "But there was a cockroach the size of a Volkswagen in the shower. Say hi for me."

I am not afraid of bugs as a rule, but the thought of one that large made me shudder and I reconsidered my suggestion. "Okay, then. There's a couch in the lobby. Maybe I can sleep there."

"Already taken," Margie shot back and pulled a pillow over, punched it a few times and tucked it under her head. "Two guys with backpacks. They smell. But don't let me stop you."

Margie patted the bed next to her. "Come-on, Joe. We have to get some sleep if we're going to get going early." She turned on her side and pulled the covers up tight. "Turn off the light, please."

Seriously. What was I supposed to do? I remained by the door trying to think of options. I could sleep in the car, but if I did that my back would hurt for days. I could sleep on the floor, but that didn't charm me. Bugs like the floor.

Finally I just gave up and turned off the light and made my way carefully to the other side of the bed and climbed in. I lay as close to the edge as possible without falling out and just stared up at the ceiling wondering how things had come to this. I was actually in bed with another man's wife. Of course it was just ... It wasn't like we were going to... I didn't really have a choice, damn it!

Margie fell right to sleep and began snoring softly and after a while I looked over at her back and without wanting to I pondered what it would be like sleeping with her every night. Yes, I know it's wrong to think that way, but you can't control *all* your thoughts. Jeez, gimme a break!

I pushed the thought out of my head and forced myself to think of Jillian and I spent a few hours trying to focus on my wayward wife while Margie continued to snore gently and occasionally made little whimpering noises like a puppy dog...chasing a bunny? Eventually I dozed off.

Clothing Optional

I woke to the sound of an electric hairdryer and slowly, carefully, I opened one eye, hesitant as to what I might encounter.

There was Margie in the bath area – naked of course – drying her hair. A true gentleman would have closed his eyes tightly and pretended to sleep, but I was getting tired of being a true gentleman so I watched her through my eyelashes. Yes, it was shameful, but in my defense it was also very enjoyable.

Margie finally turned off the hairdryer and pulled on one of my t-shirts and a pair of my shorts, which ended the show. I deemed it safe to open my eyes fully.

I cleared my throat so Margie would know I was awake. She was squinting into the mirror at an imaginary blemish that women always think is there but isn't.

"Morning sleepy-head." She looked at me through the mirror and smiled. "Do you always snore like that?"

She didn't wait for an answer. "It's after nine. I let you sleep 'cause I woke you up. We can catch the sunrise tomorrow. I have stolen some of your clothes, as you can see and hope you don't mind." She twirled to model the outfit, which was very baggy but still managed to look sexy on her. "I will not wear anything that spent the night in my room. Those roaches get into everything."

She dug in my shaving kit and pulled out the toothpaste. "I suppose I should be mad and yell at the manager, but those damn bugs ... I'm sure it's not their fault. The previous guest must have let them in."

Margie held up a toothbrush. "I found a spare one in your shave kit. Hope you don't mind. I'll buy you a new one. I'm hoping they have clothes in the gift shop. Your stuff is way too big," She yanked at the waist of my shorts to accentuate their size. "Thanks for letting me stay here. I guess it's a good thing Jillian and Jack didn't come. Think how crowded we'd all have been together in bed. Sort of like...what's that movie? Someone and Someone and Ted and Alice. Do you remember that one? It's a really old movie. I remember watching it when I was babysitting one time."

Margie was quiet momentarily as she brushed her teeth up, down, and sideways and finally spit in the sink.

"I used your deodorant. I hope that's okay. Some people are funny about stuff like that. You know, personal stuff."

I said it was fine and she started to put on makeup. Again there was quiet as I watched her. Finally she stood back from the mirror, fluffed her curls and straightened the oversized shorts she was wearing.

"Well, I'm done. I'm off to see the manager and check the store. You can have the place to yourself now and I'll meet you in the restaurant for breakfast. Don't take too long." Margie headed for the door.

"I'll be there as soon as I take a shower," I promised.

Margie shot me a smile and pulled open the door. "Love, ya," she said and slipped out quickly, leaving me as always bemused and befuddled by her comment.

I climbed out of bed and made my way to the bathroom area where I mumbled into the mirror as I looked for a new facial blemish. "What do you suppose she means? 'Love ya.' Is there something going on I don't know about? And why doesn't she even try to cover up. She's gorgeous of course but there's no reason to flaunt it in front of me. I'm a happily married man."

At least I thought I was a happily married man.

When I'd showered and shaved and dressed and taken care of all that personal business no one talks about, I went and found Margie in the restaurant where she'd secured a table by the big windows with a mesmerizing view of Kilauea crater under a brilliant sun. A cup of coffee awaited me.

"They were very apologetic," Margie told me when I asked how things had gone with the manager. "They're going to take all my stuff and have it cleaned today, and they promised to fumigate the room and find me a new one for tonight." Margie stood up and twirled. "What do you think of the duds? I found them in the kids section of the gift shop."

Whereas the stuff she'd borrowed from me was baggy, the new stuff was tight, with a capital 'T.' The shorts were scandalous and the top only slightly more acceptable but still plenty revealing – she was obviously braless.

"So what do you think of the view?" Margie asked, looking out the big plate glass window.

I was still looking at Margie's duds. "Awesome," I said appreciatively. I turned then to look out the window at the caldera where wisps of steam rose here and there about the immense depression. "Very awesome." I'm not sure whether I was referring to Margie or the prehistoric view. I think probably both.

"Well, you're certainly not a writer." Margie slipped back into her seat across from me and fluffed her napkin and put it on her lap. "Is that the best you can come up with? Awesome? Doesn't it just make you feel primordial? As if you'd been transported back in time? When it was just man versus the elements?"

Margie put her elbow on the table and rested her chin on the ball of her hand and looked at the view. "I think it's sublime." She turned to me. "That's what Mark Twain said about sunrise at Haleakala – on Maui."

"You seem to like quoting Twain," I said.

"Yes I do! I love Mark Twain. I know he wrote mainly for men and boys – Tom Sawyer and Huck Finn – but I think of him as a kindred spirit. If he were alive today we'd get along just fine. Do you like golf?"

There she was again, switching subjects without a signal.

"No," I said and shook my head for emphasis. "I think it's a game for masochists. Masochists and guys who like to wear funny pants."

Margie laughed. "I'm actually very good at it, but do you know what Mark Twain said about golf?"

"No," I said honestly.

"He said: 'Golf is a good walk ruined.' Isn't that insightful? A good walk ruined. I wish I could come up with stuff like that."

I ventured a guess. "Do you write?" I found the idea fascinating. What would Margie's prose be like? Or would it be poetry?

Margie looked around cautiously as if someone might overhear. "Don't tell anyone." She leaned toward me for emphasis. "I do write. Secretly," she said quite seriously.

"Why secretly?" I asked. "Have you been published?"

Margie seemed stunned by my question. "Heavens no! If I could get published, I wouldn't keep it a secret. But I write a little every day and I keep a diary."

"So you've been collecting rejection slips. That must be hard." I made the assumption she'd at least tried to get published.

"To be honest I've never had the nerve to send anything off." Margie gave a sigh of disappointment and returned to looking out toward the caldera wistfully.

"But how do you know if your stuff is any good or not?" I asked.

She turned back. "I don't. That's why you're the only person I've ever told about my writing."

I was stunned. "Really?" I felt privileged, but confused. "I'm the only one you've told? Why in the world...? Surely you've told Jack. Or Amanda."

"Nope," Margie said and went back to peering out the window. "I don't even know why I told you. It just popped out." She turned back to me. "You have a certain 'you can trust me with your deepest secrets' quality, Joe. Did you know that? Anyway, I told you. Promise you won't tell anyone? Not Jack or Jillian or Amanda." She stared at me hard with her baby blues. "Promise?"

Under her intense gaze, I would have stood up and taken off my clothes if she'd ask me to, so this was easy. "Okay. I promise," I said. "But I think you should send something out sometime."

Margie smiled out at the caldera, as if the thought of doing such a thing might be daring. "Maybe I will," she said and drew her attention back into the restaurant and picked up her menu. "Maybe I will."

Alona, our waitress, came and took our order. Eggs and bacon and toast for me. Orange juice, oatmeal with raisins, and tofu milk for Margie.

"So boss, what's the plan for today?" I asked as we awaited our meal.

"Well," Margie said. "I'm having the kitchen make us a picnic lunch, so we'll have to wait a little while for that. Then I thought we'd take our time driving down the Chain of Craters road. There are a number of places to stop. You don't want to be out on the lava during the hottest part of the day. We can have lunch down at the end of the road, and then we'll hike to where the lava is flowing. It's really quite a ways...." Margie, who is always talking with her hands, froze suddenly. "He's here!" she said.

She was looking past me and I turned quickly to see what she meant. Sure enough 'That Guy' was entering the dining room and a waiter showed him a table along the wall not a stone's throw from us.

"He followed us," Margie breathed softly.

I turned back quickly so as not to be spotted watching him. Margie just stared at him.

"Don't stare at him," I said.

Margie looked down at her coffee. "I'm going to go over there," she said decisively.

"I don't think that's a good idea," I said. I didn't have a reason, it just seemed like a bad idea.

"He's looking over at us now." Margie seemed shocked that he had the audacity to do so and before I could say 'leave sleeping dogs lie' she was on her feet and headed over. I sat a moment, uncertain what to do, then got up and followed her.

We arrived at 'That Guy's' table and he looked up at us timidly.

"Hello?" he said. He didn't look at all surprised to see us.

"Why are you following us?" Margie blurted harshly, accentuating her accusation by placing her hands on her hips. She has nice hips.

'That Guy' swallowed and looked quickly around, which I thought made him look guilty.

"I'm not following you," That Guy said. "Honestly. We just seem to be landing in the same places." He tried a guilty smile. "You're Margie Moore, aren't you?"

Margie dropped her hands to her side and crossed her arms in front of her. "That's my maiden name." There was less gruffness in her voice. "How did you...?"

"We went to school together," That Guy said and tried a better smile. "I doubt you remember me. I was very,

very shy and you were..." He looked up at me. "I came over on the plane with you I think?"

I said nothing.

"I was in Mr. Kinson's American history class with you Margie. I sat in the back and you sat way up front. I had a terrible crush on you. Everyone did."

Margie smiled and pursed her lips while she studied him closely, obviously trying to place him in her past life. Suddenly she pointed at him. "You wore glasses. And your hair was long."

"That's me! Andy Sommers," the guy said cheerily and looked at me warmly. "I've changed quite a bit I guess. You haven't changed at all, Margie. You're still ..." he let the sentence die. "I'm surprised you remember me. As I said, I was really shy."

Margie lightly punched my arm. "This is my friend Joe," she told Andy.

I was trying to picture That Guy – Andy – from the plane, but I'm terrible with faces so I wasn't at all troubled that I couldn't identify him.

"Well," Margie said suddenly. "It's very nice to see you Andy. And I'm glad you're not following us." Margie laughed lightly. "Maybe we'll run into you again. It's a small island." Margie tugged at my sleeve. "Come on Joe, let's let Andy have his breakfast."

We returned to our table where our own breakfast was waiting and getting cold.

"Isn't that just silly," Margie said, digging in. "Here we are worried that someone is following us and it's just an old classmate. I really can't say I remember him though, but it's been a long time. Oh, well."

"We've both been letting our imaginations run amok, Margie," I said as I scarfed down my bacon. "But I'm glad

204

you confronted him. I feel as if a burden's been lifted off me. How about you?"

Margie batted the air. "I was never worried."

I stared at her. Hadn't she been the nighttime intruder?

"I wasn't!" Margie insisted.

I continued to stare.

"Well, maybe a teensy bit," Margie said finally and called for more coffee. She avoided my eyes until I let it go. We ate quietly.

"Do we have to climb down and up the walls of any mountains today?" I asked, as we got up to leave.

"No, but the terrain is extremely rough and it's hard to make more than a mile or two an hour. It's going to take most of the afternoon to get where we're going." She held up a backpack. "I've got lots of water and I bought candy and trail mix and stuff. I also bought a brand new flashlight in case we want to stay out after dark. If the lava's flowing, that's the best time to see it."

"So what's the hurry?" I asked. "Let's get a late start and come back late."

Margie though a moment and then decided she liked my idea. "Okay. We'll poke around till lunch and then take the lunch they're making for us and have it out on the lava at sunset."

"Great," I said. "So there's time for a nap?"

Margie furrowed her brow. "A nap? You just woke up. You need a nap already?"

"It was a hard night..." – yes, I do think that was a Freudian slip – "I mean, I didn't sleep all that well. I guess my snoring kept me awake."

Margie shook her head and scowled "A nap...."

And so we left the dining room, giving a cordial wave to our old friend Andy who I was pretty certain was indeed following us, but I didn't tell Margie that.

Lava Joe

It was after three and we were far out on the lava, making slow progress over what seemed to be mile after mile of rolling lava mounds.

"Is it much farther?" I asked for the two hundredth time.

Margie scowled. "You're like a three year old. Honestly, Joe. Look, there's a couple coming. I'll ask."

The couple looked to be in their late fifties and quite tuckered out. The man had a big Kaiser Wilhelm mustache; his wife's mustache was not as impressive. They were both wearing Aussie hats.

"Hello?" Margie called. "Could you tell us how much farther it is to the lava?"

"Oh, you've got a good hour I'd say," the man answered with a thick Australian accent. "Hope you brought a torch along," he took off his hat to reveal a bald dome and wiped his face with a handkerchief he pulled from inside the hat. He looked at the sun, which was getting lower in the sky. "It'll be dark by the time you head back. Don't want to be out there without a torch. Dark as anything."

"We've got a good flashlight," Margie answered and patted her backpack.

"And give yourself plenty of time coming back. Last year it took us close to four hours to hike out, didn't it Edna."

Edna, who looked ready to fall over from exhaustion, nodded and the guy replaced his hat and they started off. "Good luck," he said and waved. His wife smiled and waved too.

"Have a safe trip," I said unnecessarily.

"Same to you, mate," he replied unnecessarily.

I turned to Margie. "I didn't even think about coming back in the dark. It's going to be hard to find our way over this stuff at night, even with a flashlight. Will that flashlight last four hours?"

"We'll be fine, Joe," Margie scoffed. "Even if it takes us all night. We don't have any appointments that I'm aware of and it's nice and warm. We've got lots of food and water. The flashlight is brand new and just in case, ..." Margie patted her backpack again. "...I have another one for backup. Besides, there's always someone else making the trip."

Of course we didn't know it, but someone was indeed making the trip. They were, in fact, making the trip 'with us.' By which I mean they were following us but far enough back so as to avoid detection, which was very easy since now that we'd met Andy, we had no reason to assume anyone was following us. Stupid us.

So we continued our journey and an hour later arrived at a spot with an incredible view of the lava entering the ocean.

Margie smiled and opened her arms like Moses parting the Red Sea. "I told you it would be worth it. Was I right?"

I took it all in. "You were right, Margie," I agreed wholeheartedly. "Are there any more of those macadamia nuts? They are so good. I suppose they have a million calories."

Margie handed me the package. "You can have the last of them. I'm going to have a Snickers." She sat down on a rock and pulled out the small bag of nuts and the candy bar.

I sat down next to her.

"Look at those idiots," she pointed to a group of people over near the water. "They're way too close. They're on the lava shelf. I hope it doesn't collapse while we're watching. I don't want to see even stupid people die."

Margie then explained that a 'lava shelf' was created as the lava goes into the sea. "Like the snow coming off your roof in the spring," she said. "It kind of overhangs the house for a while, but since there's really nothing supporting it, it eventually breaks off and falls. Here it falls into the sea."

"And takes you with it if you're standing on it." I finished.

"Of course. But it can also kill you if you're just close to where it breaks. When the shelf collapses, there's a surge of lava entering the sea and a huge plume, which contains a lot of sulfuric acid. Get that in your lungs and you're as good as dead. They found a couple dead out here a few years ago from that."

Margie had some chocolate on her lip and I motioned that fact to her. She used her tongue to clean it off. I wish she hadn't done that. It was a hard to watch.

"Are there a lot of deaths here?" I asked and turned to see if any of the other groups were doing anything stupid.

"No. But it happens because people ignore the signs and don't understand what they're doing. I think a lot of them think it's like Disneyland and the rangers will watch out for them. You didn't see any rangers out here did you?"

"No," I ventured.

"They go home at night. After dark this place is as wild as it was a million years ago."

"Okay," I said. "I'll stay away from the shelf." I turned and looked up at the sky. "Looks like it's going to be a clear night for star gazing."

Margie followed my gaze. "Yes it does," she agreed. Then she added: "You know, that's one picture you can't really capture, isn't it?"

As usual her comment confused me. "What? The stars?"

"No, silly. The dark. You can take pictures of things *in* the dark or things silhouetted *in* the darkness. And you can take pictures of the stars, or the moon, or anything light. But you have to look at those pictures in the light. You really can't capture darkness on film. Except sort of in the movies when you're sitting in the dark."

I wasn't sure she was right or that I was following, but it sounded perceptive so I gave her credit. "You know, I never thought of that, Margie. That's very insightful,"

"Mahalo," Margie said. "Would you like some trail mix?"

"No thanks. I think I'm just going to lay back and wait for it to get dark."

"So basically you're going to take another nap." Margie pegged me with an M&M. It didn't even hurt.

I did not nap. Nor did Margie. We just lay there on the warm lava and stared up at the sky and listened to the waves and the hiss of the lava as it entered the sea.

I imagined myself a Hawaiian warrior just back from the hunt a million years ago. Of course I had access to flashlights and trail mix.

We lay there while the sun set and the stars grew so bright it seemed you could reach out and touch them. We alternately watched the glow of the lava entering the sea, but as time wore on it began to get cool and I suggested that perhaps it was time we head back.

"We've outstayed nearly everyone else," I observed. "I think those people over there are going to make a night of it but I don't like the look of that dark line coming from the east. I wouldn't want to be out here in the rain. I'm betting this smooth lava – what did you call it?"

"Pahoehoe," Margie answered.

"I'll bet this pahoehoe gets pretty slick when it's wet."

Margie laughed at me. "You are such a worrywart. It's not going to rain, Joe. We'll be fine. But you're probably right. It'll be past one before we get to the hotel. Do you want to lead or do you want to follow?"

"I make a good follower," I said honestly.

We gathered up our stuff and set out slowly and carefully with the light from the flashlight to guide us.

A half hour later...

"I thought that flashlight was new!" I grumbled in the darkness.

"It is! I just bought the damn thing!" Margie shook it for the umpteenth time. "It said right on it. 'Lasts up to four hours!'" Margie dug in her backpack. "We'll have to use the spare. I don't know if it will last all the way back, so we'll have to use it sparingly."

I was going to say, that's why they call it a spare, but I decided to be nice. Besides, it wasn't all that clever.

Margie looked up at the sky. "I wish those clouds hadn't rolled in. The starlight helped a little."

"Maybe we'll meet someone when we get closer to the road," I said encouragingly. "We could team up."

"That's still a long way, Joe." Margie cautioned.

Twenty minutes later....

"I think you got cheated," I said gloomily.

Margie angrily flicked the switch on the second flashlight back and forth a dozen times and beat it in the palm of her hand. I won't repeat what she said because only sailors would understand. She finally handed me the flashlight. I performed the same ritual – I didn't know some of bad words she knew, I think they were Spanish – but to no avail.

"Well, what do you want to do now?" Margie asked. "We can try to go forward blind or we can pitch camp where we are and wait till morning. Personally, I don't think we can make it across the lava safely without a flashlight."

I agreed and suggested we try to find a place with a little protection from the wind. "Someplace that might offer shelter from rain," I said looking skyward.

"Don't be such a pessimist, Joe. It *isn't* going to rain!"

The accuracy of Margie's comment was accentuated by a clap of thunder.

"I think there's a spot over there," Margie said nervously. "Now go really slow."

Sometime later...

"That last shower soaked me pretty good," Margie said and rubbed her arms briskly. "I wish I'd remembered to pack my space blanket. You know when you live in the tropics, you hardly ever think of being cold. But I'm cold now what with that wind and all. How're you doing?"

"I'm wet," I said. "And cold." I sneezed twice to prove it. "Move to the left a little. I think the wind's shifted."

Margie moved to the left and I moved with her.

"Is that better?" she asked.

"A little," I said, trying not to let my teeth chatter.

Margie wriggled close to me. "We need to huddle, Joe. To conserve our body heat, I mean." Margie put her arms around me and leaned her head on my shoulder. "There. Isn't that better? Put your arms around me."

I did as directed.

"I read a story once about these people that froze to death hiking up...I think it was Mt. Whitney. That's in New York state isn't it? Anyway, I remember the article

211

said that if they had been less modest and huddled together to conserve their body heat, they would have survived easily," Margie pulled me closer.

I had my cheek on Margie's head and could smell her shampoo. Mango, I think.

"Joe?...Did you hear me?" Margie jiggled me to get my attention.

"Yes. I heard you," I said and breathed deeply. Where my body touched hers the heat was intense and the chill I'd felt before was all but gone.

"You can still see the stars over there," Margie pointed toward the horizon. "Aren't they lovely? Sometimes I lay out by the pool with all the lights out and stargaze for hours. Do you ever do that, Joe?"

I pulled her closer. "Not in Chicago. Not this time of year." I repeated what I'd said earlier about sledding with my friends.

Margie gave me a squeeze. "You're quite a guy, Joe. You really are. Here I've led us out onto this God forsaken lava and we're almost freezing and you haven't even yelled at me."

Margie looked up at me and smiled.

I looked down at her. "I'd never do that, Margie," I said softly.

And then I did something that was so stupid I can't believe I did it; something I realized I'd been wanting to do for days but hadn't had the guts to even let myself think about doing. What I did was close my eyes and lean down to give Margie a kiss.

At least that was the plan, but that's not what happened.

What happened was the following in very rapid succession: One, Margie pushed me roughly away; two, Margie wriggled free of my arms; three, Margie slapped me hard enough to loosen my filling; and four, Marge jumped to her feet and stood there with her arms over her chest and I gave me the tongue lashing of my life.

"What was that, Joe Thomas?" Margie roared. "Just what was that? What do you think you are doing?" She stomped her foot hard. "Are you trying to take advantage of me?"

I recovered my senses and backpedalled as fast as a circus bear on a tightrope. "No. No. Of course not!" I hollered and struggled to my feet. "I only thought..."

"What did you think?" Margie was fuming. "I'll have you know I'm a happily married woman," she took a step away from me. "And you're a happily married man. Just what..."

I put my hands up to avert the barrage of angry words and butted in. "I'm sorry Margie, I misread what was happening and what you were saying..."

"Just what did you think I was saying?" she sounded shocked. "'I'm easy?' Is that what you were thinking? I most certainly am not! I don't believe in extramarital affairs, Joseph Thomas. Is that the kind of person you are?"

"No, no. Of course not," I said, pleading my case. "Listen Margie, please. Calm down. I'm not trying to ...." I stopped to choose my words carefully. Even though it was dark, I could see the hurt on her face and I didn't want to make it worse. "What I did wasn't like me at all, Margie. It's just..."

"What? Just what?" Margie's voice softened somewhat.

I felt I had a chance to smooth things over. "I'm...I'm...not sure I can explain," I said slowly, gently. "Will... will...you accept my apology and my promise not to do that or anything like it again? I swear, I am not a.....a...philanderer. Please forgive me, Margie. Please?"

Margie let her arms fall to her side.

"Here things were going so well, and I was feeling so close to you and enjoying your company so much and you have to go and do something so incredibly stupid."

Margie sounded so disappointed I felt as if I should find a rock to crawl under.

"Oh, you make me so angry, Joseph Thomas." She stomped her foot again.

"It's not like me, honest," I reiterated softly.

Margie took a deep breath and stared at me a full minute without saying a word. Then she offered an olive branch.

"Okay, I'm going to excuse you, Joe. We're going to pretend it never happened. Although it did happen. But we're going to pretend it didn't happen. Okay?"

I jumped at the chance to normalize things. "Yes, okay. That's all I want... Thank you, Margie."

"Then that's that," Margie clapped her hands together as if dusting off flour. "Under the circumstances, I don't think we should huddle anymore."

"No," I agreed softly. "Maybe we could do some exercises." I suggested. "You know, get the blood circulating. If it doesn't rain again, the air is warm enough to dry our clothes."

"That's an excellent idea, Joe. It's too dangerous to run in place; deep knee bends ought to do it." Margie started to do knee bends.

"Yes," I agreed and started to do deep knee bends. "Deep knee bends, and maybe some pushups," I said, eager to win back Margie's approval.

"That's the idea," Margie said, her voice level again and even playful.

Margie was doing deep knee bends and I was doing pushups when a man's voice came out of the darkness and

214

a light swept over us. "Sure is a strange place to be doing calisthenics."

We stopped our labors instantly. Salvation! I shielded my eyes from the light to see who it was out there but the light from his flashlight was too intense.

"Where on earth did you come from?" Margie asked. "Were you looking for us?"

There was a moment of hesitation, then he answered. "No, I was just making my way back and I saw your shadows and I thought that's not right, so I decided to see what was up."

I noticed he had a bit of an accent, but I couldn't place it. A Texas twang? I thought it impolite to ask.

"Well, thank goodness, you did," I said. "Boy are we glad to see you. We're a little damp, but if you lead the way, we'll be happy to follow you back?"

Another slight pause, then: "Name's Lou, Lou Forester." *Yes, it did strike me as odd that there are so many Lou's in the world, but what do I know?* "Come on, folks, follow me. It's a good thing you didn't keep going the way you were headed. There's a big shatter ring up over there, you would'a never made it through without falling. We'll have to circle up that a way to avoid it." Lou started walking slowly, holding the flashlight so we could see the terrain.

"Well Lou, we're very glad to meet you. I'm Margie and this is Joe. If you're hungry, we've got some candy bars and trail mix."

"No thanks ma'am. I'm fine." Lou kept going as we joined up to follow close behind. Margie behind him and me in the rear.

"Watch your step," he cautioned.

We tried to make small talk as we went along, but Lou was not a talker so after a bit we just trudged along single file careful not to fall and twist an ankle.

215

After a while I voiced a concern that had been welling up in me. "Lou, are you sure we have to go this far around. It seems to me we're going way out of our way." We were heading away from the ocean and up toward the line of trees that marked the edge of the last big eruption.

"I think Joe's right," Margie agreed. "As long as we have a flashlight I don't think we have to worry too much about that shatter ring do we?"

I was reluctant to show my ignorance but eventually I caved. "What exactly is a 'shatter ring?'" I asked.

Margie gave the answer. "Remember when we were in the lava tube? Well a shatter ring occurs when a tube gets blocked. The lava pushing through the tube creates pressure and someplace there's a rupture to the surface. They call it a shatter ring because it looks like a pile of shattered glass when the lava pushes through."

I thanked Margie for her succinct explanation then suggested we take a rest. I was thirsty and tired, though I was almost dry and not nearly as cold as before.

"And lets discuss going another way," I ventured. "We're getting a long way from the ocean. I seem to remember some pretty heavy country up ahead."

Lou agreed to stop and we found a spot where we could sit; Lou turned off the light to save energy. I was curious to *see* Lou, but I thought it impolite to ask him to shine his flashlight on his face.

We drank our water and sat quietly a few minutes and then I started to suggest a new course. "Now what I suggest we do..."

I was rudely interrupted by Lou who suddenly didn't have any accent at all.

"Stuff it buddy. I don't care what you suggest. You're gonna keep going where I tell you to go."

I glanced at Margie. I could just barely see the alarm on her face.

"What's going on?" Margie asked.

"You too, lady, can it. You and me and your boyfriend here are going for a hike up to the foot of those trees there."

"Now just a minute," I started. Who do you think..."

My outburst was interrupted by a sound I'd only heard on TV detective shows: the sound of a gun being cocked.

"What was that?" I asked anyway.

"That's a Walther P88," Lou said.

"A what?" I had no idea what a Walther P88 was.

"It's a gun, Joe. He's got a gun," Margie reached over and put her hand gently on my knee.

"Listen," she said. "If it's money you want, we'll be glad to give it to you. And you can have my car keys. My purse is locked in the trunk. Joe, you've got your wallet. And the camera. It's a very expensive camera."

"I'm not here for money," Lou barked, then after a pause. "How much dough you got?"

"I've only got a hundred in my purse. But I've got diamond earrings...."

"No jewelry," Lou spat. "I'm not a pawn broker. What about you, lover-boy, how much you got?"

"A couple hundred in cash. Some traveler's ..."

"Traveler's checks? Give me a break. Gimme the money both of you."

Margie passed over the car keys and I gave him the money from my wallet. He took the camera too.

"Now you, Blondie. You're gonna lead the way. He handed Margie the flashlight. Go slow. Lover boy here is going next. Make sure you stay close together. Anybody tries anything I'll shoot you on the spot." Lou took the camera by its strap, whirled it over his head, and smashed it on the rocks. Pieces flew everywhere.

"Why'd you do that?" Margie asked.

"Never mind," Lou said. "Just get moving."

Lou warned Margie that if she pointed the flashlight at him, he'd shoot her, which was smart since as I said we hadn't seen Lou yet and couldn't identify him. Assuming we were going to live to identify him.

We'd only gone a little ways when Margie stopped. "You know if you shoot us, everyone will hear. Sound carries forever out here."

Lou chuckled. "Nice try, Blondie; maybe you never heard of a silencer?"

"Oh, I see," Margie said softly and began walking. "Joe, watch your step. It's very tricky here."

A few steps further on and Margie had a new comment. "Well, if you're not here to rob us, Lou – if that's your real name – what are you doing? Where are we going?"

"I've answered enough questions," Lou snapped. "You'll see soon enough. Now move."

"Are you going to kill us?" I asked cautiously.

Lou said nothing.

"Joe! If he wanted to kill us, he could already have done it."

"Yeah," I said. "But then we'd be lying out on the lava. All those helicopters flying over every day. It would only be a matter of hours till they found our bodies and knew what happened. If he kills us in the woods, it could be days or weeks before they find our bodies. Isn't that right?"

Lou chuckled. "Your boyfriend's a smart guy, missy," Now shut up. Both of you.

Margie stopped. "Well, if you're going to kill us, I'm not going any further. If you're going to kill me. Do it now."

I wasn't sure Margie was thinking straight. "Margie, I don't ...."

"Okay, Blondie. If you're going to be difficult. But I don't think I'll shoot you. I think I'll shoot your boyfriend here, and you can drag him along. How's that?"

"Margie?" I said, my voice displaying more distress than I intended.

"Okay. Okay," Margie caved. "I'm going. But, why do you want to kill us? You could at least tell us that. We have a right to know."

"It's a job," Lou said lazily.

"A job?" Margie perked up. "You mean somebody hired you to kill us? Who? Tell me who? If you're going to kill us, what difference does it make? Maybe we're not who you think we are. Maybe you're here to kill some other people..."

"Lady, be quiet. I'm not answering any more questions. Just keep moving."

Lou sounded weary and things were looking absolutely hopeless. I was beginning to wonder exactly how much getting shot hurt and the idea occurred to me that maybe I should make a grab for the gun even if it was a long shot.

But just as my brain was wrestling with the idea of trying to grab the gun, fate intervened.

We were coming down a particularly steep mound of lava and heading up a new one when I heard a very loud 'crackling' sound that was followed almost immediately by a noise that sounded like rocks falling. This was followed quickly by Lou shouting "What the hell...l....l...l." Which was followed immediately by the sound of a muffled gunshot.

I screamed. Margie screamed. Lou howled a muffled expletive.

Margie spun around and flooded me with light. I was temporarily blinded. "Where'd he go?" Margie yelled.

I turned around. All I could see were spots. They faded quickly. Lou had magically disappeared.

"Are you okay?" Margie asked.

"I'm fine," I answered. "You?"

"I'm fine." Margie trained the light back on the ground. "Where on earth did Lou go?"

"I fell in a f...king hole," Lou howled from someplace beneath us. "I broke my f...king arm, that's what happened. Get me the hell out of here!"

I took Margie's hand and shined the flashlight back where Lou should have been. All that was there now was a big hole. Lou continued screaming expletives from the hole.

Margie swept the light over the ground and trained it on something else. "The gun! Get the gun, Joe! There, see it?"

I spotted the gun and walked over cautiously and picked it up.

"I've got it," I said, holding it between thumb and forefinger as if it might bite me.

Margie came and took the gun more convincingly and tucked it in her shorts. She seemed to know how to handle a gun.

"What should we do, Joe?"

"I don't know." I answered. "We've gotta get to the police and get help."

"Right," Margie said and turned the flashlight on the ground and started to walk away.

"Wait a minute," I said. "We can't just leave him."

Margie stopped. "Are you kidding me? Why in the name of hell can't we leave him? He was going to kill us," Margie was disturbed with my suggestion.

"I know, but we can't..."

"I say we leave him here to rot. We'll go back to the car, get help, and let the authorities come back for him."

Margie walked over and shined the light into the hole; Lou covered his face with his arm so we couldn't get a look at him.

I came over. "His left arm does look a bit mangled," I said. "You really think we should just leave him?"

Margie's tone was incredulous. "Yes, Joe. I'm sure we should just leave him. He's not getting out of there with a bad arm. For Pete's sake, Joe, he's a hit man! You can't be sympathetic to a hit man!" Margie shined the light back into the hole and again Lou shielded his face.

"Andy?" Margie quizzed cautiously.

"Who the hell is Andy," Lou growled.

"Okay, listen Lou, if that's your real name," Margie said. "We're going to leave you right where you are, so get comfortable. Someone will be here in the morning to arrest you. Here. Have some candy." Margie dropped the rest of the candy bars into the hole. "And here's a bottle of water." She dropped a bottle of water as well.

She turned and shined the flashlight on the ground and took my hand roughly and started to lead me away in the direction we both wanted to go an hour ago. "Come on, Joe. This way."

"You can't leave me here!" Lou yelled.

"Wait," I said, taking the near empty backpack from Margie and tucking it in a crevice to lock it in place. "Let's leave this here to mark the spot. It should be easy to spot from the air."

"You're way too soft, Joe," Margie said. "I was thinking I should put a couple of slugs in him just for fun."

"You were not!" I said confidently.

"Was, too!" Margie snarled. "It'd serve him right! Hey, wait a minute." Margie stopped and turned and backtracked to the hole and shined the light at Lou, who once more shielded his face.

Margie pointed the gun at him. "Who hired you to kill us?"

"Eat a booger," Lou responded.

"Come on buster, tell me. Otherwise, I'm going to count to ten, and then I'm gonna shoot you full of holes," Margie sounded quite convincing. She would have made a good gangster.

"You aren't going to shoot me," Lou said, still holding his hand up to cover his face.

"I will!" Margie said forcefully and began to count. "One...two...three..."

"Margie. No!" I said.

"You aren't going to shoot anybody," Lou said boldly.

"Four...five...six...seven...eight...nine..." Margie cocked the gun.

"Margie!" I pleaded. "Margie, don't shoot him!"

"Ten!" Margin finished. There was silence for a moment, then Margie turned toward me and uncocked the gun and stuffed it in her shorts. She took my hand again and led me away.

"How did he know I wasn't going to shoot him, Joe? I could have. I really could have. But how did he know I wasn't gonna."

"Because you're not a killer, Margie," I said.

"I know that. But how did *he* know?"

I decided to humor her. "Lucky guess, I suppose."

222

"Yeah," Margie said disappointedly, then: "Who do you think is trying to kill us, Joe. I mean first it was you, and now it's me, too. What's going on?"

"I don't know," I said honestly. "Let's just get the hell out of here and let the authorities deal with it."

"Yeah," Margie said sadly. "Watch your step. It's really rough here."

In the distance we heard Lou. "Come back you assholes. Get me out of here!"

"You're sure we should just leave him?" I asked again.

Margie squeezed my hand hard and shook her head. "Joe! Honestly! Who are you?"

How Did *This* Happen?

I was sitting across the interrogation table from Detective Lo. He wasn't happy, but then neither was I.

"You're going away, Mr. Thomas, unless you start talking now! I've got an officer missing, and you've got his gun. A bullet's been fired from it..."

I shook my head. "I'm not saying anything until my lawyer gets here. Where the hell is he anyway?"

"Must be having trouble in traffic," Lo mocked me. "What did you do with officer Koi?"

"I already told you. You're officer was going to kill us!"

Lo sneered at me. "Gimme a break, Mr. Thomas. I've known Koi for twenty years. He's a highly decorated member of this department. You and the lady cooked up a bad story. It might have been believable if it had been someone else. But it isn't going to fly. Now tell me, where did you leave officer Koi?"

"I already told you. We marked the spot! Did you even look?"

"Yeah, we looked. There was no marker. We didn't find no collapsed lava tube. Nothing."

"Then he must have climbed out!"

"You said his arm was broken! Do you think he crawled out with a broken arm?"

"*He* told me his arm was broken. I didn't examine it!"

"So you just left him with a broken arm..."

"He was going to kill us!"

"Why was he going to kill you?"

"He wouldn't say. Only that he'd been hired to kill us."

"Who hired him?"

"He wouldn't say."

"He wouldn't say...he wouldn't say. You're beginning to repeat yourself, Mr. Thomas."

Lo leaned back in his chair. "Listen, why don't you make it easy on yourself. You lead me to the body and you testify against Mrs. Geanosa, and you'll still have some life left when you get out of prison."

Detective Lo paused. "You know you don't do prison time here on the island. Oh, no. We send all our big losers to Texas. Down south where boys know how to make life miserable for one another. Maybe you'll get a cute cellmate..."

"Now just a moment..." I interrupted. I was sweating like a steam room attendant.

"Don't 'just a moment me' sonny boy... You don't want to make a deal? Okay. Let's see if your partner's ready to talk. Maybe she saw you pull the trigger. Maybe *she* didn't have anything to do with it. If she talks, maybe she'll only get a year or two for aiding and abetting."

Detective Lo stood up. "Wally, come in and sit with Mr. Thomas. I wouldn't want him to get lonely."

A big crew cut with bulging muscles came in and sat down. Evidently this was Wally. "Okay, boss," he said. "The woman's in number five."

Lo started to leave, then stopped. "Be back real soon," he said menacingly.

Before he got the door shut, I yelled out. "Where's Frank? I want to talk to my lawyer! You're violating my rights!"

I found out later that Lo tried a 'good' cop approach with Margie, whereas he'd been the bad cop to me.

"...so you see, Mrs. Geanosa," Lo said softly. "If you tell me what *really* happened, then you get to make the deal. *You* do the easy time."

Margie pursed her lips and looked up at the ceiling. "So, if I confess and tell you what *really* happened, then I only get a couple of years?"

The detective could all but smell confession and got excited. He leaned forward and smiled. "Maybe less. Maybe just probation. I've seen it happen. Judge decides you've been misled by some sleazy guy and they all but let you walk. What do you say, Mrs. Geanosa? Do you want to make a deal?"

Margie looked down at the table and muttered. "I don't know, detective. I'm not a squealer. I don't want to rat out Joe."

Lo was sweaty with anticipation. "Don't think of it like that," he said gently. "Think of it ... as clearing your conscience. Confession is good for the soul."

Margie sat up straight and looked him in the eyes. "Okay. Okay. It's a deal. Here's what *really* happened..."

***

It was a half hour later when Margie and I tagged along after Frank from the police station. The cool mid-morning air felt incredibly good after the long grilling and time in the slammer.

"So how come we didn't have to post bail?" I asked, surprised that we were free.

"Because they never charged you," Frank said. "They don't have anything to charge you with. Based on your statements, all they have is a missing police officer who you claim tried to kill you. They don't believe that, but they have no evidence. They can't charge you unless they have some evidence of a crime."

Frank paused and turned to Margie. "And you young lady. Never ever play games with these guys. If I hadn't shown up when I did and you'd told that story of yours to Lo, you'd both be behind bars, without bail."

Margie put her fists on her hips. "But he was such a dick! 'Just tell me what *reallllly* happened.' I wanted to smack him!"

Frank wagged his finger. "Don't ever do that either. These guys don't know how to take a joke. When they think they've got someone, they bite down hard and don't let go, like a pit bull. I've seen it happen. That's why you don't say anything. Nothing. Now I'll repeat that again. Nothing."

Frank paused by his car. "Listen, I've got to get back to the courthouse, but we need to talk. Can you come by my office this evening. Say about six-thirty?"

"Do we have a choice?" Margie asked.

"Frankly no," Frank said. "Unless you want to wait around until Lo digs up enough evidence, real or manufactured, to arrest you. He's working on that now. Believe me. He's working hard on that now."

Margie looked as if she wanted to refuse, so I butted in. "We'll be there, Mr. Bonza." I turned to Margie. "You know where his office is?"

"Of course I do." Margie took my arm and steered me to the Volvo. "Bye, Frank. Thanks," Margie called over her shoulder. Then to me she added: "I think we should stay together until after we talk to Frank."

I agreed but only if Margie agreed to swing by my condo so I could pick up some things.

"I'm starved," I said when we got to Margie's, suddenly aware that I hadn't had a square meal in almost a whole day.

"Yes, and a drink sounds utterly marvelous," Margie added. "Take the guestroom and make yourself comfortable. I'm going to fix a drink before I do anything else." She made a beeline for the bar.

"I'm with you there," I said and then saw there was a light blinking on the phone. "Light's blinking. You've got a message."

"Play it, please. I can hear from here." Margie pulled out bottles and glasses from the bar. I suspected Ice Tea would be on the menu.

I pressed the message button.

A perky and sultry female voice filled the room. "Hi Margie. It's Daisy. Sorry I couldn't get back to you sooner. I'm back from Honolulu, so bring that photo stick by anytime. I won't know if I can help until I try, but I should be able to salvage it unless you shot a lot of pictures afterwards. You know the number." *Beep*.

I looked up at Margie who was coming at me with a tall Mai Tai. "I'd almost forgotten about the photo from the airport," I said. "It may be more important now than ever. What's Daisy's number."

Margie handed me my drink and I took a hit. It was heavenly.

"It's in the address book there," Margie pointed to a little black book on the table near the phone. "Daisy Blake. Do you think there really is something in that photo? We sure could use a break." Margie gulped half her tumbler.

I found the number, set down my drink and dialed. "Yes, we certainly could," I agreed, taking another long pull on the ice tea. "Maybe you should talk though, I'd have to explain who I am and...."

Margie took the phone just as someone picked up.

"Hi, Daisy, it's Margie...."

Daisy

An hour later we were at Daisy's apartment near Waikoloa. It was a nice place with an ocean view but since it also served as her office it was a hodgepodge of computer equipment and furniture. It had a big sofa, a small kitchenette, and a big lanai.

Daisy herself was a lot like her place – a hodgepodge. She was not the geeky persona I'd imagined, but she did wear big 'Harry Potter' glasses and had a tattoo on her neck of a gecko wrestling a cockroach. She also had the shortest hair – a remarkable florescent shade of green – I'd ever seen on a woman. A buzz cut I think it's called.

She was feminine enough to pull it off and was dressed in half a sweatshirt with the arms torn off. By 'half' I mean it only reached just past her breasts which I'm pretty sure were unsupported by a bra, and she had the shortest short shorts I'd ever seen. They were even shorter than those Margie bought in the kid's department back at the volcano.

Overall, she was quite stunning, and had I not been informed that she was a lesbian, I wouldn't have guessed it. But then what do I know about such things. I'm still trying to figure out straight women.

At the moment she was in front of a computer screen, typing faster than that secretary I had had many years ago before they became obsolete. There are no secretaries anymore. They are now executive assistants and people of my status don't have them. I have to type my own correspondence, which is why I had to learn to spell.

"What are you doing?" I asked.

"It's a program I use for screening deleted information," Daisy explained. "Whenever information is deleted on a computer, whether it's in memory or on a disk or, as is the case here, on a memory stick, the information is not deleted. Just the pointer to that information is removed. Generally, the information itself is still there until it's written over."

It sounded logical to me.

"I'm going to pretend I understood that," I said. "Do you think it's still there?"

"We'll see." Daisy typed some more and we waited patiently. "Even if only part of it is here, I should be able to get something."

"Isn't she a wiz?" Margie offered, clearly impressed with Daisy's computer knowledge.

"Definitely," I agreed. "Someday I suppose I'll have to join the computer world. I only..."

"Here's one," Daisy said excitedly. "I'll bring it up on the monitor."

A nice picture appeared on the monitor.

"That's it!" I yelled loud enough to startle everyone.

Margie leaned over to see. "And look, Joe. Look who the dead guy from the pool is shaking hands with!"

Daisy spun around in her chair. "What dead guy?" Obviously she had missed the local paper when she was in Honolulu.

"It's officer Koi!" I said happily. "Our friendly neighborhood hit man. This is it Margie. This is the proof we need. Wait till Detective Lo sees it! Daisy, can you print this out?"

"Sure. But what's this about a dead guy in a pool? And a hit man?" Daisy looked troubled and puzzled.

Margie gave her a shoulder hug. "It's very complicated, Daisy. I'll explain it all to you later." Margie grabbed the printout from the printer and picked up her purse. "Let's go, Joe." She took my hand and dragged me toward the door, then stopped and pondered a moment. "Maybe we should call Frank first."

I considered her idea for a second and agreed. "I think you're right. We probably should do that."

"Daisy, where's the phone," Margie looked around the crowded apartment.

"Right here," Daisy pointed to the computer. "What's the number?"

Margie gave her the number and Daisy's fingers danced over the keyboard; I heard ringing.

"Just speak into the little microphone." Daisy got up to give Margie her chair. "Joe, can I get you a beer?"

"Sure. But I'd rather have an ice tea. Do you know how to make an ice tea?"

"A Long Island Ice Tea?" she asked.

"That's the one," I said.

"Me too!" Margie crowed as Frank's receptionist answered mechanically.

Well That's a Shocker

It was just after six-thirty when we pulled into the lot outside Frank's office.

We'd spent the afternoon at Pete and Amanda's enjoying each other's company and trying not to drink too much or tell them the good news about the photograph.

Frank had insisted we *not* share the news with anyone till after we got together with him and detective Lo had seen it. He claimed it had something to do with 'tainting' the evidence. I found this puzzling but Margie insisted it was something she'd heard of many times so I played along.

Frank had also insisted we bring Daisy with us to the meeting since he had questions for her about how she'd 'resurrected' the photo.

When we picked her up, Daisy was wearing a very different ensemble from the earlier visit. Her sweatshirt had been replaced with a rather loose fitting blouse that was buttoned up to her neck but tied just above her navel. She had baggy cargo pants that hung way down on her hips, and I was pretty sure if she bent over I'd spot a 'whale tail,' assuming she was wearing underwear which I suspected she didn't wear. She had a thin sweater on but it wasn't buttoned. You might think that odd, – the sweater not the whale tail – but I'd already learned that the locals start to get chilled when the temp dips below eighty. Thin blood I guess.

In the tropics it's pretty much dark by six so when we arrived at the parking lot it was empty except for a big Lincoln – Frank's – and an old panel truck with black windows – which I figured had either been abandoned or died there.

232

"Thanks for coming along, Daisy," Margie said again. "I hope we didn't spoil any plans you had."

Daisy had been quiet on the way over, which contrasted with her enthusiastic afternoon persona. I assumed she was tired. In any event the plan was to meet up with Pete and Amanda after the meeting and then the five of us would have a celebratory dinner. Margie told me she also intended to give Daisy a sizeable reward. "We'd have been lost without her." A fact I agreed with wholeheartedly. Thankfully it was not my money.

"Not a problem, guys," Daisy said with a bit of enthusiasm. "I wouldn't miss this for the world. A real who-dun-it."

We'd explained the circumstances and importance of the photo, so she was up to speed.

We parked the car and entered the building through the back as Frank had directed and found the lawyer alone in his office; he came forward to greet us with his hand out and a big smile.

"Aloha, Joe, Margie," he shook our hands even though we'd been seeing him almost every day since I arrived. "And you must be Daisy?" He gave Daisy a big two-handed hand shake and looked her over thoroughly. "It's very nice to meet you."

He motioned us toward a big leather sofa and we sat down and then he sat on the edge of his desk and looked down on us.

"I'm glad you called me before you took that photo to detective Lo. That would have been a terrible mistake. Do you have it with you?"

Margie pulled the printout from her big straw purse, the same one she'd had when I first met her, and handed it to him.

He looked at it carefully. "Thanks. And the ... what's it called?"

"The memory stick?" Margie said, handing that over as well.

"Yes. The memory stick." Frank turned the little nothing over in his hand and slipped it into his pocket. "So tell me, did you make any other copies, or manipulate the data in any way?" He looked at each of us in turn and landed finally on Daisy.

"The reason I ask, is that the police are going to want to know. Digital photography, as I'm sure Daisy can tell you, is not bullet proof."

"All I did was bring it up on my PC." Daisy answered.

"So there is a copy on your PC?" Frank asked.

"No. I just brought it right up with the browser from the memory stick."

"Good." Frank smiled. "One last question. Did you discuss the photo with anyone?"

"No," Margie said emphatically. "I wanted to tell everyone of course, but you said not to, so we didn't."

"Good. Very good," Frank smiled again.

He folded the photo and we sat waiting for his next question.

"I'm just going to run across the hall and show this to my partner. I'll just be a minute."

Frank disappeared, closing the door behind himself.

We sat silent a moment.

"Nice place," Daisy said, glancing around at the spacious office.

"Yes," Margie said. "I think Frank does pretty well. I know Jack pays him a small fortune every year for this and that. And he's got lots of clients. Jack's dad was a client, too."

To fill the void of Frank's absence, we discussed where we should go for dinner and decided on a Japanese place Daisy was fond of. I like sushi so I was on board with that. And sake. I like sake.

It wasn't more than a few minutes before I heard the door open behind us and turned to look, expecting to see Frank.

I was astonished to see someone else.

"You!!!" Margie shrieked.

Margie and I jumped to our feet. Daisy just sat there and looked confused.

In the doorway, armed with a revolver aimed straight at us, was Jimmy Koi, aka 'Lou,' and he looked very unhappy.

Margie overcame her shock first. "What are..." She started but never got to finish.

"Put your hands in the air and keep them there," Jimmy said sharply.

We did as told. He pointed the gun at Daisy, who was still sitting on the sofa looking quite befuddled.

"You too," he barked.

Daisy stood up next to Margie and raised her hands. "What's going on?"

She got a quick "shut up" from Jimmy.

"It's the guy who-dun-it," I whispered gloomily. "And it looks like we're next."

Daisy looked perplexed. My comment was a bit obscure, I'll admit, but I didn't try to clarify it. My mind was reeling with questions but no answers came with them. *What in god's name did Frank and Jimmy have in common?*

I wasn't thinking for long before Jimmy was joined by a second man with a gun. He looked vaguely familiar, but I couldn't place him until Margie put a name to his face.

"Jack?" Margie's voice cracked with astonishment.

I glanced at Margie. She was staring incredulously at the duo in the doorway. I recalled a photo of Jack and Margie I'd seen at her place. So this was Jack? Now I was really confused.

"What the hell....?" I started, but Jimmy cut me off.

"Quiet." Jimmy ordered and stepped aside to let Jack into the room.

Jack took a few steps forward then stopped. He looked at Margie, ignoring Daisy and me.

"Sorry, honey. It's just the way it is. Put the handcuffs on 'em, Jimmy."

He held out his hand and Jimmy gave him his gun and then pulled a pair of handcuffs from behind his back and came at us.

We should have had plenty to say, but I think we were stunned into silence.

Jimmy handcuffed me first, my hands behind my back, then he handcuffed Daisy the same way. While he was cuffing Margie, she finally found her voice.

"Jack? Do you mean you're the one that hired this...this..thing?" I could sense Margie was on the verge of tears. "Why, Jack? Why? I don't understand."

Jack made a face that said 'no comment' and ignored her question. He turned his attention to me.

"So, you're Joe," he said, grinning in a very distasteful sort of way. "Sorry to meet you under such unpleasant conditions. Jillian sends her love."

"What does Jillian have to do with this?" I asked quickly and naively. You've no doubt figured it out by now so don't be too hard on me. You know the old saying 'hope springs eternal.' I'd been hoping Jillian loved me for a very long time.

236

Jimmy decided he didn't want us standing around so he pushed us down one by one so we were again sitting on the sofa like three birds on the fence.

Jack came around and sat on the corner of Frank's desk. He smiled at me.

"Are you kidding? It was her idea, hubby."

I have never liked the word hubby, especially used in this context, but I couldn't think of a good retort so I said nothing. Besides, I didn't follow him at first. I think my brain was numb. I couldn't put two and two together. "What do you mean?" I asked stupidly. "What was her idea?"

Margie gave a disrespectful snort and shook her head. "Don't you see, Joe. Jillian and Jack..." she choked up and couldn't finish. She didn't need to.

My brain thawed and everything fell into place. How could I have been so blind. All the signs were there. The eagerness to spend time in L.A., the... It was suddenly crystal clear that Jillian and Jack had been having an affair. Probably for a very long time.

"You mean you and Jillian..." I started.

"That's right, Einstein," Jack mocked me. "And we finally decided the best way for us to be together was to kill you. Or to be more accurate, to have you meet with an accident. But by golly Joe you are one hell of a lucky guy. If you was a rabbit I'd lop off one of your feet and carry it with me everywhere."

I thought about things. "The helicopter ride?" I asked.

"Jillian planned that. Months ago," Jack said testily. "I made arrangements with friends to shoot it down so it looked like a random act, but it was her idea. Only *you* chickened out and gave up your seat to some poor schlock. Not that it mattered. Who'd a thought the pilot could fly like that!

237

"And when that failed, guess who came up with the idea to fill my scuba tank with bad air?"

I said nothing.

"That's right hubby. Jillian! Who would have thought that stupid scuba instructor would take my tank? Dumb luck again.

"And then the limousine and the bike? It was just chance that you decided to take a bike ride. But it was Jillian who thought of running you off the road with the help of Jimmy's brother-in-law. Unfortunately he is just about as incompetent as ..." Jack stopped. "Are you starting to understand Joe? Jillian ain't your girl anymore."

He turned to Jimmy. "Gag 'em, and let's get 'em out of here."

We'd all been quiet all this time, letting Jack do the talking, the explaining, but now Daisy piped up. "You'll never get away with this," she said with what I mistook for confident bravado. We had no cards to play.

"Sure we will," Jack said sinisterly. "Because we're holding all the cards."

See, I told you.

"You think so, asshole. The truth is..." Daisy started viciously, but was cut off by Jimmy, who shoved a rag in her mouth from behind. All that came out of Daisy after that was "mmmmm mff nmfnm..." and such. Not much of a sentence.

Jack obviously didn't want complainers.

"Shut up and sit still or I'll put a bullet in your head!" He brought the revolver up to Daisy's temple for emphasis and Daisy stopped. Jimmy followed up the gag in her mouth with a generous amount of duct tape.

Then it was Margie's turn to spout off.

She repeated the same question she'd asked before. "Why Jack, I don't understand why? I thought we were doing so well. I thought we were making progress. Why didn't... "

Margie did not get to finish her sentence either because Jimmy stuffed a gag in her mouth just as he had done with Daisy and he sealed it in with duct tape as well.

But Jack did answer Margie, at least to some extent.

"Margie, Margie, Margie," he said, shaking his head pitifully. "There are so many reasons. You're a heck of a lot of fun, but you're not what I'm looking for anymore."

He gave her the once over and shook his head disagreeably. "Look at you. You're closing in on forty and you still dress like a high-school flirt ... or a two-dollar hooker."

That was hitting below the belt, and when I glanced over at Margie I saw a tear form in her eye and streak down her cheek. He was going too far.

"Just a minute, asshole." I jumped up and lunged at him. Jimmy grabbed me from behind and pulled me roughly back onto the sofa and quickly stuffed a gag in my mouth. I too got the duct tape.

Jack shook his head and scowled at me. "That's real sweet of you, Joe, defending Margie's honor. But you're not in any position to do anything. Are you?"

Jack stood back and examined each of us and shook his head and settled on Daisy who was once again trying to communicate her displeasure with the circumstances.

"As I said before, young lady, we'll get away with it, so long as we take care of all of you. It's too bad Jimmy screwed up at the volcano. If he'd done his job there, you'd never have gotten involved. But like they say, 'that's the way the cookie crumbles.'"

Jack turned to me again. "By the way, the volcano deal was Jillian's idea as well. She is a very creative lady."

Then Jack turned on Margie again.

"The truth is we never planned to kill you, Margie. Had the helicopter ride been deadly, or the scuba dive, or even the bike accident, you would have been just fine. After Joe was gone and Jillian got the insurance money..." He turned to me and smiled. "Did you know there's a two million dollar policy on you? Double indemnity. Thanks to Frank that is."

He turned back to Margie.

"Anyway, Margie, after Jillian collected the money, I was going to get a divorce. It's too bad you two got so close. But it's probably just as well. It's a lot neater this way and there's more money for me. You've got an insurance policy too. Didn't know that did you? Of course when you two just disappear it'll take a long time before the insurance pays off. But we can wait. It won't be forever."

Jack stood up. He seemed to have finished with us. "Okay, on your feet," Jack ordered. Then to Jimmy: "Let's get 'em to the car."

Jimmy took Daisy by the arm and guided her toward the door. "You first, honey."

We saw nothing of Frank as we were ushered down the hallway and down the stairs and told to wait at the side of the building while Jack went around the corner and got a big Lincoln and pulled it close. He popped the trunk, which made me miserable right away since I'm terribly claustrophobic, but I was pretty sure no one cared about that.

"Okay, one at a time," Jimmy said. "Anyone tries to make trouble, you're dead on the spot. You first!" He poked me with the barrel of his gun.

With help from Jack, I got loaded in the trunk. Once inside my feet were secured with duct tape.

240

"Don't want anyone kicking anyone," he said with a little laugh.

They piled Margie and Daisy on top of me and we did our best to scoot around and make room for one another. It was a tight squeeze and when they dropped the lid, I was laying on Margie's stomach looking up at her and Daisy was contorted around us with her butt close enough for me to kiss. Not that I thought of doing so at the time.

Things looked horribly grim of course, but had I known what else was happening, I would have had some hope.

For at that same time, my old friend Detective Lo was with officer Wally in that dilapidated van across the parking lot watching everything. They had also heard everything.

"Should we move in now?" Wally asked. "We got a confession. We can add kidnapping and ..."

"Shush," Lo snapped. "The confession won't hold up. We don't have a court order for that wire Daisy's wearing and they'll argue it's attorney/client privilege or something. We also don't know where Mrs. Thomas is. Let's hold off and follow 'em. I don't want any loose ends. Mrs. Thomas is somewhere out there and I'm betting they're going to meet up with her before anything goes down."

"Okay." Wally shook his head. "We got cars waiting in all directions to cover whatever route they're gonna take. We follow way back, right?"

"Right," Lo said. And have a car pick up Frank Bonza as soon as we're out of here. I've been waiting a long time to catch that shyster."

Meanwhile, in the trunk of the Lincoln, I was about ready to scream – if I could scream, which I couldn't because of the gag in my mouth and the tape over that. I kept thinking there must be something I could do. But

241

what? My mind raced with all the usefulness of a mouse on a wheel.

It was a bumpy ride at first and I would have apologized to both Margie and Daisy had I been able to, but finally it smoothed out and I could tell we were moving fast – highway speed. Margie and Daisy were both restless, trying to free themselves from their bonds. I figured that that was a waste of time, so I put all my effort into my cranium. Yes, I know *that* was a waste of time.

After about twenty minutes or so, I felt the car slow and we took a turn and the ride got really rough. We bounced around like fish in the bottom of a boat and more than once my head hit the lid and more than once Daisy's butt hit me in the face. It would have been quite funny if I didn't suspect we were going to die when the car stopped. Which it finally did.

I heard the car doors open and close but no one came to let us out. I prayed: "Please, dear God, don't let them be firebugs!"

God heard me and after a bit the trunk sprang open and cool air rushed inside. I could smell the ocean and hear the surf, but I didn't have a clue as to where we were.

One by one our feet were freed and we were helped from the trunk and then we were herded down to the water where a dinghy waited just off shore in a small, calm lagoon. Jack was nowhere in sight and I wondered if he'd left us.

"Okay, in the dinghy," Jimmy said. "It's going to be a tight fit, so don't make trouble. I doubt if any of you want to try to swim with your hands behind your back, so do just what I say."

I certainly did not want to swim with handcuffs!

We did what Jimmy said and after the four of us were in the dinghy, Jimmy began to row.

I was just beginning to wonder where the hell he was rowing to when I saw it – a big cabin cruiser – waiting darkly on the water just beyond the shallow breakers, a stone's throw away.

Jimmy approached from the rear and I read the name across the back "Jack's Lady." So this was Jack's toy. Very impressive.

We pulled alongside and Jack, who was already on board, helped us aboard, none too gently. Jimmy must have taken Jack out first and then come back for us.

We were seated across the stern and our handcuffs were unfastened and reattached to a railing that ran around the stern of the boat. I don't know what it's called but it looked pretty secure. I was on the port side with Margie in the middle and Daisy on the starboard side.

Once we were secured, Jack yelled out: "Okay, skipper. Let's do some night fishing."

"Aye, yea, captain," came a response from the shadow at the controls.

I almost swallowed my tongue! It was Jillian's voice. I glanced at Margie. She knew who it was as well, and her eyes flashed angrily.

I could make out her shadow now. The hair, the broad hips, the curve of her butt. I would have yelled at her, but I couldn't yell. I just had to sit there and stew as the boat picked up speed and we headed out into the dark and the deep, deep ocean, away from anything safe, to God only knew what horrible destination.

Meanwhile, back in the police van, Detective Lo was furious, probably as much at himself as with anyone, but he was taking it out on Wally.

"A boat! Where are they going with a boat? Where the hell are they going? Call the f–king coast guard. Call the airport. We need a chopper! Get me out there!"

Wally was on the radio to the coast guard in nothing flat and then he called the airport.

Had I known how things had screwed up, the optimism I might have had earlier would have been lost. But since I didn't know, I wasn't disillusioned. I was just plain scared. Lucky for me, my bladder was empty.

We cruised diagonally out from the shore for at least ten minutes. No one said anything to us but Margie and Daisy and I shared eye contact for all the good that did. Nobody looked hopeful. Daisy was constantly working her mouth, but that tape is a bitch.

When we first started out, there were some lights on shore, but as we got further along the lights ended and all I could spot in the starlight was the surf pounding hard and white against tall cliffs.

The boat eventually slowed until we were just chugging along, holding our own, the swells more noticeable now that we were no longer plunging through them. "Dear God," I prayed, "please don't let me get sea sick with this gag in my mouth."

Jack had been sitting all this time in what I believe is called a 'fighting chair,' which is a chair that faces the stern from which you fight the fish you've caught on the line. I guess in this instance, we were the fish.

Jimmy took over at the wheel and Jillian came back to join Jack. She glanced our way but turned so her back was to us.

"Can I go below?" she asked Jack. "I don't see why I need to be here at the end."

"No," Jack said firmly. "We're in this together. There's not going to be any deal making later on if..." He didn't finish the sentence.

Jillian shifted her weight, and turned and looked at us. "Margie," she said softly. "I want you to know I didn't mean for this to happen to you. Really I didn't. But it can't be helped now." She looked at Daisy. "And you, whoever you are, I'm sorry you were in the wrong place at the wrong time. I really am."

Finally Jillian looked at me and opened her mouth to say something but stopped. She turned away and returned to the wheel.

Jimmy came back by us. "Where are the chains?" he asked Jack.

"In the dry tanks," Jack answered.

I wasn't pleased at the thought that ran through my mind. Not pleased at all.

Jimmy crossed the boat to what I assumed were the dry tanks and pulled out three heavy lengths of chain and threw them at our feet.

"How will we explain their disappearance to the police?" Jillian asked from her position at the wheel.

"We're not explaining anything," Jack called. "We just got off the plane, remember? If they ask us, we just say we came back and don't know nothing about anyone. If we're lucky, they'll figure they ran off together. Jimmy can tell Lo that they spent the night together at the Volcano House. Anyway, they won't find anything. It's deeper than shit out here. Their bodies aren't coming up. Ever."

"And the pool boy saw them together!" Jillian added eagerly.

"Exactly. They'll look, but they won't look too hard. The cop's'd rather have a missing person's case on the books, than a triple homicide."

"But aren't they going to wonder how they got off the island without being seen?" Jillian was no dummy.

"How hard was it for us to get on and off the island? They know it ain't that hard."

"It'll be a long time before the insurance companies pay," Jillian said sadly.

"We can manage till then, sugar."

As this conversation was taking place, Jimmy was dutifully divvying up the chains at our feet. Time, as they say, was running out.

But Daisy wasn't playing dead. She'd decided enough was enough; she had something to say and by God she was going to say it.

So while Margie and I sat like lumps who had accepted their fate, Daisy was struggling like mad to work her gag loose and finally she succeeded enough so that I heard her mutter something that actually sounded like words. And the words I thought I heard were: "Why me?"

In addition to working on her gag, Daisy had been throwing her chest around quite violently and I know it seems odd to say it but it reminded me of someone trying to shimmy. I had no idea what that was all about but it did draw Jack's attention.

Jack stood up and came over to Daisy: "Why you? I already told you. You just got caught in the middle. Now sit still and shut up."

But Daisy continued her gyrations.

"Won't the police be suspicius if Daisy disappears at the same time as Joe and Margie?" Jillian asked from the wheel.

"Don't worry about it, sugar," Jack answered. "It's just another mystery. Does anybody know she's involved besides those of us on this boat? It's just a coincidence that she disappears at the same time. They'll never put two and two together."

Daisy was shimmying really hard now and her muffled voice came through again louder and clearer. "Why me?"

Jack snapped at her. "I already told you. Now shut up!"

246

Obviously her antics had triggered his anxiety. But Daisy wasn't a quitter and continued more violently than before and now Jimmy took a sudden interest. He stood up and leaned over Daisy. He watched and listened a moment.

"Holy shit!" he swore. "She's not saying 'Why me?' She's saying 'I'm wired!'"

Daisy stopped thrashing and let her head fall backward. I heard her exhale deeply through her nose as a sigh of relief.

I stared over at her. Could it be?

Jimmy reached out and ripped open Daisy's shirt, exposing a microphone and wire and a transmitter attached to her bra. Okay, she was wearing a bra, so I had that wrong.

"Holy f...king shit!" Jimmy howled and ripped Daisy's bra off unceremoniously and stood holding it as if was something evil.

For the record, Daisy had very nice breasts.

"What is it?" Jillian left the wheel and came back. "Oh, my God! Get rid of it!"

Jimmy started to throw it overboard, but Jack grabbed his arm. "Wait!" He took the bra from Jimmy and stared at it in disbelief.

Meanwhile, Detective Lo had managed to contact the coast guard who had a boat in the area and it was steaming as fast as it could in our direction. He had also managed to get a police helicopter in the air, but they had been way up on the north end of the island so it was going to take some time to get south. Not to be left behind, he had also managed to commandeer a very fast boat from the small boat harbor and was headed our way just as fast as the cavalry in a 1950's shoot-em-up!

Of course we didn't know this so I figured we were still dead. Except for Daisy. She seemed pretty confident about things.

As the conspirators were trying to comprehend what the wire meant – it couldn't be good – dire warnings began to take shape.

Jillian was the first to panic. "What's that?" She pointed to a pinpoint of light far up the coast.

"It's no one," Jack answered sharply. He was trying to stay calm, but I could sense apprehension in his voice. "Just someone out fishing."

Suddenly a light from that distant boat searched out across the water and stopped when it hit on us. A flare shot up high. It was too far away to illuminate us, but I was certain it meant that help was coming.

Jillian pointed skyward. "A helicopter," she whined.

Jack ripped the tape and gag from Daisy's mouth and put the gun to her temple and held her bra up to her mouth. "Tell 'em to stop or everyone dies."

Daisy shook her head no and closed her eyes. I expected brains to fly at any moment.

"That won't do any good, Jack," Jimmy scolded. "You can't take hostages on an island! Where would we run?"

That distant boat was speeding our way and I could almost hear the motor now. If we could just last a few more minutes. Just a few more minutes.

Margie kicked me to get my attention and I turned to see her nodding at the chain by our feet. Margie had managed to get her foot under a length of it and was getting ready to kick it at Jack; I shook my head no. I was certain it would only make him mad and he might start shooting. Our only hope was if they saw the futility of continuing with their plan. Margie must have figured it out too 'cause she let the chain fall back to the deck.

But we weren't out of the woods yet. Jack was frantic now and irrational.

"Jillian, take the wheel," he shouted. "Turn us around and take us toward shore. Full throttle. Jimmy, get 'em chained up. No body, no crime!"

Jillian ran to the wheel and hit the throttle. A second later we were skimming over the waves, this time toward those distant cliffs and the white surf and away from the approaching boat. Jack had binoculars and was looking back and forth from the boat to the helicopter.

Jimmy hadn't moved and Jack noticed.

"Get to it Jimmy!" he ordered.

But Jimmy had his own plan, and pulled out his gun and aimed it at Jack.

"Sorry, Jack. It ain't going to happen that way. I haven't killed anyone yet. I may be going to prison, but not for as long as you. Give me your gun."

Jack dropped the binoculars and turned on Jimmy, trying to grasp the double cross. He sputtered: "You lousy no good..." and he brought his gun up and fired at Jimmy.

It was a true shot and Jimmy grabbed his chest and fell back. But as he fell, he returned fire and the bullet must have struck Jack in the stomach for he doubled over and stumbled backward.

Fate intervened and the boat hit the crest of a wave. Jimmy was thrown to the deck and Jack was thrown hard against the gunwale. A second wave hit harder still and Jack suddenly flipped over the side of the boat.

"Jack!" Jillian screamed and left the wheel. She took a quick look at Jimmy, then at us, and then without a moment's hesitation she dove over the side after Jack.

My first thought was this: We're saved! My second thought was this: She can't swim!

These were not my finest thoughts however because we really weren't saved at all. We were handcuffed to the back of a pilotless boat that was heading full speed ahead toward a bleak, rocky shoreline with no one to intervene. What's that old saying? 'Out of the frying pan into the fire?'

Jimmy, who might have been able to save us, was either dead or unconscious. In any event, he wasn't moving.

Margie was taking a more proactive stand.

"Daisy, can you reach the throttle?" Margie shouted

I looked over at Margie who had somehow managed to flip herself around so her handcuffs were in front of her and she was facing the stern. She had torn off her gag. I wished I'd seen her do that. I knew she was flexible, but still... Houdini could probably have learned something.

Daisy, who was closest to the wheel and the controls, had managed the same feat as Margie and was at this point stretching to reach the throttle control with her foot; unfortunately, her toes were toes. Had they been fingers she might have been able to reach it. She was inches short.

"I can't reach!" Daisy cried, and continued to try mightily.

I egged her on, but since I was still gagged all that came through was "aaaaaaaaaaaaggggga aaaaaaaaaaagg."

Margie took pity on me. "Hold still, Joe," she said and saddled me and used her teeth to tear the gag off my mouth. I thanked her and realized that her lips were only inches away; I thought briefly of kissing her, but the moment didn't seem right.

Don't judge me. I might not get another chance. I could be dead in a minute!

"Joe!" Margie said. "The keys. Can you get the keys from Jimmy's pocket?"

She meant the keys to the handcuffs of course, and since I was the closest to Jimmy it sounded like it was my duty to try.

I maneuvered my handcuffs to the end of the run and kicked off my shoes and used my foot to tear off my sock and reached out my foot toward Jimmy. I could just touch his pocket, but I couldn't get inside.

"I can't get at it." I yelled desperately.

"Try harder!" Margie yelled as if her encouragement might lengthen my leg. I did try harder, but my foot always came up short. Daisy for her part was still stretched out trying to reach the controls.

Margie decided to try something new and turned around and was standing on the back of the seat, pulling at the railing that ran around the stern with all her one hundred plus pounds of muscle. She turned to me. "Help!"

Since I am not made of rubber, I was still turned the wrong way, but I gave up my attempt to reach the keys in Jimmy's pocket and followed Margie's lead and pulled as best I could. Daisy saw what we were doing and joined us. So there we were, the three of us, tugging and grunting and swearing just as hard as we could.

Why do they build things so well. If it'd been a safety bar for a baby carriage it would have yielded by now.

"Joe!" Margie yelled. Yes there was a lot of yelling. The engine noise was loud and we were excited. What did you expect?

I looked at her. She nodded and I looked where she indicated. The shore loomed very close off the bow and we were moving very fast.

Suddenly we were bathed in light from above and I thought that God had sent an angel to rescue us until I

251

remembered about helicopters. It was right over us but I hadn't a clue as to how that was going to save us.

Behind us, that boat that had been coming our way had gained precious little ground. At the rate we were going we were going to beat it to shore by a good two minutes, not that two minutes mattered. Any seconds meant certain death.

It was at this point that Margie stopped pulling and tugging and dropped back onto the seat. I thought she'd given up, but that's not her style.

Instead, she reached out with her foot and caught the engine compartment latch. With one motion she unlatched it and kicked the cover so it toppled end over end toward Jimmy. The noise increased dramatically.

Margie looked at me and gave a nervous little smile. Then did the bravest thing anyone has ever done. She stuck her bare foot into the dark engine compartment!

I expected to see chucks of skin and bone and tiny manicured toes shoot out like so many pieces of shrapnel. But they didn't.

Margie moved her leg around, then stopped; she pulled hard and her foot appeared with a thick wire dangling from her big toe. I waited expectantly a moment, but nothing at all happened! We shared a dispirited look.

"Damn," Margie swore and stuck her foot back into the blackness.

I abandoned my attempts to dislodge the railing and returned my attention to Jimmy. I was attempting to force my leg to grow so that I could get the keys from Jimmy's pocket but I was having no luck at all.

The shore loomed ever closer.

Daisy had also resumed her former attempt, and she too was willing her leg to grow. "Damn it," she spat, her toes only millimeters from the control throttle.

Margie had her foot in the engine compartment and was moving it around more than before. I kept praying for her.

"What should I do?" she asked, as if I might have an answer.

"Pray!" I answered truthfully.

And as soon as I said that, Margie pulled her foot out of the darkness again with a second wire firmly grasped between her toes.

This time something did happen! The engine started to sputter. First once, then again. We lost speed quickly. We looked at one another delightedly.

Could it be?

But no it couldn't. A second later the engine caught and we were thrown about wildly as the boat again raced forward.

But for only a second.

As quickly as it raced forward, the engine sputtered, once, twice and then it died.

We were dead in the water!

For a brief moment we shared tentative looks of astonishment and relief then war whoops were the order of the day and tears streamed down my face and Margie's and Daisy's too. It was a miracle.

But as quickly as we launched our celebration, we were forced back to reality. The rocky shore and the thunderous waves crashed only yards away and we were adrift!

And then, to prove that God really did care, a rope fell from the sky and a voice called from above: "Tie it around the rear cleat. We'll hold you till the coast guard arrives."

Moses couldn't have been more delighted to serve the almighty than I was, so with Margie's help we quickly accomplished the feat and with no time at all to spare the line pulled tight and the chopper stopped our forward motion and ever so slowly pulled us away from the cliffs and the crashing waves.

We should have shouted for joy again, but I think we were too astonished. And maybe a little afraid to tempt fate.

I dropped down on the seat and took a deep breath. Margie and Daisy did the same. We said nothing, though Daisy did try to close up her blouse, but since her hands were still handcuffed... Well, you know.

"Well, Margie," I said after a bit. "You did it. You found the right wire. You saved us all."

Margie shook her head and smiled and laughed softly. "I'd like to take the credit Joe, but I think you're wrong."

"What do you mean?" I asked. "You were in there pulling wires and ..."

Margie stopped me. "I'm pretty sure that wasn't what happened, Joe."

I looked at her and waited. "Then what *did* happen?"

Margie smiled and shook her head till her curls danced. "I'd bet anything we simply ran out of gas. Jack never filled a tank in his whole life."

I started to really laugh at that thought. And Margie started to laugh hard, too. And finally Daisy joined us and by the time the coast guard boat arrived we were laughing uncontrollably.

They must have thought we were absolute bonkers.

The End of My Favorite Vacation

I tried several times the next day to reach Margie but all I got was her answering machine and later a callback from Amanda who told me that Jack's body had washed up in the morning and that she – Margie – was out making funeral arrangements. Amanda said she'd tell her I called.

I stayed in my condo all day, just lazing around and having a drink now and then. But I didn't get drunk.

We'd been up late the night before. After our rescue we were taken to the police station where we spent a couple of hours giving statements and getting answers to some of our most nagging questions. Like how did it come about that Daisy was wearing a wire?

The answer to that one was actually pretty simple. Daisy, as you may recall, did freelance work for the police department and after we'd left her place with the printout of the picture she got a call to come in and help fix a problem. While she was there she casually asked one of the officers about some guy who was found floating in a pool. One thing led to another and Detective Lo put two and two together and ... well I don't suppose I have to walk you through it. We got lucky. Just plain old lucky.

I got a call from the police late in the day. They'd found Jillian, alive, paddling around out at sea, headed toward Japan – she never did have a good sense of direction.

I was surprised she survived at all, since she is a lousy swimmer, but the salt water helped I guess. I wasn't sure how I felt about her surviving. It was going to be hard on her parents when they found out what she'd done. John and Lisa were okay as in-laws go.

Of course I'd given quite a bit of thought as to what had happened to make her hate me so much that she'd

wanted to kill me. Yes, our marriage wasn't perfect, but...
What was it exactly?

She certainly had loved Jack. Diving overboard as she
did made that obvious. I know she wouldn't have done it
for me.

And I thought how hard all this must be on Margie.
She'd been *so* certain her marriage was strong and happy.
At least she spoke about it that way. Maybe that was just a
facade she kept up for everyone's benefit. But to have Jack
show up suddenly and say what he said and ...

I got angry all over again thinking about what Jack had
said to her. How he'd hurt her. There was nothing wrong
with the way Margie dressed. Most men I know would kill
to have beautiful wives who dressed the way Margie did, or
looked the way Margie did. So she was a flirt? So what?
She was smart. And yeah she could play the dumb blonde
when it suited her, but she knew a thing or two and she
was the most approachable woman I've ever known and
she cared about everyone and took pains to show it. Jack
had been a damn fool not to appreciate her.

As it turned out, Margie didn't call me back at all that
day, which was understandable. And I got no phone call
from her the next day, although Amanda did call to tell me
that Margie was sorry she was so busy and would call me
soon.

To stay occupied during this period, I sat on the lanai
and watched for whales and drank some more, which is
not a good thing to do because it makes you melancholy
and I was pretty certain that if I read between the lines
when I talked to Amanda the truth of the matter was that
Margie didn't want to see me.

Which was understandable. I'd made an ass of myself
at the volcano and hadn't been much of a hero the night

we almost got killed. 'Brown shoes don't go with Size Five Sandals,' I told myself, although I didn't want to believe it.

The next day was my last in Kona, and I packed and cleaned a little and went and sat by the surf and watched the ocean. Hawaii's a nice place – even if someone tries to kill you there. Go if you get the chance. Take someone you love, you'll have more fun.

It got to be late afternoon and I hadn't heard anything from Margie so I let it go and decided I'd write a nice letter to her and to Amanda and Pete and thank them for everything. I thought of stopping by, but I didn't feel comfortable with that.

I took a taxi to the airport and got in line with all the other travelers and started to think what I had to do back in Chicago and at the office and about Jillian and her parents and a whole lot of really boring stuff I'd managed to block for the last two weeks. I tried not to think of the snow and cold, but I was just thinking of the snow when Detective Lo surprised me with an appearance.

"What brings you here, detective?" I asked suspiciously.

He offered a little smile, the first honest one I'd seen on his face. "I just wanted to make sure you got on your plane." Then he added: "I'm kidding. I just wanted to say aloha and make sure there are no hard feelings. I leaned on you pretty hard a couple of times."

"You were just doing your job," I said. "I understand. I know I'm a little late on this, but who was the guy in the pool? No one ever told me."

Lo smiled again. "The guy in the pool was a hit man that Frank put Jack in touch with. Frank in case you haven't figured it out, is not a very nice guy. I'm not sure if we've got a case against him or not. It depends on whether Mrs. Thomas or Jimmy Koi will testify against him.

"Anyway, the guy was supposed to work with Jimmy to make sure you had an accident, but he got greedy. He decided he wanted more money. I assume Jack invited him up to the house, ostensibly to pay him off, and when he got there Jack shot him. The slugs in Jack's gun match."

"But weren't he and Jillian on the mainland?" I asked.

"Everyone thought they were, but what with cell phones and so many actors eager to play any part in Hollywood, creating that illusion was easy.

"So Jack was never a suspect, and of course we couldn't connect Mrs. Geanosa to the murder. But as luck would have it, we *could* connect you to the dead man. Lucky, huh?" Detective Lo finished.

"Yeah, lucky," I said wistfully. I was still trying to sort it all out in my head. "What about Norman? Was he involved?"

"That I can't tell you," the detective scratched his cheek. "There's still the prowler out by the pool. But whether that was Norman I couldn't say. I guess it'll remain a mystery."

I nodded my head.

"Have you talked to Margie... I mean Mrs. Geanosa lately?" I asked. Secretly I was hungry for any information I could get about her.

"Haven't you?" Detective Lo seemed genuinely surprised. "I expected she'd be here. You two were pretty tight as I understand ..."

I interrupted. "Detective, we only just met. Despite what you think, there was never anything between us."

I looked down at my feet. Yes, I think that was true. We'd just been friendly. Margie was friendly with everyone.

"Yeah?" The detectives response sounded phony.

I didn't like his inference so I set him straight. "For the record, detective," I said sharply. "Mrs. Geanosa may dress like a bit flashy and she is certainly the biggest flirt I've ever known, but she's an amazing lady. And she was not unfaithful to Jack!"

Lo put his hands up defensively. "I didn't mean to imply..." His voice softened. "I never said otherwise," he said apologetically.

We looked at one another a moment and then detective Lo gave me a pat on the shoulder and we shook hands and he said aloha and reminded me that I might have to come back for court, but it was his opinion that Jillian and Jimmy and possibly Frank as well would be smart enough to make a plea to lesser offenses and then he was gone.

It was busy at the airport and the line was moving at a snail's pace so I took out the new camera I'd purchased the day before and reviewed the pictures I'd taken on the little screen. The cops had found my shattered camera so I got my memory stick back. That was one small triumph at least.

All of the images were of Margie or me or me with Margie. I smiled as I reviewed them and thought of the fun we'd had. I especially liked the one the Japanese tourist took of the two of us. I'd get that one framed for sure.

A well-dressed little old lady behind me peeked over my shoulder at the pictures.

"Did you get some nice memories?" she asked and gave me a pleasant smile.

"Yes, ma'am. Yes I did," I answered.

"That's nice," she said. "It's very beautiful here isn't it?" she took a deep breath and looked around.

"Yes," I agreed. "Very beautiful,"

"Are you on your way home?" she asked.

"Chicago," I answered.

"Oh, my," she feigned a little shiver. Well those pictures won't keep you very warm, will they?" She winked at me. "I think it's sad we satisfy ourselves with pictures of the things we love and don't try hard enough to actually get them. I'm just going over to Honolulu to do some shopping. I'll never leave the islands again.

"I fell in love with Hawaii the first time I came here but it took me twenty years before I made the move. Why I didn't do it right then and there I can't imagine. It's an easy place to fall in love with, isn't it?"

I looked off toward Kona. I could just make out the stack of a cruise ship in the harbor. "Yes. Yes it is," I said distractedly. "It's very easy to fall in love with."

And suddenly everything became clear to me.

I stepped out of line.

"I'm sorry, ma'am. I've forgotten something very important. Have a pleasant trip." I rushed away toward the line of taxis.

She called after me to tell me I'd forgotten my luggage but I ignored her and jumped in the first taxi I found and tossed a wad of twenties over the seat and yelled: "drive like crazy."

"Where to?" the cabbie asked.

"To Margie's," I hollered.

"Yes, sir," he answered, and took off like a bat out of hell.

As we flew down the highway I tried to figure out what I was going to say and how I was going to say it. I turned it over in my head this way then that way and then the other way, but by the time we got to Margie's I hadn't a clue what I would say. I'd just have to wing it.

I didn't bother to knock; I just pushed open the door. Magoo looked up at me, wagged his tail happily and then quickly returned to eating the strap off a pair of Margie's sandals.

It was quiet in the house and at first I thought Margie was out, but then I heard the shower running.

I paused a moment – but *only* a moment – and then made my way through the house and entered the master bathroom.

There she was, all soaped up and using a big luffah sponge on her back. She was humming quite happily, but then she must have sensed my presence because she stopped and turned around and smiled at me.

"Hello, Joe," she said cheerfully; she made no effort to cover herself.

Obviously, the ball was in my court, so I walked over close enough so that the spray was splashing off Margie and soaking my clothes. She stood silent, looking at me expectantly.

"Margie," I said finally. "I have to ask you something."

Margie cocked her head slightly and waited patiently. *God she was adorable.* "What is it, Joe?" She looked genuinely concerned.

"I need to know why you slapped me that night at the volcano when I tried to kiss you?"

She stared at me a moment. I waited expectantly.

"I'll tell you on one condition," she said seriously.

"What's that?" I asked eagerly.

"You have to tell me why you wanted to kiss me."

That was easy. I knew the answer. I'd figured it out at the airport. "I kissed you because I'd fallen in love with you," I said truthfully. "I love you Margie! I'm madly, passionately, crazy in love with you and I can't imagine living my life without you."

I stepped into the shower and took her in my arms and stared into her eyes.

261

Again I asked: "Why did you slap me?"

Margie smiled and just stood there under the shower looking up at me and let the water cascade over her. Her curly hair wasn't so curly and she reminded me of one of those models you see in a magazine that sells bath products – except the women in those ads typically aren't naked.

Margie reached out and in a very coquettish manner she slowly began to unbutton my shirt.

"I slapped you because I'd fallen in love with you too and I didn't realize it till that moment and I got scared."

"Scared? What were you scared of?" I couldn't imagine Margie scared of anything.

My shirt was unbuttoned now and Margie helped me out of it and tossed it onto the bathroom floor.

"I was afraid you were kissing me for the wrong reason," Margie said and began to loosen the belt on my pants. "I thought you were just missing Jillian and..."

I didn't let her finish. "Are you still scared?" I asked.

Margie stopped what she was doing and put her arms around my neck. We were nose to nose. I puckered up and we kissed. Bubblegum.

"But why didn't you return my calls?" I asked when we came up for air. "I was at the airport..."

Margie pushed me away playfully and shook her head at me. "What were you doing at the airport?"

"My ticket... It's for today."

Margie giggled and kissed me lightly several times.

"What's so funny?" I asked.

"Did you try to use your ticket?"

"No, I was in line but..."

Margie put her finger on my lips to quiet me.

"I cancelled your reservation, Joe. I told you that didn't I? I wasn't going to let you leave."

Then Margie kissed me like I'd never been kissed before and when we came up for air again, Margie helped me take off the rest of my clothes.

"Now," she said playfully, "I need my back scrubbed properly," and she turned her back to me.

"Okay," I said mischievously. "I'll do your back if you'll do mine."

I took the luffah and started to gently scrub her back and a moment later she turned around again and faced me.

"Joe," she said softly.

"Yes," I answered tenderly.

"Nice woody!"

Acknowledgements:

I would like to thank the following friends and relatives for their efforts in ridding this book of typos, bad grammar, and lapses of logic. Any remaining boo-boos are the author's and should not be attributed to those who helped.

Jackie Peterson Dahler, Kathy Matson, Richard and Priscilla Stimmler, Richard Swanson, my wife Paula, and daughter Elizabeth.

A Note on the Volcano House

The Volcano House does NOT have bugs. I have stayed there several times and it is clean and neat and has the most amazing location and views you can imagine.

Margie's bug was either a figment of her imagination or a device used by the author to get her into Joe's room. You decide.

Go and stay at the Volcano House and see for yourself.